FROZEN DREAMS

Moe Lane

Flying Koala

ISBN-13: 978-1-7350982-1-0

Cover art by Shaenon Garrity (http://www.shaenon.com/).
Map by Robert Altbauer (https://www.fantasy-map.net/).
Printed in the United States of America

To Andree Rathemacher:
Because I said I would.

Cin City

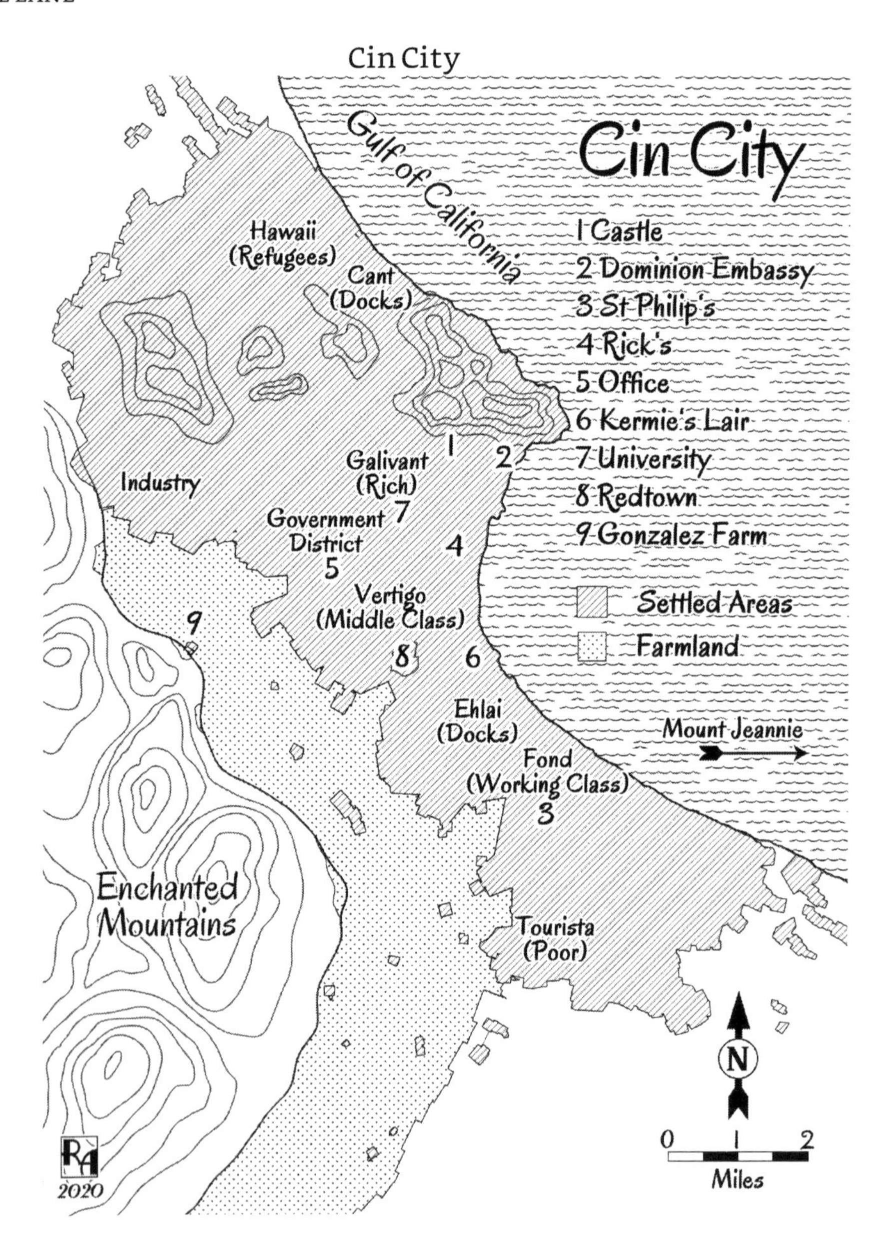

Cin City
Gulf of California
1 Castle
2 Dominion Embassy
3 St Philip's
4 Rick's
5 Office
6 Kermie's Lair
7 University
8 Redtown
9 Gonzalez Farm
Settled Areas
Farmland
Hawaii
(Refugees)
Cant
(Docks)
Industry
Galivant
(Rich)
Government
District
Vertigo
(Middle Class)
Ehlai
(Docks)
Fond
(Working Class)
Mount Jeannie
Tourista
(Poor)
Enchanted
Mountains
N
0 1 2
Miles
RA
2020

CHAPTER ONE
Living In Cinderella

I woke up in the night, ripped from a dream of Jeannie – and it wasn't an easy wake-up. I went from sleepy time to crouched-by-the-bed, staring-out-at-the-darkness while still blinking dream-grit out of my eyes. The darkness stared back at me for a while before it turned itself into my bedroom. Which was also my office, *abracadabra, alaka-zam*! I should take it on the New California vaudeville circuit.

I shook my head to clear it of the sleep-thinking and realized my left hand was full of gun. I must have grabbed my revolver from the shoulder holster (carefully draped over one chair, as per the Lore) while I was waking up. That made me shake my head, but in a different way. A Shamus wakes up with his gun in his hand: something's up and it's never gonna go down easy.

But there was nothing in the office. Or bedroom. Not even in the kitchen, which was barely able to be its own thing.

I tossed the revolver back on the bed in a way that would have made an Old American wince, but back then they had bullets that actually worked. Ours tend to explode whenever a mage sees them. Not that New California has any mages.

Okay, one mage. But he didn't count. And he wasn't a New Californian, and would never be.

I fumbled with the string for the lightstone on the ceiling; I was rewarded with a second or two of light, and then a flash and pop as the magic inside the artifact short-circuited. Guess I should have gotten a new one from the Adventurer's Guild after all.

Well, I preferred the light coming from the bay-facing window anyway. I opened the curtains to see if there was something going down on the street, but it was just Cin City out there, as quiet and drowsy as it ever gets. And above it, standing watch between us and what was now war-torn Sonora, was Mount Jeannie.

The magical stars hovering just above the iceberg's crest shone as brightly and reassuringly as they always did, and if the window was open I'd be able to feel the cool, wet *beso* breeze from Mount Jeannie that makes this town livable. Nothing was wrong, in other words. So why did I wake up with a gun in my hand?

I didn't know the answer yet. But I figured I would, pretty soon. And I didn't waste any time wondering whether I'd like it.

#

It was a morning right out of the wizards of Central Casting when that old rat-a-tat-tat started vibrating my office door. Whoever was in charge of making the local weather today had earned their beans; we had sunny skies to go with the ice-kissed breeze coming off of Mt Jeannie, out of the east in the Gulf of California. The calendar said it was September 9th, 2534 AD; my eyes told me it was going to be a pretty day.

But it's always pretty. Everything in New California is pretty. Even the sins. If the sins were ugly, there wouldn't be a need for Shamuses like me to rip off their masks.

All that banging on the door kept disturbing my morning litany. How's a Shamus supposed to do an internal monologue because somebody can't open a door? "Find the doorknob," I yelled. "You'll scuff the name on the glass!" It was in nice, big letters, too: 'Tom Bannion Vargas.' With 'Shamus' right beneath it. Just in case people were lost.

As the door finally opened, I recognized a Flatfoot from the Castle, still dressed in his ceremonial Old American uniform. I sighed. If a cop shows up at my door, then trouble's either on its way, or it had already showed up and was waiting to surprise me.

The Flatfoot awkwardly bowed to me, actually clutching his police cap in both hands. "Sh-shamus," he stammered. "There's been a murder."

I shook my head sadly as I took my feet off the desk. "And here I thought that you were selling tickets to the Policeman's Tourney, copper." I reached for my jacket and hat, then looked at the Flatfoot. "Do I need a nichols for the horsebus, or did somebody kindly leave the body close enough for a walk?"

The Flatfoot shook his head nervously. "Neither, Shamus. It's up at the Castle. The King bade me bring you. By automobile."

I stopped, blinking. This was serious stuff. The King protected his automobiles like he'd protect the virtue of his children, if any of 'em had any. He wanted me there fast.

Too fast. I looked at the Flatfoot. He was young, but that happens more often these days. The breastplate and badge still gleamed, and the kid didn't look like he'd taken too many hits to the soul yet, either. Not the kind of seen-it-all street monster you'd send if you were planning to entangle some poor old Shamus in the latest round of court shenanigans.

I put on my hat, and peered at the Flatfoot. "Well," I said. "Let's not take the scenic route, then."

#

So you're wondering who the Hell I am, and why I have an office. Well, the name's on the door: Tom Bannion Vargas. Half of my ancestors were here in Cin City a few centuries ago when the other half came down from Old California to carve out a new kingdom, and after the dust cleared and the blood got wiped up, the survivors all made the best of it. New California's got a nice thing going, down here in what they used to call Baja.

But sometimes things still get messy. Not the regular kind of messy, where it's damned clear from the start who killed who in the room with which weapon; from time to time you get Cases. When that happens, you call in a Shamus. We clear the Cases, usually getting slapped around a lot in the process. Not many people love us, but they know they need us around.

And we don't stop working the Case until it clears. Ever. You can kind of say that's our calling.

#

When we got to the street, the sun was busily rising above Mount Jeannie as if it couldn't wait to get away. I don't blame it. The higher you go in Cin City, the rougher the people play. There are days I think I wouldn't stay, if it weren't for the Mount.

And there are days I think that I still would. Cin City: Cinderella, jewel of the crown of the Kingdom of New California. 'Course, the jewel is plastic and the crown is tinsel, but when was the last time anybody made either of those, anyway? There's a half million souls here, where the desert shoves at the sea, and we're all caught up together in something bigger than us. Some people call it a dream, other people call it a pack of lies, and neither know what the hell they're talking about.

I whistled as I saw the car waiting for me, which pleased both the Flatfoot walking with me and the one waiting behind the wheel. This was one of the Castle's joyrides, and no mistake: the Old Americans called it a 'Jaguar,' and if it was a horse I'd have said somebody had the job of brushing its mane with ten thousand strokes every night. But no horse ever smelled like the fry vats at the local greasy spoon, which reminded me: I hadn't eaten breakfast. I hadn't even drank it. There had better be a feed on at the Castle.

Cinderella didn't look much different in the back of a lovingly preserved four-door sedan than it did by horsebus or just plain horse or even the carpets or broomsticks the wilder kids were night-racing now (though you'd never get me on one of those things, even if they suddenly became legal). It was the same old Cin City out there, just whizzing by faster. Bumpier than I expected, too; the wheels found every rough spot on the road when you traveled at – I snuck a look, and was impressed despite myself – fifteen miles an hour.

The Lore suggests I'm supposed to wise off in a situation like this, but I stopped before I started. The Flatfoots were both kids, and they were having too great a day. Here they were, driving a car on a mission for the King. Just like in the Lore! Yeah, this was what they had signed up for. Seemed hardly fair to spoil their fun by pointing out the shudders from all the cobblestones.

Besides, there were plenty of locals there to gawk at the Royal automobile. It was mid-morning, and they didn't see cars every day. You could tell who was who by the way they looked. The ex-peasants, newly in from the south and still learning the ropes: they just thought it all was a spectacle and a half. Their more jaded cousins, the ones who'd been in Cin City long enough to for the aw-shucks to get ground away a little: they respected the car, but resented that it was in their way. They weren't shy about telling the Flatfoots that, either – and the Flatfoots gave as good as they got, with big grins. That was also part of the Lore.

There were also plenty of foreigners. Half-dressed ken mercenaries from the barbie kingdoms of Old California jostled Sonoran traders looking anxiously at the latest broadsheet about the war east across the Gulf, between Sonora and the orcs, and Grand Panaman traders just looking smug for mostly the same reason. Every corner had Deseret cart vendors selling food. We weren't that close to the docks, but there was still a sailor off of one of the Dwarvenwood ships, clearly lost and getting inexorably pulled into a modeling agency. He'd be fine, though. The working girls would send him back to his ship. Eventually.

And then there were the smart ones in the crowd, both domestic and foreign. They were the ones who used Court English as much as they did Spanglish. They saw the car, and they saw me, and they wondered what message the Castle was sending. And, you know, so did I. But if I'm so smart, why was I working out of an office downtown when I could be up here in the Castle district, smelling of vegetable oil?

#

The Castle dominates the skyline; you're not really in Cin City if you can't see at least the spires. They say that the first kings built it just like the holiest of the Old California shrines up in the north, but I don't believe it. The Old Americans had to've had better taste than that, although some of the Lore I've seen argues against it. The Castle's still the beating heart of the Kingdom, all done up in carefully salvaged glitter and sequins and schmaltz.

It takes people a while to realize how the walls are *really* thick, and the battlements are fully manned. When half my ancestors came down here a few centuries ago, the other half weren't real happy to see them. To this day, no matter where you go in the Castle, there's a guy or gal slouched at attention against the wall, sporting brightly-colored but very serious arms and armor. A few of them tensed when they heard the car arriving, and didn't relax when it parked in the courtyard. If anything, they got stiffer. Something was, as they say, up.

The staff got me out of the car nice and smooth, I'll say that for them. I was halfway across the courtyard and up the steps before I realized that the breeze I felt was somebody cleaning the dust off my suit with a little brush. That seemed harmless enough, but I glared away the courtier with the spray bottle of cologne until he went somewhere else. A Shamus smells how he smells. If a court flunky just starting out didn't know that, it was high time he learned.

I've been to the Castle before. Shamuses had a habit of visiting places of power, usually at inconvenient times. It always paid well, but there were just too many people lying to each other with not enough elbow-room to keep it down to a dull roar. Usually I worked the lower to mid levels of the court, which had to jump when the higher-ups yelled '*Rana*.' Now I was going to where the upper kept its crusts, to quote the sage, and I had a treacherous hope that the air would be cleaner. Or that at least the lies would be more interesting.

The air may have been cleaner, but there was still a whiff of something underneath. There was definitely a Case starting up, and I could feel my head starting to shift gears like a Dwarvenwood sasquatch clock. Something serious was going down. Not that my future employers were ready to tell me what it was right away. And when they eventually did, they'd just lie. Everybody tries to lie to a Shamus, even though it never helps. You get used to it.

#

But at least I was being given the heady privilege of being

first lied to by the Court Producer herself. Dorothea Fleming Toro wasn't immediately on hand for my arrival, but I didn't have to wait long before she descended upon me with a flurry of grips and fitters in tow. We've butted heads in the past, but usually to a mutually satisfactory result. And were we anything else? Well, a gentleman never tells.

The cigarette in her holder was conspicuously unlit, so I leaned in and obliged. "Let me get that for you, dollface. You look good." *That* was no lie. Dory stood out in a too-pretty court by choosing to age with dignity. More than one idiot had decided that was weakness, only to find out that Dory knew where all the bodies were buried — and the best way to swing a shovel.

But the strain was showing along with those fine bones of hers as Dory inhaled smoke. "Flatterer," she said. We were speaking Court English, naturally. We also pretended that this meant we had privacy. "You at least haven't changed at all."

"If I had known I was coming..."

"You'd have baked a cake?" She smiled, gamely. "I thought I'd spare us both that."

"Ouch," I said. "I've cooked for you before."

"Oh, yes, you have. It was... memorable."

"That bad or good?"

"I'll let you guess."

I did not like the sound of that. She looked tired, and not just from whatever happened last night. And her patter was dull; I remembered Dory as quicker on her feet than this when it came to banter. So maybe it was time to switch gears. "So, where's the corpse?"

That got a flash of — maybe relief? — from Dory, which was definitely *not* what I was expecting. "You'll see the girl in a moment, Shamus," she responded, and now it sure looked like we were being going to be formal about the whole thing. "The scene's been kept safe for your examination. But first I must impress upon you the need for discretion."

I rolled my eyes. "Because this happened at the Castle and the King is *very concerned* and things need to be handled quietly.

I've heard it all before, milady."

"Not like this, Shamus," (I noted the lack of 'Tommy.') "This one is serious. Serious enough that a Shamus had to be called in." Dory looked at me very directly. "And we need you focused. The Crown needs you fully engaged in this. Do you understand?"

I opened my mouth, closed it. "Yeah, I understand. I should clear my calendar. Or just throw it out. So go ahead and check telling me off your little list."

Dory smiled, briefly. "Excellent, Shamus. If you will wait here, someone will come shortly to show you to the death scene."

"You're not coming?" Which surprised me. Dory's no ghoul, but she's got a real bad case of work ethic.

"Not coming? Shamus, I am not even here." And Dory was off, without even once trying to haggle over my fee. Which was downright unnatural; haggling and grumbling over a Shamus's daily rate, plus expenses, has been part of the Lore since the very beginning. If she wasn't even trying, something was wrong.

That's when I realized what that smell was. Politics. On the whole, I'd rather it was necromancy.

CHAPTER TWO
Cast A Deadly Spell

There are a lot of things that I *have* to do as part of *what* I do. Closing the Case is a big one, obviously. So is putting my nose into places where they don't like seeing noses, or the snoopy people wearing them. But I hate seeing the body for the first time – because I also love it. I love puzzles. I love solving them. But the human ones, when you put them back into the box, they never get to come out again.

The victim was just a kid, but everybody looks like a kid at my age. Maybe in her mid-twenties. Dark hair, dark eyes, and if she wasn't dead, I'd have said her complexion was someone who hadn't gone out much in the Baja sun lately. She was dressed respectably in a long skirt, plain shirt, and heelless boots; this wasn't a refugee from the Hawaii slums up north. Not nobility, though. Her hands weren't roughened, but there were more calluses on them than just from a fountain pen.

The girl was settled down on the floor, like she'd gotten lost in the woods on her way to her grandmother and was just taking a little nap. Only the Big Bad Wolf had shown up, and the kindly woodcutter hadn't; she was cloaked in her own clotted blood, in a way that made you wonder whether the Old American fairy tale had been cleaned up for the kiddies. The murderer had arranged her corpse neatly, with her hands in her lap, her long skirt smoothed over her legs, and – this made me grimace – a pillow for her head. It was going to be one of *those* kinds of murders, then. No ring was visible on her fingers, so I was assuming unmarried unless I discovered otherwise.

At first glance, the murder weapon was a knife. Judging from the stains, it had been wiped and left on another pillow that had been carefully set to the side of the victim. It was the kind of knife everybody pretends not to recognize in New California, because pretending keeps us out of trouble and war. But if I *did* have unlawful thaumaturgical knowledge of wizardly tools, then I would've said that the blade was a mage's athame

– and that it probably belonged to the corpse. There was an empty sheath inside one boot, at least, and the athame was about the right size to fit.

The doc finally straightened up from her preliminary look at things. I've worked with Remy before; she's all right, if you don't mind them morbid. True to form, her first response was sardonic, even for a Cin City medical examiner: "Well, she's dead."

"Thanks for the expert opinion, Doc."

"That's why I make the big simoleons. The cause of death," Remy visibly decided to dumb it down for the Shamus, "was getting stabbed in the heart from under the ribcage. I think the death itself was quick, at least. There's nothing showing up right away on the hands or underneath the fingernails, but I'll look some more, back at the lab."

"Time of death?" That earned me a look from Remy.

"11:57 PM, September 8th, 2534 AD."

That was a lot more specific than the 'sometime last night' I'd been expecting. "For real, Doc?"

Exasperated sigh. "No, not for real, you lummox. This isn't the Lore. In real life, she died sometime last night; this room was being used yesterday evening, and the body was discovered by the morning staff. That's as good as you're going to get, Shamus."

"Fair enough." I took a quick look-see of the room. It was just me, the victim, and the obligatory two guards keeping an eye on everything. Because it's the Castle; they do that. No windows, a skylight that looked like it didn't actually open, and only the one door. The whole place was set up as what the court primly calls a 'conference room,' Sultan's Seraglio edition; New Californian nobles have a real problem keeping track of where their own beds are, and sometimes in a crisis they don't have time to remember. A look at the walls confirmed that none of the, ah, *devices* on the walls were sharp, and the only decorations that looked like they could be removed from their settings were a set of flimsy-looking handcuffs. Excuse me:

'manacles.' I privately resolved not to actually touch anything. "What else you can give me, Doc?"

"Well, Shamus, the guy who did this was lucky." The doc gave me another look; the one that New Californians give when discussing magic in public. "Really lucky."

"How so?"

"I'll need to look at her on the slab to be sure, but the victim here didn't react to being stabbed. It's a clean puncture wound, all the way through. No signs of a struggle at all. Not even an attempt to strike back."

"What about drugs?" I asked.

"What *about* them?" replied Remy. "If there's something out on the streets that can make somebody walk *and* not complain when you steal their own knife and stab them with it, I'd run across it every Saturday night. And I don't believe in secret poisons. If they're any good, they don't stay secret for long."

I frowned. "Fair enough. You said that she got stabbed in the heart, Doc?" Remy nodded. "There's no blood spray, though." It's never as gory as the Lore suggests, but there's usually some from a stabbing.

"I think the murderer covered the wound area with a cloth, and only took the knife out after she died. It's consistent with the wound."

"But how did she manage to arrange herself on the floor like this?" Again, the blood evidence was strange. This was far too clean a scene for anything involving knives.

Another New Californian look. "Gee, Shamus, I'd hate to guess how she ended up on the floor, with her limbs arranged and her head raised, and the knife used to kill her gently dripping blood on a nylon pillow next to her body."

"Real nylon? Damn. That's going to piss off the cleaning ladies." Enough that I was glad it wasn't me. Nobody likes to annoy an old-school *bruja* by contaminating their work spaces with blood rituals. Not that *brujas* exist, either.

I went back to looking through the victim's purse. It screamed 'illegal mage,' if you knew what you were looking for.

There was a small makeup bag, but the lipstick and eyeliner were both extra-wide enough to double as crayons, and the victim wasn't wearing either — I was willing to bet that the powder in her puff wasn't for her face. Several keys on a chain, a couple of dull-looking library books about meteorology, a small coin-purse with some cash in it — mostly gippers and chaplins, with a monroe or two in there for swank — and a wallet with some identification cards.

Our victim's name was Elizabeth Gonzalez-Hernandez. I stopped for a moment, to fix the name in my head. Age 27. Graduated from UNC-Cinderella three years ago, but she still had a current library card. The street address listed on the card was back in the sort of okay part of Cin City, the place where you never saw desperation but you could hear it partying down the road at night.

And then I stifled a groan at the other identification card. Elizabeth was a paid up member of the Alliance of Theatrical Stage Employees, otherwise known as 'ATSE' – and never, ever called 'The Mages' Guild.' Great, they'd be invisibly breathing down my neck on this. It was already clear that the victim was one of the magic-users that we don't have in New California, but her belonging to the group that officially and loudly denies that it represents magic workers? Made this scene even more serious than it already was.

None of this explained why the victim was *here*. The Castle was no stranger to illegal mages, but they're usually of a certain kind. Elizabeth looked just a little too straight-laced to be offering most of the services that the court might need done onsite. I looked at the books again. Still boring, not really magical. Yeah, when the King decides he wants some variety in his sunsets he idly tells somebody, who then sends word. He doesn't bring in someone to do that in person.

Obviously, I needed more to go on — and why hadn't I been briefed better, anyway? — so I glanced at the doc. While I was looking through the victim's belongings, Remy had been finishing up physically examining the victim herself. At my look, she shrugged, and answered the question I didn't want to ask. "No sign of any outrages done to her before or after, Shamus. This looks like it was just straight-up murder. Whatever her killer wanted, it wasn't that." She sniffed, a little. "There's a smell, though."

"That's politics."

"No, under that. You notice how it looks like she was that way? I think that her killer was, too."

"A full-up you-know? Not just a *sicario* who found himself an" – I flicked a look at the guards – "edge?" We get those. Usually for not very long, though; the local bad boys either wise up real quick, or get grabbed by the cops, or just disappear one night after one too many flashy magical crimes. The powers-that-be want Cin City to be nice and quiet about magic. I'd be upset about that more if my own boss didn't agree.

"Nah," Remy replied. "You got a docile victim, a pristine crime scene, and an uninterrupted murder. And in the Castle, no less. You can get a black market gizmo for any one of those, maybe. But if you have all three, suddenly you're one of those costumed guys from the Lore. And they didn't go around randomly murdering people."

"Could be just a regular murder," I said, but I couldn't make myself believe it. If it had been a regular murder, the Castle wouldn't have sent for me. And everybody was hinting that there was magic involved, although it would have been nice if they had come out and told me, instead. Even for New California, this kind of deniable talking around the subject was pretty strong.

I grimaced. Mages killing mages were the worst kind of case. Things could get out of hand, once somebody decided there was no percentage in keeping the spell-slinging private. I might have to have a chat with somebody in the ATSE over that. If this was the first move in a mage-on-mage fight, it would need to be the last one before people started feeling that they'd have to actually notice things. Nobody wants that to happen, except our enemies.

I kept coming back to the mystery of what the victim was doing in the Castle, anyway. I had already decided that she wasn't here to professionally assist in any hanky-panky, and I was pretty sure that if the victim was on the staff, Dory would have found some way to tell me. And Elizabeth would be wearing better boots.

I looked around at the room, which was admittedly tawdry with potential, and wondered if this was a clue. Had the murderer brought her in for something jaded and sweaty, my gut feeling to the contrary, and then something went wrong? No, that didn't make any sense. This wasn't that kind of court. The New Californian nobility, starting with the King and working down the list, collectively had the morals of a jackalope, but they were damned careful of their playmates. And Remy had said that the corpse hadn't been messed with in that way. Besides, the Castle had gone and gotten a Shamus, which is the absolutely worst thing to do if you're actually trying to do a cover-up. It just didn't feel like a crime of passion.

Which is a shame; those kinds of Cases are usually easy to Clear. People in what the Lore calls 'the throes of passion' get real dumb, real quick. I sighed at the thought of the coming legwork. "You got anything more for me, Doc?" I asked – and then managed not to start as another voice answered me, silkily arrogant.

"She doesn't, but I do. The killer is five-nine, two hundred pounds, left-handed, black hair, red eyes, has a bloodline that puts all of you New Californian mongrels to shame, and is standing behind you."

I turned. It was a fair-enough self-description of the man, although I would have added 'goatee that didn't quite work' and 'no fashion sense.' And there he was, holding out his hands in mocking surrender, considering that eldritch serpents of green fire were writhing all over them. The flashy spellcraft alone would have told me that this *escoria* was a mage from the Universal Dominion; nobody local would have dared to be that blatant in public. And since the Universal Dominion ambassador was the only official mage in New California at all, I figured I knew who I was dealing with.

The guards certainly did; they tensed slightly, in that way that can suddenly turn into spiky death. The mage treated them like they weren't even there as he sneered at me.

I'll grant that he had a pretty good sneer, if nothing else. "I, Wolfstone Aconite of the Ninth Circle, Consul over your pathetic little kingdom, killed Elizabeth Gonzalez-Hernandez, for the crime of being an unregistered mage. As is my right. Arrest me, if you dare."

CHAPTER THREE
Taking The Tour

I deliberately waited long enough for the smug look to flicker a bit, then pulled out a cigarette. I lit it, shook out the match, and said "Not 'Ambassador'? What, did your guys demote you?"

"What did you say?" the 'Consul' almost shouted. Yeah, but didn't that question just set off Wolfstone Aconi- ah, to hell with it; his name was now 'Wolfie.' Dominion mages are like that; they'd rather be cut with an acid-dipped knife than not be taken seriously. Though since they currently rule most of the old American Midwest and the entire Mississippi river, most people *do* take them seriously. As seriously as they would any other plague.

So, I decided to start there. I helpfully repeated, louder, "I said, 'They demote you?' Sorry about your hearing problem, Consul," I went on, slowly and loudly enunciating each word. "I guess you were too close to a fireball when it went off? You gotta watch out for those lab accidents."

"I DO NOT HAVE BAD HEARING!" he yelled. I blinked.

"Oh. Sorry. My mistake," I went on in a normal voice. And as Wolfie looked like he was about to open his mouth, I interrupted, "So. They demote you?"

The mage gritted his teeth. "What are you babbling about? Speak, before you rip out your tongue at my command."

Right then, twin rattling sounds cut through our little discussion. The two guards that we had all been politely ignoring had come to noisy attention at the direct threat. The Kings of New California might have ripped off the costumes from the Lore — 'Beefeaters,' with full head masks and gloves added — but they had carefully replaced the halberds with seven foot long bear spears, not that there were any bears around here. Which is why the guards now called the weapons 'magestickers.' They did the same job they did before, though: keeping dangerous things safely out of grabbing range.

That was enough to make even Wolfie pause for a moment. To help him along, I said, "See, yeah, the Castle isn't real big on mages casting spells here. And, hey, that's backed up with a signed treaty and everything. The same one that lets you guys *capture* any mages you find here, if we had any. Which we don't.

"The Dominion ambassador" — I emphasized that word, slightly — "would know that. So would a consul. If we had those, either."

Then I grinned. "But I must have misheard you the first time. You're just the new Ambassador, huh?"

I could tell he wanted to keep going. But publicly casting spells in the Castle without the King's leave really was a no-no, and his own Circles would take apart whatever part of his hide the guards didn't perforate. So, sourly, he said, "Yes." His eyes promised later murder.

"Great! Good for you. Nice to see young people working their way up in the world." I paused. "So, what were we talking about, again?"

I could see Wolfie visibly trying to get back in control of anything, including this little talk of ours. "I am announcing that I killed this renegade mage! Arrest me!"

I considered my cigarette, then shrugged and said, "Nope."

Wolfie drew himself up. "Then this investigation is ove–" Just then I broke in, *again*, and he did not like that at all.

"Didn't say you won't get arrested, *vergo*, but it's not gonna be by me. I'm no Flatfoot; I don't slap the cuffs on nobody. But if you want to go to the nearest police station and turn yourself in, be my guest. Maybe they'll even send me a report about it in a few days. Until then, you're in my crime scene."

"It is *my* crime scene!"

"I'll get to you, I'll get to you. Later. Once I'm done here." I blew smoke, as close to his face as I thought I could get away with. Wolfie here looked like he was about to forget about the magestickers. "Meanwhile, I'm working the job. You want to make a complaint, go find the landlord. Can't miss him; he's the guy with the dimpled chin and the crown that goes 'ting.' Now amscray!"

I thought for a moment that may have been a shade too much, but Wolfie managed to keep from going completely purple. "I will remember you."

"Great. Hold on. Okay. Ready to get a good look? Because this is my best side."

"You'll regret telling me that." And then he, well, Dominion mages never retreat. Just ask 'em. But he left in what would have been unseemly haste, if it had been anybody else. I considered the two guards. Their costumes covered everything about them, including the face, but that wasn't going to be enough.

"You boys better switch out with whoever's on backup today. Dump the gear, too, and get new ones from stores. Tell 'em the Shamus said so."

I turned to see Remy barely avoiding either whimpering, or laughing in panicked terror. Couldn't say that I blamed her, because I wasn't sure how I felt about what I just did, too. The Universal Dominion gets throws-fireballs-around touchy about two things: anybody who made light of the Dominion's 'right' to take ownership of every mage in North America, and anybody who sassed them. I had just done both.

Remy shrugged off her own leather coat and full-face plague doctor's mask, for the exact same reason that I just told the guards to: all of us had to leave the Castle sometime, and you can count on a Dominion mage to try to put the whammy on anybody who saw him get embarrassed. I just hoped she had gotten the mask up before Wolfie had really noticed her. "That was a Dominion mage!" Remy hissed. "I know you're a Shamus, but why poke that troll?"

"Why did I do it, or why did I get away with it?" I took a final drag of the cigarette and flicked it at the ashtray. "I did it because I'm a Shamus. I tell people what they don't like hearing."

Remy was packing her bag pretty quickly, which was fair. She said, "Can't say I wanted to have a ringside seat for that, Shamus. Can't say I didn't mind watching him almost stroke out on the spot, either. You took a big risk, there."

"Yeah. I got away with it for the same reason that I'm looking at this instead of a cop detective. Something's going on here, under the surface."

"I'm supposed to ask 'What?' right? And you say something like 'I don't know, but I'm going to find out.' That's how the Lore goes, right?"

I beamed. "That's right! But first I gotta go have a chat."

"With a man about a horse?"

"No. With a King about a girl."

#

Well, not quite. First I had to have a chat or two with the people who used the room last, and the people who cleaned up after them. Preferably, without going into too much unnecessary detail.

Ah, the new Californian nobility. The couple that had used the room last night were desperately eager not to be publicly linked to this Case, to the point where they came disguised to the interviews. I couldn't figure out why until I heard their names, and then realized that the two had set up what they thought was a little adulterous interlude, only to discover when the masks went off that they were actually married to each other. As the husband sheepishly pointed out, this sort of thing was a lot less socially embarrassing when it happened in the Lore.

At any rate, neither of them had invited Elizabeth along, and they were fairly adamant that they didn't kill her, either. This got backed up by the two cleaning ladies, who both made it clear that they were really *just* regular cleaning ladies. I believed it with the younger one (Florence), but not the older one (Rose). But, in New California: when a witch tells you that she's not a witch, you agree with her.

"Those two?" said Rose, referring to the nobles. We were all taking the opportunity to punish the royal coffee pretty hard. "Forget them. They were gone by sunset. Florence and me, we straightened up, tossed the wastebaskets, and locked up afterward."

"Locked up?" I straightened a little at that. "Why keep the room locked?" Rose's face set a bit primly at that, but Florence seemed more willing to talk.

"Oh, all the conference rooms are kept locked. If we didn't, we could never keep them clean! It's enough of a scandal as it is. Ah, this court."

Truer words were never spoken. You can't call the Castle 'decadent' — and not just because they'd all complain that, no, really, they have all their teeth. When you're decadent, that implies that you used to be higher up. New California's nobility started out in the gutter, and decided to stay down there and just keep everything reasonably clean. Almost the only thing you can say about it is that it seems to work for them.

"So, you know the victim?" I asked. Florence shook her head: she didn't know Elizabeth. I noted that Rose did not do the same. But I didn't try to push the not-a-witch right that moment; if Rose wasn't taking to me about the victim, it was because she wanted to clear it with somebody first. I wasn't going to have any say in that decision at all.

But at least I had a better feel for the times involved. Elizabeth's death must have taken place after full night had fallen, which would eliminate a lot of suspects. Assuming that it wasn't Wolfie, after all. I don't trust it when people go ahead and flat-out confess to the damn crime without a qualm, but weirder things have happened.

I decided enough time had passed for word about my little encounter with Wolfie to climb all the way up to the top of the Castle. Which meant it was time to consult with my client. And his chin, and his crown that went 'ting.' I didn't expect the king to tell me anything, but hopefully he could tell me what some of the nothings were.

#

What can you say about King Ronald the Ninth? He's got the crown, and the chin, and the smarts to get and keep somebody like Dory to do the heavy lifting. His vices were easy enough to stomach, too: he knew what 'no' meant, even when he had been drinking, but he hated to ever say it. Ronnie even paid his markers on time. We've had worse monarchs.

But Ronnie probably still didn't want to see me on general principles as I used a Shamus's privilege to 'barge into' his lunch. At least the king *was* still eating: he wouldn't have an excuse to just leave right away. And Queen Salma was there, which meant that I could get a straight answer from my monarch, for once.

The king *did* do his level best to forthrightly forestall me. "We did not know the girl, Shamus." Ronnie's got the right voice for a King, too; I wanted to believe it, although I didn't (on general principles).

Ronnie and I have one of those interesting kinds of relationships; back when we were both starting out our respective careers, he got in a little bit of a jam with a torch singer who turned out to be a Grand Panama spy. I got him out of that little problem without his parents ever quite hearing about it, and he's never quite forgiven me for that. One reason why I don't work at the Castle.

He probably knew why I had stopped by during lunch, too. Ronnie's not a bad guy, for a king, and I didn't think that he killed the girl; but when somebody young and out of place dies under your roof, you can't really expect the cynical old Shamus to just believe you when you say you never met the victim before in your life. But I did believe Queen Salma from the way she *wasn't* saying anything, because she absolutely would have spoken up if the King was fibbing about who his playmates were.

I gave the Queen a discreet sidelong look, decided that she was just in the dark about how the victim got here as everybody else, and nodded. "She didn't work for you either, your Majesty?"

Salma responded to that one, as I expected. "She wasn't employed at all by the Castle, Shamus." The Queen gave her husband an indulgent look. "In any capacity. I have made inquiries among the staff, and Ms. Hernandez had no liaisons or understandings with any of them, either. Personal, or professional."

That was a mild surprise. "Not even a steady sweetie? I

mean, I believe you, your Majesty," I hastily tacked on. "But if she wasn't seeing someone at the Castle, then why was she even here?"

"I don't know, Shamus." Queen Salma seemed a bit upset, but not at me. "Whoever did this showed no interest in respecting Our Royal hospitality. It was inappropriate."

That sudden shift to the royal We felt unforced, the way she said it – but kings and queens of New California learn how to act, really early. Still, if Her Nibs was lying to me I'd be better off figuring out why on my own. I looked back at Ronnie. "I'm on the Case until it clears, Your Majesty. That's official." *And I go where it takes me, whether you like it or not.* I didn't say that aloud, but I didn't have to. He knew it already, and I was looking for any sign of guilt from him over it.

I didn't see any, which was nice. You hate to see that kind of thing in a sitting monarch with the right of High Justice. But there was one thing I did have to mention, right away. "Ah, yeah, your Majesties. You talk to the new Ambassador yet?"

The King looked at me, over a half-raised cup of coffee. "No. We do not expect to, until *after* you have taken Our leave." His mildly quelling look was enough for me to stand up, put my hat back on, and mumble the usual wiseacre pleasantries at my dismissal. As I stood, I found a servant at my side, with a bag containing my standard retainer, a surprisingly bulky envelope labeled 'expenses' – and one of the sandwiches being served from the Royal buffet. The Queen smiled, regally. "We assumed you had missed lunch, Shamus."

As I said: we've had worse monarchs.

CHAPTER FOUR
Devil of a Case

Before I left, I had to have a little bit of a chat with Lt. Foster, of the Castle Flatfoots. More like she had a little chat with me. And at her convenience, not mine.

I haven't exactly worked with Lt. Sharon Lenina Foster in the past. It's more like every so often she shows up when I'm working a Case, and when she does, I'm supposed to take it as a hint that the Castle is *very concerned* about what's going on and I should *get cracking* with my inquiries. It was a little weird seeing her so soon; I was just talking with Themselves, right? I had already cleared my dance card, is what I'm saying.

Turns out the Lieutenant was just there to tell me who to cross off my lists. "None of our regular consultants were involved," she said in that charming way of hers. Eh, I should be nicer; it's not her fault. Foster was just born centuries too late. She'd have been in her element as a Drowned Manhattan police detective, busting Old American perps and wearing a bulletproof vest to the john. Chain mail and a broadsword was the burden she shouldered to do her job.

But I had my own job to do, and I'm not going to take a Castle Flatfoot's say-so on the first try. "That's great, Lieutenant. So I guess they won't mind sayin' so to my face?"

Foster actually laughed. "You want to interview 'em, Shamus? All of 'em? Be my guest." She leaned back in her chair. "My people already have. They all say they don't know the victim. I got a stack of statements, back at the office. You want those? Swing by and grab 'em so I can get my desk back. Spoiler alert: the executive summary for the whole stack is 'I don't know nothing, copper.' You think you can get more out of them, go ahead and try."

I considered that. Was there a point to trying? Well, maybe not. I'm good at grilling people, but so is Foster and she's got the law to be the stick to her carrot. Me, I'm lucky if I even have a stick. "Fair enough, Lieutenant. Gimme the list of names, though. If one of them comes up later on, I may have different questions to ask."

"No sweat, Shamus." Foster handed over a tri-folded sheet of paper – ooh, the names were typewritten! She *was* taking this Case seriously. "You understand that list shouldn't get passed around?"

"Memorizing and burning it now," I said, after I had done the first and got out my lighter for the second. "Don't worry, I know what secrets to keep."

"Good," she said. "Get this taken care of, Shamus. The clock is ticking."

"Sure," I said as I grabbed my hat and stood up. "It always is. When it stops ticking, it ain't a clock no more."

"This is serious, Shamus." She almost sounded worried, which was surprising. Foster doesn't get rattled easy.

"It's always serious when somebody ends up on the slab," I said as I walked out the door. "That's why it's a Case."

Foster usually reserved herself the last word. I realized that she hadn't, this time. Great. Now *I* was nervous.

#

The nice thing about being hired by the Castle is that you can expense a lot. In this case, I could take a private cab to the victim's apartment, downtown. The only drawback was that I had to listen to the cabbie argue with himself, or maybe his horses, about the Insidious Haidan Threat the entire time. It's not that I love Commies, but they're a thousand miles north. Let Vancouver worry about them.

Well, that's what I said at the time. But we'll get there later.

Anyway, I took my revenge for the monologue by being stubborn about signing off on the bill to the Castle until the cabbie stopped trying to jack up the price. Then I relented and over-tipped him anyway. Still, it's the principle of the thing.

Elizabeth Gonzalez-Hernandez lived near the Elhai docks, in the sort of place where people stop for a while on their way going up the ladder, or else coming down it. It wasn't a bad neighborhood, but it wasn't the kind of place where they left the doors unlocked, either. But I had Elizabeth's keys.

I looked around for the nosy neighbor. There's always one. And sure enough, here she was, coming along now. Pinch-faced, disapproving, yappy little dog: perfect. Just the sort to complain about the youngsters, with their loud parties and flashy ways.

Did I say 'their'? I meant 'our.' Within a minute of yapping and growling (the dog was pretty aggravating, too), the old harridan had made it clear that, the way she saw it, I was just as young and irresponsible as the rest of those wild kids running through the streets every night after curfew. Which we haven't even had since the last war scare, thirty years ago. I wasn't sure whether to be flattered or insulted, so I just asked her if she knew Elizabeth.

"The mage?" she said, maybe just a bit too loudly (older folks are like that). "That..." she struggled for a moment, then sighed. "No, Elizabeth is sweet. She is a good girl. Her parents shouldn't let her live here!" she went on, triumphantly; she couldn't in good conscience slander the victim, but by her Virgin she'd say something nasty about the family.

"You going up there?" asked the woman. She got a gleam in her eye. "Maybe I should go get a policeman, have him find out your business."

"Go right ahead, lady," I said. "That way, if something tries to eat our faces, you got a one-in-three chance of it not being you."

That got her attention. And then she really *noticed* my Shamus getup. Some people are like that. "You official?"

I touched my hat. "Nah. But I'm on the job. Ma'am."

She sniffed at that. "You'll regret it. Nothing good ever came of disturbing a *brujah*'s home. You'll see." She huffed off; I was mildly surprised that the dog didn't yap the whole way. Mini Gran Pomeranians are supposed to yap.

The super wasn't in, so at least I didn't have somebody nosing over my shoulder as I tried keys until one hit in the apartment's lock. I paused, at that point. If Elizabeth really was a mage, well. So I removed my hat, and announced to the empty air: "My name is Tom Bannion Vargas. I am a Shamus, investigating the death of your mistress. Let me pass, please." Nothing happened as I went through the doorway, which could have meant anything, either way.

You could tell right away that Elizabeth was into magic; sure, lots of people have books these days, now that we have mechanical type again, but loose paper with funny stuff written all over it is still what we in the Shamus life call a 'hint.' The apartment was full of diagrams, drawings, scribbled equations, and everything else you'd expect from a mage in a town where people wink at the existence of mages. What it didn't have was any sign of somebody else living there. Which was a shame, for both her and me. A roommate or special friend could have told me a lot about this case, starting with whether or not he or she was the killer.

I didn't know why I cared; somebody had already done his best to confess. But the little professional voice in my head that doesn't trust easy answers wasn't about to let Wolfie claim credit for this murder right away. Some more digging was needed.

Now I'm no mage, although I ain't exactly normal either; but I know enough of the patter to be able to get the summaries. Elizabeth was one of our weather mages, it looked like. She had a lot of papers and reference books (also boring) about water and air currents and how to tease the best moisture out of Mount Jeannie. Which was probably one more reason for the Castle to be upset. Without people like her fiddling with the winds coming off of the glacier, this part of the coast would be almost too hot and dry to live. The court would hate to have to pack up court and move to Tijuana. Or worse, Esmeralda.

Ten minutes later, I was a little confused. Elizabeth didn't hide the papers and books that yelled that she was a mage to anybody with even half a clue to how things worked. But she didn't have any of the *stuff*. Mages need the stuff, like ingredients and bowls and circles and the rest of it. This apartment didn't have any secret rooms; it barely had a closet. So where did Elizabeth do her thing?

I looked at her key ring. There were three keys that I hadn't identified yet; one of them was probably to her secret mage's lair, or more likely temporary storage space. Tracking down the locks in which the keys fit would be the trick. What I needed to do was find who Elizabeth worked with. Mages like to socialize; even the Universal Dominion likes to have other mages around to sneer at, or sneer at the rest of the world with. Find her friends, find her lair. Or else find her lair, find her friends. Ouroboros has nothing on me.

Elizabeth didn't have an address book, or she didn't have one anymore, so I settled for grabbing her opened mail, and reminded myself to check the box downstairs (that was probably one of the keys). As I stuffed her probably meaningless correspondence in my satchel, I suddenly got the faint prickling of my neck hairs that I'd been expecting for the last hour and a half. So I threw myself across the room without thinking.

#

Which was the right move, but only by accident. I'd been assuming that old Wolfie would have thrown a deniable curse or remote shock ball my way, once I was away from the Castle and had stopped moving. Part of the job, and he'd only get one free shot, and I figured I could duck it. But what I got was something else entirely: a sand-devil materialized in what I'll politely call Elizabeth's living room. A damned summoned sand-devil.

If you've never seen one, you haven't missed much. Cursed things look a little like a gargoyle from the Lore, only about half as big (which is good), made out of whirring sand (which is bad), and with vibrating teeth and claws (which is absolutely worse). They're not smart, they're not all that tough, but they can carve through steel like it was wood. What sand-devils do to flesh, you can imagine.

Fortunately, the damned thing spent its first few seconds on this plane attacking the first thing it saw, which was the fold-out bed in one corner. The sound of claws ripping through bedding and mattress drowned out my hasty retreat to cover. I do too much of my best thinking under pressure, and I was spending the time trying to remember anything else about sand-devils.

This one at least wasn't too fast; it looked like it needed to gather up its sand before it could strike with its claws. If I could time it right, I could get outside – and, dammit, then there'd be a demon stalking the streets of Cin City. Crap, I had to get rid of it now.

Or maybe it'd get rid of me; I heard the whine as the sand built up and was just able to dodge the claws as they ripped past me and into the bathroom. Mostly. I came this close to losing the arm instead of just a gouge out of the suit and a whole lot of skin. If this thing was sent to deliver a message, the message was 'die.'

Can't complain, though; the door and the cheap sink behind it both got hammered but good. I have to admit, the spray of water from the sink kind of warmed my heart. Both because it was straight out of the Lore, and because it gave me an idea. I scrambled and almost skittered away from the bathroom and into the kitchen. Moving like that would only buy me a little time, but I was hoping I'd find what I needed there.

To be clear, I spent my time in the kitchen *not* looking for a door or window to burst out of. There was no time. I didn't try to pull out my gun, either. A Shamus's gun is good for keeping regular demons away from your throat or out of your head, but it wouldn't stop anything physical. And I can't actually shoot it; no gunpowder in the bullets. I'm not *insane.*

Instead, I went right for the icebox.

Okay. So, there's a reason why 'Shamus' gets a capital letter. It's a little because we *do* get more deference from those in power than the ones in the Lore ever did, at least in New California. But it's really because we can see things, that other people often don't. Sometimes it's a little esoteric, but a lot of time it isn't; Shamuses do connections pretty good. But the big thing is, about us? When we're on the Case – and this was a capital-C Case – we sometimes get lucky.

Now, Elizabeth had one of the iceboxes that used a chunk of the glacier bits that fall off of Mount Jeannie on the regular; it'd probably keep the box supernaturally cold for another five years. I opened it up, and sighed in relief. The distinctive green bottle was there, right where you'd expect a mage to keep it. Looked like Elizabeth was a girl with a healthy sense of paranoia; a shame that had failed her, just when she needed it most. I grabbed the bottle and started to shake it.

So, yeah, this made some noise. But it took the sand-devil a few seconds to notice, and turn, and charge right at me, scouring the apartment and sending papers (including the ones I hadn't looked at yet) in a fragmenting whirlwind behind it. But I had all the time in the world to painfully pop the bottle-cap off with my thumb and send the fizzing brown soda inside at the sand-devil.

I don't remember the name of the lunatic Adventurer from the Kingdom of Virginia – but I repeat myself – who went questing into the swamps for the recipe for this stuff, back in the wild and woolly days of the Twenty-Third Century. From what I hear, the only thing harder than getting into the ruins of Atlantis to find the formula was getting back out again. But she did, and the Virginians then made sure that every civilized realm in North America learned the secret of the syrup. New California was the first country to restart full-scale production; it's an integral part of the Lore. Which makes it very, very holy.

"Have a Coke and a smile, *gilipollas*," I snarled as I directed the spray.

The sand-devil tried to dodge the soda, with about as much success as you'd have dodging a hive of angry wasps. Only these were exploding wasps, and the sand-devil was doomed within seconds. And wanting me dead all the more, dammit; it lunged for me, I dodged and fell right on my ass, and then it was a mad crawl across the floor as I wiggled back and threw things at it for a few frantic seconds. It did one last desperate reach that managed to tag my sleeve, I somehow levitated my way up on top of the sink and against the window, and then the sand-devil shuddered and collapsed in a heap of itself.

Which heap then started to get bigger and bigger, because why shouldn't it? Damned demons can't ever lose gracefully. The window was barely large enough for me to crash through it, and onto the fire escape outside. Unfortunately, the fire escape was just there for the look of it, and it was apparently loose anyway. There weren't many rivets holding it in place, and I could hear every single one of them pop out of the walls as the escape swayed, collapsed a little, shuddered a couple of times for the look of it, and then finally enough of the soft iron bars snapped that I suddenly didn't have a fire escape to hold on to.

Fortunately, there was a pile of trash to aim at. And it was all, well, soft stuff. More Shamus 'luck,' although my back felt that the luck was pretty theoretical in this case.

As I lay there, the light was obscured for a moment. I focused, to see the harridan and her dog. She sniffed again. "Told you so." And then she stalked off.

I yelled after her, "You gonna call in the Flatfoots now, at least?" She deigned not to answer. Typical. Always minding everybody else's business, except when it'd be useful.

The sand stopped magically multiplying while I pulled myself out of the trash pile, and what was on the remains of the windowsill was already blowing away. From what I remembered about sand-devils, the sand still inside would probably all vanish before the floor collapsed. A quick look inside the front foyer didn't show any incipient disaster, but it *did* reveal the apartment mailboxes. And, happy day! In Elizabeth's mailbox there was a package, addressed to her, in what looked like Elizabeth's own handwriting. So I left a note for the super warning him to check the third floor for damages and went quickly on my way.

I didn't whistle, although I had the urge. There's something reassuring about somebody trying to kill you when you're on a Case. Means you're doing something right. But being attacked, and getting a mysterious package? That meant I was on the right track.

Two wrinkles, though. First was that the Universal Dominion hates even the *idea* of demon summoning. Demons imply that there are gods, and the idea there's anything more powerful than a Dominion archmage out there will make your average Dominion mage froth at the mouth. It's one of the few forms of magic they're all inept at, and Wolfie didn't seem the sort to apply himself towards learning that sort of parlor trick.

The other wrinkle was that demon summonings are real serious business. The kind of business they hang you for after a quick trial, so once you start using it as a weapon, you might as well keep trying till your victim's dead or you are. I didn't want to spend the rest of this Case looking for more bottles of holy soda – which meant I was going to have to consult a specialist.

CHAPTER FIVE
Back to School

San Felipe Church is in the Fond district, out where the working Josés start being careful that they don't wind up living in the Tourista part of town. The streets are clean, but there ain't much on them that hasn't been washed and repaired a few dozen times. The church itself looks the same, but that's just because every time Father Miguel gets something new, he ends up giving it away.

Some places in Cin City, I get looks by people who wonder what I'm sniffing after, and whether I think it's coming from them. In Fond, I get looks from people who wonder why I'm wearing an Old American necktie. They're not real used to Shamuses around here; the Catholic Church has a pretty good lock on things in this part of town, for all that they're always not-quite butting heads with the Crown. The Church thinks of the Lore as competition, and she doesn't always like Shamuses, either.

But Father Mike was all smiles to see me, and when an orc smiles, there's a lot of teeth in it. "Tommy! Good to see you! What do you want?" Then he got a good whiff of the supernatural reek that was being masked by the stink of garbage on my suit, and got a lot more serious. "Inside, Shamus. Now."

Perforce, I went inside. Mike wasn't fussy: he had an open bucket of his own church's holy water by the door, and I got hit with it the moment I was on presumably consecrated ground. I would have minded, except that I knew it was coming. He peered at me, and when I didn't explode or melt he led me back past the altar and into his own working area.

Mike pointed at a basket as he went to a dresser. "Clothes in basket. Shower's over there. You have anything have that can't stand a Christian exorcism?"

"Come on, Father," I protested. "I wouldn't bring something like that in here. There's some special documents in the satchel." Which is waterproofed, and has its own protections.

Or so I've been told. "But they're clean. Anything unholy on me, I want it off, too." I was already stripping down and heading for the showerhead. You want to clean yourself up after meeting a demon, you go to the Catholics and you do what they say.

The shower felt like it was piped in right from Mt. Jeannie, which was a nice change. Hot water's all the fashion in Cin City these days, and never mind that we live in a tropical desert. And the soap was a little tingly, in that special way that meant that I probably needed to sluice the sand-devil dust off of me more than I had thought.

When I was done, toweled, and dressed in your basic simple robe and bandages, Mike was already looking over my clothes with an experienced eye. "Sand-devil, right?"

"Yeah. Took it down with the Real Thing."

"Well, it worked. This time." Mike's good about not being stuffy about competing faith traditions, but he'll always pitch his own side. "You got lucky, Tommy."

"Tell that to my suit jacket."

"That?" Mike snorted. "I got somebody coming in a few minutes. You wait around an hour, it'll be back, cleaned, patched, and smelling of orange blossoms." And also warded in a distinct sort of way that neither of us would talk about. Mike's Church had made its own peace with the *brujas*. "What's going on here? Shamus business?"

"Yup. Which reminds me." I pulled out the expenses envelope, whistled at all the orsons, and tossed a few in Mike's collection plate. "Lemme know when that runs out; the Crown's paying the bills this time. I'm going to need some serious protection, Mike. That demon went and jumped me, out of the blue. I don't want another one latching onto me."

"Why not just kill the demonologist summoning it?" Did I mention Mike was an orc? His parents were refugees from the other side of the Gulf; they converted, Mike decided he had a vocation, and who was going argue with a six and a half foot mass of green-skinned muscle about it? Good guy, had a real placid temper normally, but some things are just bred in the bone.

"That's the problem, Mike. I don't know exactly who sent it." And not knowing that bothered me. For a whole lot of reasons.

#

After I got my clothes back, I still had time for more investigating before the day ended, so the University it was. I expected that it'd be more than once, too. Mages are just drawn to books, the way that mice are drawn to grain, or like flies are drawn to shi– yeah, they like books, okay?

It was a nice afternoon, as always, so I decided to walk a little until my feet started hurting. The Lore says that Old California sprawled so much, they had to take cars everywhere, but Cin City's the kind of place where you can walk anywhere, including to trouble. But I'd be fine as long as I stuck to the docks; the trouble you could find there wouldn't care about a Shamus as long as I was just ambling along.

No sooner did I think that before I felt quick fingers brushing against my belt pouch. I swung around and grabbed, mostly by instinct; my hand found a skinny wrist, which was apparently attached to one of the foulest mouths that I've ever heard.

Especially on a kid that looked, what, twelve? I knew that they send the local rogues-in-training out early to try their luck, but why wasn't this kid in school? Thieves need to read, too.

I looked him up and down. He looked thin enough to be from one of the Redtown alleys west of here, but he was far too clean. "Where's your mother?" I asked.

"Oh, you found my baby boy! Thank you, Shamus."

I turned to see a senior dipper. She looked as nondescript as you have to be in that job, and at the sight of her my would-be pickpocket relaxed just a little. I'm a kindly man, and I don't pick fights with the Thieves' Guild for fun, so I let him go before we made more of a scene.

She moved closer. "Sorry, Shamus," the dipper said in a low voice. "Kid's a Redtown runaway. He's a good kid, he just didn't notice the suit."

"Redtown, huh?" I scratched the back of my head. "They having another 'purge'?" They do that sometimes. Mostly it just means a few more dead bodies in Redtown.

The dipper waved one hand. "Sorta," she said. "They got a new Red Hood claw his way to the top of the crab bucket. But the kid here was gonna take a runner anyway. Says he wants to do some honest work for a change. Sorry again." She prodded the kid until he muttered an apology himself. It wasn't exactly surly; more like he had to remember how to be polite. Which, if he grew up in Redtown, he probably did.

I shook my head after I started walking north again. Man. Kids today.

#

There were other kinds of entertainment out and about, too. Cin City doesn't go in much for street theater, but when one of the bums starts ranting, he can sometimes draw a cloud. As I passed this one guy, busily yelling away about the iniquity of this treacherous strumpet of a city, I was surprised to see he was old (surprising for somebody that poor) but still kicking. The streets get harder, the closer you are to them. His accent was faint, but there; I couldn't tell where he was from, but it wasn't around here.

I looked at his weathered face and wondered if the old guy thought it was worth it, to come here. We get a lot of people from all over the west half of the continent, and even a few from the east. All want a taste of the tinsel, and never mind that it'll make your teeth ache.

That last line made me grimace a little as I climbed the steps of the library, stubbed out my cigarette, and gave my best grin to the best scowl of the guards. I was definitely in the throes of a Case. The cynical metaphors I was firing off were proof of that.

#

Now, I got nothing against libraries, in their place. Which ain't my place. The books themselves seemed to draw back as I walked through the slightly gloomy stacks, which suited me fine. It wasn't like I looking for the card catalog; I wanted to find the assistant librarian. Always look for the assistants – they have to know just as much as their bosses and they usually can't wait to let *you* know it.

I found the guy I was looking for rearranging the magazines. Frederico Baldwin-Cuaron was one of those sprigs of the mid-tier nobility, out there grimly doing Good Works among the peasantry while secretly enjoying it. In Freddie's case, that meant being always disheveled, and constantly drinking from a hip flask that I knew was full of water. Still, Freddie knew the stacks, and he knew the illegal mages. He'd be one himself, except that he's got the magical sensitivity of my left shoe.

And Freddie thought he knew why I was there, and he wasn't happy about it. "Not here, Shamus!" he hissed, and would have made just the memorably 'stealthy' scene he wanted to avoid if I hadn't put my hand on his shoulder.

"Freddie," I sadly mused, looking at him like a world-weary uncle, "Never sneak. Never run. Just act like I'm your bookie for the canoe races and you want to count your winnings in private." That's good advice, by the way. It also calmed him down enough for me to get Freddie to his office. Well, desk. He sat there, trying too hard to look at ease, but nobody was around to stare at us; besides, they'd be more shocked to see a Shamus around a bunch of books.

Freddie leaned forward. "You here about the deaths, Shamus?"

First rule is, never say no when somebody asks you a question like that. "What do you think, Freddie?"

He almost looked happy, like if he had a treasure map to Rodeo Drive and I showed up with the fedora and the bullwhip. "Yeah. I knew somebody else would notice! I mean, somebody like a Shamus. Here, this is my list." He fumbled in his desk, then pulled out and handed over a sheet of six names. Ms. Hernandez wasn't on it, but I was getting that tingle in the back of my head anyway.

Freddie went on, "Those are all" – quick sidelong New

Californian look – "illegals. The first four, they looked like accidents, you know? Drowned in the bathtub, ate some bad fish, stuff like that. Those last two were a married couple, the Pumas. Four days ago the husband supposedly killed the wife and then himself. Open and shut case, right?"

Four days. And Elizabeth's murder last night. Too close for comfort. "But it wasn't." I made it sound like a statement instead of the question I really meant.

"But it wasn't. I knew Estaban and Diane; they were trying for a kid. There was no way he'd do that. So I went looking for the people they worked with, doing, you know, stuff" – the look again – "and turns out that their little 'working group' had started losing people suddenly. It's gotta be murder!"

"Quiet down, quiet down. What was their group working on? And why didn't you go get a cop, or talk to the ATSE?"

Freddie looked abashed. "I didn't think that I had enough to tell the Flatfoots. And, you know, 'Do not meddle in the affairs of wizards'..."

"'...because you can't outrun a fireball.' I get that, Freddie. But maybe duck and weave next time."

"It wasn't that simple, Shamus. I don't think, ah, I don't think that they were really following the ATSE's lead on this. Or anybody else's. You know what I mean?"

I did, and I didn't like hearing that. In Cin City, you had two paths to magic: the ATSE, and the Syndicate. You didn't have to belong to either, in the same way that you don't have to have a job. Nobody's going to force you not to starve to death. But it's a bad old world out there without help. Most mages pick one or the other, and switch off as they have to. But a *bunch* of mages doing their own circle without any oversight at all, from either side? Well, that didn't sound all that great.

"So, tell me about the people who died?" I said. "Were they all right? They behave themselves?"

Freddie's face scrunched, and cleared. "What? Oh, yeah. These were a good bunch. None of them were doing anything nasty, or anything. They were just trying to figure out Mount

Jeannie. The usual: how it works, why it works, how to make it work better. Real basic stuff, nothing worth dying over."

"What were their names?" I asked.

"I got a list, Shamus. Hold on." Freddie started rooting in his desk, which looked suspiciously full of actual paperwork. He pulled out a folded piece of paper. "It's not everybody, though. Just the ones that died."

I looked at the list. I didn't recognize the names, and Elizabeth wasn't on it. But from the stuff about the Mount, I had a bad feeling that this list meant something to the Case anyway.

"You know if they had a workshop somewhere in the University, Freddie?" I didn't think that was likely. Based on his quick head shake, neither did Freddie.

"Not for something like this, Shamus. Too risky for the University if they got caught. One of the guys, Billy, he had a place close to the docks. Big enough for a lab or two. I can give you the address, more or less."

"This Billy had rich parents?" Buildings ain't cheap.

"Nah," said Freddie. "It ain't his. It's a warehouse. He said that somebody was letting him use the top half in exchange for keeping an eye out for crooks. Seemed reasonable."

I guess that it would, if you were a student or a New Californian noble. But then Billy hadn't made up that excuse for me, had he?

Freddie stood up, started to pace a little. "I'm glad you got here. I was trying to figure out who the rest of the group was by what books they had all checked out, to warn them and everything, but a couple of books are still out and the cards are missing anyway."

I stood up too, and took out the books that Elizabeth had been carrying when she died. "These the books?" I asked.

Freddie looked at them. "Yeah." His face clouded. "Oh. That's how you got here."

"'Fraid so, kid."

"Who was it?"

Freddy's face had a look on it that I figured needed

squelching right away. "Why?" I asked. "What's it to you?"

"It's a murder case, isn't it? I can help you with it!"

"Freddy, you know it don't work like that." Yeah, he knew and he didn't like it. "How it goes is, you find out things, you tell somebody like me, then you go back to your life. So do yourself a favor and tell yourself that the Shamus is handling everything. Not your problem anymore. Thanks for the info; now forget it, and me."

"What if I don't want to?" asked Freddy. "What if I'm tired of letting other people handle everything?" He threw up his hands in frustration. "It's always the same! Damn it, why won't any of you people ever let people my age *do* anything?"

We do, I carefully didn't say. *We just don't get why rich kids like you would want to.* Instead, I headed to the door. "Look, this just isn't your turf. It's mine."

Well, it was my turf, and the cops'. And weren't they going to be thrilled when I walked through their door. Nobody likes somebody showing up and changing the story. But that visit could wait; I suspected that first I needed to see a dame about a Case.

CHAPTER SIX
Trouble in Paradise

When you have a problem in this town, you go to Rick's.

It's above the lower harbor; shoot, it's always just about to fall into the harbor. Rick — you gotta be a Rick if you want to run the place — says it was the last bar closed in Old Felipe, and the first one that reopened in Cin City. Rick's is a joint everybody knows and nobody talks about, and I mean everybody. People come from all over Cin City to trade in their worries, so if you're lucky you can get rid of your old problems and at least have something new dragging you down. Or you can meet someone. Or you can drink.

I was there for all three, and I had managed to check off the third reason a couple of times before the second sidled through the bead curtain. When she was out on the town, Dory dressed a whole lot less fancy but looked a whole lot better. I got no personal beef against the king, as I've said, but the Castle's costuming department still thinks that it's 2035.

I figured that she would be coming, eventually. I guess so did she. Call it luck or the Lore: it didn't matter as I stood and Dory sat. This was where she was always going to end up, and maybe now I'd get more details about this Case she had me on.

This time she lit her own cigarette. "You're looking good, Tom." Dory had eyes the same color as the smoke curling around her cheeks, but I could still see the worry in them.

"Only in dim light."

"That's the best kind." She was better at the patter than this morning, but her banter was still off-key and forced.

"Why?"

"Because then you don't see what you are."

"What are you, Dory?"

She looked at me. "A woman who needs you to not solve a murder, Shamus."

I looked at her, honestly shocked. "Dory. You know the Code. I can't walk away from a murder. Some goon dead in an alley with blood on his knife, sure. Punk pulled out of the Gulf after an icemold deal went bad, well, that's a shame. A room full of stiffs after they all tried to rob each other, aw, too bad, somebody know who their mothers were? But this is a murder. There's a dead girl on the slab, and whatever she was mixed up in, that's too much."

"I know." Her voice could have been used in a Drowned Manhattan, it was so bitter. "But I need you to walk away anyway. The Kingdom needs you to."

I raised my drink. "The Kingdom needs me to be a Shamus."

"Yes, but what if there's no Kingdom?"

My eyes swiveled to meet hers. "That sounds like politics. I don't ante up for that kind of game."

"Oh, it's a game, all right. And for high stakes. Don't you ever read the papers?"

"You know me, Dory. I only read the funnies."

"Yeah, well, these days the funnies are on the front page. Only nobody's laughing at the punchline." She leaned forward. "Hermosillo got captured by the orcs, Shamus. Hell, it got razed to the ground. The entire damn country of Sonora's been overrun. They got a general up in Old Tucson trying to put something together, but nobody expects her to last long. That makes our border up there pretty damned scary right now."

I did know that, sort of. The Hawaii neighborhood up at the north of town was full of refugees these days. But they didn't make any kind of fuss that I would be involved in, and didn't we have nobles to deal with that? In fact: "What's the Army doing?"

"Grabbing anybody willing to march, drill, and lie about how long they've been enlisted. Too many regiments only existed in the muster list, so now the generals are scrambling to get the border forts back up to strength before it matters. They'll get away with it, too, as long as nobody fights us in the next year. And nobody might, if the orcs decide to take their time eating Sonora." Dory looked unhappy. "I let the state of the Army go, and I shouldn't have. But so did the rest of the court, so nobody can use it against me. At least the Navy wasn't playing games. They're solid."

"And this is important because?"

"It's important because we're all alone in the world right now, Shamus. Or will be, soon. And the Universal Dominion knows it."

I sipped my drink and thought about our neighbors. Without Sonora to the east – and they weren't bosom buddies; they just weren't the Dominion – New California didn't have a friend in the world closer than Deseret up north, and they were never real friendly, either. And Deseret had lost a war with the Dominion a couple of generations ago, bad, and lost territory; these days an archmage satrap ruled from what was left of Salt Lake City. If Old California wasn't an everlasting mess, we'd still be up there. And trying to ally with the orcish tribes? When Sonora fell, we'd probably be next on whatever orcs use for lists.

Which told me why that little *cabron* ambassador was so smug. "You think that Wolfie decided to kill the girl to see what you'd do."

I grinned to see Dory's involuntary snort of laughter as she heard the nickname, but she sobered too fast to be in a bar. "Right," she said. "We don't go along with helping the Dominion enslave every mage in the world, but we don't wave the cape in their face, okay? We know it's not smart. And they know it's not smart to start something when we're still too far away. Especially since they're still digesting parts of Deseret."

Dory shivered, which is a trick in Cin City even when the icebreeze was flowing. "But this Wolfstone – he's from the Circles that want to start conquering again. The Castle relaxed when he didn't start throwing his weight around, but now that Sonora's about to get replaced with a raging orc horde? Well, maybe he sees his chance."

"So you think he murdered the girl?"

"It makes sense, doesn't it? If Wolfstone gets arrested for killing a mage in the wrong place, the king's got enough to worry about with Sonora going belly-up without starting a fight with the Dominion over something the Dominion's allowed to do. So he'll release him because of 'diplomatic immunity,' then try to have him recalled. But it's for certain that the Dominion won't do that, so Wolfstone will think he can just do it again and again until either the illegals or the king make a deal. And if we sweep the whole thing under the rug, the same thing happens. That's why *I* called you in, Shamus."

"Because we never solve a Case on the first try, and we don't go for the easy answer. But we do solve the Case, so Wolfie would have to play it smart, which means slow. Even his bosses wouldn't like it if he went on too much of a murder spree." If only because the Dominion wanted those mages shipped up to Grand Moingoana, alive, unspoiled, and ready to be brainwashed.

So Dory was going behind the Castle's back to get me to just go through the motions on the Case until she could figure something out. Well, this was her lucky day, because she wouldn't have to. "I got maybe good news, Dory," I said.

"What's that, Tom?"

In answer, I pulled out a small glass vial filled with sand. The evil was all gone, but even Dory could feel the unpleasant scratches and patterns it left behind on the glass.

"That," I said, "came from a sand-devil. Ambushed me at the girl's apartment. Almost wrecked my damned tie, too."

Dory had been Court Producer long enough to know what that means. "A demon summoning? Targeted? But the Dominion doesn't do that."

"Exactly." Demonology is a big no-no for the Dominion. The kind of no-no that gets mages recalled, and killed, and sometimes not in that order. "So tell the court they don't need to try to arrest Wolfie just yet."

"My hero," breathed Dory, almost well enough for me to believe it.

"We're not back from the sea yet," I said. "If Wolfie's claiming to do the murder, either he knows who *did* do it, or he's one hell of a gambler. I need to figure out which."

"So what else are you going to do?" Dory asked me.

I leaned back. "I'm doing it now; working the Case. Somebody wants me off of it and just plain offed before I even start doing legwork, I gotta keep going. That means figuring out the players. What can you tell me about that *esbirro* ambassador? And what happened to the last Dominion guy, anyway?"

"Old Cackle?" His name was actually Grackle Toadstone from the Nightmare Stalkers, which was yet another of the million mage's Circles that the Dominion had. Nasty old sort, but he only ever showed up in public when rumors circulated that he'd explode if exposed to sunlight. "He left," Dory said. "You know how those people are. They don't tell us anything, like why one of them comes and the other one goes. This Wolfstone just showed up three months ago, pitched the usual fit about not being able to kidnap some new servants, and got quietly frozen out at all the right parties until he got the hint."

"You think Wolfie here had Cackle offed? Or maybe his faction did?"

Dory looked wistful. "God, I hope so. I would have sent a nice fruit basket, and had the King's Bookie sign it. But Cackle could have just been called back home. The Dominion thinks that being ambassador here is worth something. They squabble over who gets to come here and insult us."

That fit with what I'd seen myself. The Dominion rules over half the continent; they smacked around and cursed into the mud what was left of the Old Americans after magic came back in the world, and they could start a war with any of their neighbors and win. But there's just something about New California that keeps them from feeling superior to us. That's dangerous – but there are angles there, if you know how to play them. Usually, somebody at the Castle does.

"And Wolfie's pals, back home?" I asked.

"It's like every court." Dory shrugged. "There's always somebody who wants another piece of pie. Wolfstone's made the usual lot of noise about us doing more to help him nab mages. Not that we have any, of course."

"Of course."

"But the Dominion only really cares about that if they think they're going to be in another war right away. Their armies go through a lot of new mages burning themselves out, you know? And the King remembers how his great-grandfather had to let the mage-slavers 'fill their quota,' back when the Dominion broke Deseret. This Ronnie won't stand for that happening again." Dory looked annoyed and pleased at the same time about that, the way we all do when our ruling class keeps insisting on doing the right thing. They're supposed to be corrupt, bed-hopping cynics performing for our entertainment. It's all in the Lore. But lately it's like they've all decided that the nobility is supposed to be *helpful.*

Well, at least they're still corrupt and bed-hopping. Which is good for the economy and the newspapers, but maybe bad for right now. "The king's talking about pushing the fight?" I asked. "Maybe giving old Wolfie the bum's rush, and telling off the Dominion in the process?"

"Yeah, Shamus. It's the dumb play to make, sure. That treaty we have with the Dominion has teeth in it. Literal, magical teeth. But some people in the Castle don't think that the Dominion can reach this far down. And some people don't care if they do."

"So what's *my* play then, Dory? Because this ain't a typical Case."

Dory's smile was sad. "Are they ever?" She threw back her drink in one quick movement and stood up. So did I, and accepted her hand to kiss.

"Just find some way to stop this, Shamus," she said. "Before the Castle decides to do something noble and stupid. And do it fast, because Wolfstone – or whoever else did this – has the look of somebody who likes his work."

#

It was getting late when I let myself back into my office. Cin City does sleep, but not all at once. At this time of night, the streets belonged to the partiers just off their first flush and the dealmakers and the vampires who could behave themselves (friendly warning, *amigo*: don't come here if you can't). I visit the nightlife but I don't want to live there. I like seeing what's coming to get me.

I settled down and went through Elizabeth's papers again. The envelopes had some names in them, but they wouldn't be the names I needed. They might lead me to better clues, but I was looking for the names she wouldn't write down where anybody could see or scry – and who weren't currently down with a bad case of dead. The library books weren't much better. Riveting stuff, these: all about Mount Jeannie and 'theoretical' ways the spells keeping it floating in the middle of the Gulf 'might' have been cast. I hoped mages found it better going than I did, because it was curing my insomnia better than tequila.

It was clear; I was going to have to find that place – who did Frankie say it was? Billy? – used to have. With any luck, it was where Elizabeth had kept all of her paraphernalia, too. With my luck, I'd have to look through half the docks to find it.

Legwork and paperwork. Sometimes I envied the private eyes from the Lore: they could clear Cases just by getting hit on the head often enough. I had to actually put in the effort, trying to find connections in this wreckage from a human life. But then, this was real life, not the Lore.

#

Before I unfolded my bed, I stared at the Mountain for a while, like I expected a sudden answer back. Sure, like that's happened, ever. Or ever would.

Answers would have been great, though. Mount Jeannie's seen everything Cin City's ever done or pulled, right from the start. And I mean the start; the mountain was here to kiss the faces of the scruffy conquerors led by old Ronnie the First himself. They say he fell in love with Mount Jeannie on the spot, or maybe with the genie who lived at the crest. Probably it was the second one; if there's one thing that Ronnie's dynasty is good at, it's finding warm beds to sleep in.

But the Mountain's seen it all. Everything we've ever

done, all the bad and the good, and She takes it all in and never gives anything back. I wish sometimes She *would* give some of it back. Give us a clue whether She's happy, sad, pissed, whatever; just give us an idea of where we stand. But if wishes were horses, Deseret might have had enough cavalry to hold off the Universal Dominion.

And if you get too upset about the Mountain not talking back to you, you don't become a Shamus in the first place. Talking to yourself is part of the job. But at times like this I envied Mike; at least he had people higher up on the chain to gripe to. Shamuses tend to be one per town – even in the capital of New California. It's a lonely life.

At that thought, I grimaced. The grave's even lonelier. And there was one right now, all ready and waiting for a girl who got killed for a reason I hadn't worked out yet. But I would. And when I did, I'd make sure that the bastard who had put her there ended up wishing I'd never taken this Case.

CHAPTER SEVEN
Back to the Farm

The Gonzalez family worked a farm west of the city, just next to Cottonton and right up against the Enchanted Mountains. It was weird, being that far out. I've been near Mount Jeannie my entire life, and though I'll always know where the mountain is, I'm not used to being that far from Her. The Lore says absence makes the heart grow fonder, but sometimes the Lore likes to be ironic.

Cottonton was pretty enough, if you like crowded rural. They pack the farms in pretty tight between Cin City and the mountains; the farther west from the city you get, the more it rains. And the more it rains, the more likely there's going to be somebody there with a pot, trying to catch it.

It was starting to rain now, in fact. But I had a rented tricycle that some magical delinquent had 'vandalized' into pedaling itself, so I wouldn't be caught outside for too long. The trike still wasn't much faster than a horse, but at least I wouldn't get there tired. Another perk of clearing a Case for the Castle — and if I didn't Clear it somehow, I'd be answering a lot of pointed questions about the expenses I was racking up. This would bother me more, except that all my clients did the same thing when I *did* Clear a Case and hadn't bought anything besides a pack of gum. Everybody loves to second-guess the Shamus when the bill's due.

I got the trike to the Gonzalez homestead before the mountain cried too much on me. It was a neat, tidy place, without being packed. Clean gutters and fresh paint on the walls at the house; the fields of corn were corn. Everything looked like it was doing well, at least. That included the workers, some of whom were looking at me with interest as they did farm things. Chores. Work. Look, I'm a City boy at heart.

I parked the trike under an awning that looked and smelled like it usually entertained visiting horses and climbed the steps to the front door. When the door eventually opened to my diffident knock, I could see the reflection of Elizabeth in her mother's face, in more ways than one. And she already knew who I was, even if the suit and hat didn't give it away. Her black mourning dress told me somebody else had already passed along the news, at least.

I took off my hat. "Good morning, ma'am. I'm Shamus Tom Vargas. I'm afraid that I'm here about your daughter."

The mother's name was Diane Hernandez. Her husband was George Gonzalez; he'd been working in the back fields and had come in at a run when she sent word that I was here. Now he was standing awkwardly behind his wife's chair. The two of them had almost fallen over themselves to make me comfortable. I was even offered coffee, which was quite civil to do for a stranger. Or someone who had come to ask about the worst news of their lives.

Being a Shamus ain't always easy. You see a lot of hard things, and sometimes they stick to your sleeves. But the hardest thing of all is sitting down with a couple after they've been told that their daughter isn't coming home. The worst is when they don't even blame you for it.

"Elizabeth was a good girl, Shamus," George assured me. "She wouldn't have gotten mixed up in something bad."

Yeah. When I talk to a parent who's lost a kid, the kid's always one of three kinds. There's the Good Girl (or Boy), and the parents always say that they wouldn't have gotten mixed up in something bad. They say it loudest when it's obviously not true. Then there's the ones who were Good, But A Little Wild; there's usually a story behind the phrase that's full of private pain. But the worst ones of all were the Bad Seeds Who Got What They Had Coming To Them; even then, if the parents have an ounce of love in them, they still want justice for their wayward kids. But they'd always think they couldn't just come out and ask for it.

That's why I could usually get parents to talk to me. They knew that, to a Shamus, the Case was the Case. I wasn't there to judge the victim, only the person who put her in the ground.

Still, I thought maybe George was right and his daughter

really was one of the Good Girls. A lot of times, you could look at where somebody'd come from and understand how they ended up somewhere bad. But not here. This was a house unprepared for murder, and they were scrambling to make sense of the senseless thing that had been done to them. Even the air itself seemed slow, like it was trying to figure out what happened.

It could have been worse. It turned out a flunky from the city government had been sent out to give them the news the day before (I didn't tell them how out of the ordinary this was, but I think they knew anyway), so they were ready for my visit. I wished I was.

The details of Elizabeth Gonzalez Hernandez's life were normal enough: born and raised in Cottonton, had three siblings (smallish family, but that's not as strange as it used to be). Her brothers and sister were all older than her; the oldest would inherit the family farm, while the other two were off on their own homesteads with their own spouses. Elizabeth had gone to the local school, where she was good enough to get a scholarship to the University. She had no husband and no steady boyfriends; she'd talk about dates she had (usually only with her mother or sister), but they just stayed dates. Elizabeth wrote regularly back home and visited several times a year, and always during Christmas.

"So, George, Diane, I have to ask. What did you and Elizabeth fight over?" Because there isn't a family in the world that doesn't squabble with each other.

"We didn't fight!" said George.

"We didn't fight about bad things," corrected Diane. I had her pegged as the parent more eager for this Case to end with the villain's blood on the floor. There was something about her eyes and her voice. Not cruel, and nothing directed at me, but there was less weeping and more cold calm than I had been expecting.

"I wanted her to think about finding a nice person, to settle down," Diane continued. "She said that she had too many books to read first. I told her, then marry a librarian! And then we both laughed." Diane blinked away both a tear and a still-born smile. "She was loved in this house, Shamus. I know that you must ask these things, but this was Elizabeth's home. She did not flee to Cinderella; she went there to learn the things that she needed to know."

"And which things were that, Diane?" My voice was calm. The parents looked at each other; then George went to a cabinet, and pulled out a music box. He wound it carefully, and started to play.

I recognized the tune: 'La Guadalupana.' Christians believe that if someone sang the song or played the music, any spell used to spy on them would hear the music instead. Would it? Well, I guess it's worked so far.

As the music played, George murmured, "You know that our Elizabeth, she was one of the mages, yes?" At my nod, he smiled, shyly. "We first knew when she was a small child. She whistled for the clouds one day, and they came to her! And rained where she asked." His face became set. "But those *magos* from the Dominion would have come for her, so we had to be careful. She studied at night, with the music boxes playing. Not a paper left the room where she read her special books."

"She loved the clouds," said Diane. "She would look at them through the window when she was studying. Soon Elizabeth wanted to learn nothing but the weather-magic. We spoke with the mayor, and she spoke to someone, and we were given books for our daughter to read. And when she was a woman grown, there was a place for her at the University. We were proud. And sad. But Elizabeth would return, if even only to visit. And if she could not come, she would send the rain-clouds in her place. But now only her body will come back to us."

The music box stuttered to a stop in the room. Before the silence could get too heavy, I stood. "I thank you for your trust. May I look through Elizabeth's room and study? I don't need to see anything private or intimate, just what she liked and thought about." I didn't add that those two things could be the most private and intimate things of all.

"Certainly, Shamus," said George. "I will show you." Diane

stood up with the jerky movements of a woman who wanted to go somewhere else to cry, nodded sharply, and left. The look she gave me on the way out almost made me feel bad for the poor murdering bastard it was actually aimed at; it was a stare that promised stone knives and blood grooves for the wicked. Then again, I was safe from that pitiless stare, so the murderer would just have to hope that I found him before Diane Hernandez did.

Elizabeth's old room and study were connected to each other, and had the feeling of being gradually taken over by the people still living in the house. But there was still her bed, dresser, and (most importantly) her old books. I looked over at George. "If you'd like to stay, go ahead and sit down, sir."

"There is no need, Shamus," replied George. "I have much work around the house. You will ask me if you have questions, please?"

"I will, George."

"Thank you. Also, Shamus? I have something that must be said." He gestured me in to come closer; I obliged. In a low tone, he continued, "I have two sons, another daughter, and eleven nephews and nieces. Every single one of them will wish to find you and insist you let them help seek a bloody revenge."

He raised a hand to stop me as I opened my mouth. "I know you would not. But they're young. And we live outside of Cinderella, so they don't see what Shamuses do every day. What we here know about you and your calling, we know from the Lore. So I'm not worried that you will let these kids be foolish." George's mouth set, hard and angry. "But if you do need some-body, you will damned well take me. Not somebody else just starting their lives."

I nodded, but felt compelled to point out, "Now, I'm not going to let a bunch of kids walk all over an unCleared Case. But if it did come down to revenge; you understand that your wife might disagree with you on who got to go?"

"That's my worry, Shamus. She's a good woman. Too good for me. But she can't understand this." He stepped back. "Thank you for taking this Case, Mr. Vargas."

"You can call me Tom, George. I'm here for her, after all." George nodded, and left the room.

That happens, too. When a man – or woman – gets angry enough over the hole that somebody just punched in their nice, rule-following lives, they'll start thinking about punching some holes of their own. Most won't. They still believe in the rules, even torn and tattered ones. But a few will get mad, and then they'll get mean. And when it's all over, they'll have to face what they did when they were mean. Some can't, and you can't know who will snap from the strain.

So George was wrong: it wasn't his worry, in the end. It was always going to be mine. All part of being a Shamus, friends.

Looked at one way, there wasn't any reason for me to look through the things of Elizabeth that she'd abandoned; the girl who lived here had been discarded by the woman who left, and who only came back to visit. But the girl and the woman had parted on good terms, and that doesn't always happen. Elizabeth wasn't running away from home, or herself – and I could use that.

So: first, the room itself. Sunny by the window, with tall, healthy-looking plants on the windowsill. Some stray hairs on the bed hinted of a cat around the place. The dresser was larger than it should have been – the Gonzalezes were prosperous farmers, but not nobles – but it was clearly of modern make. There were a few ornaments on the walls and the dresser, including a music box, but it was mostly honest wood and plaster. The room was also a bit big for one child. The Gonzalezes had put up a new wall to make a study, but it was still a size you'd expect for an adult's bedroom, not a child's; and if Elizabeth shared this room with her sister, it didn't show.

The study was *dark*, too. There were no windows, and no candle marks on the walls, either. The books on the shelves were the kind you'd expect of a studious kid; some modern stuff, some obviously assigned by school and kept, and a couple of classic texts. I opened up one of the last at random, and raised an eyebrow. It wasn't a translation: apparently Elizabeth could read C.S. Lewis in his original Old American.

I went back to the main bedroom and looked at the walls. There were a couple of hurricane lamps, which didn't surprise me. We *were* out in the countryside. But there was something about the light that still bugged me, until I figured it out: the window was smaller than normal. It didn't seem all that odd, since sheet glass isn't the cheapest thing in the world, but then I saw it. You couldn't see inside the room from outside. I took a closer look at the plants. Yeah, those pots were carefully put in other pots that had been glued to the sill.

There wasn't a closet, and a peek under the bed just showed a forlorn dust *cabra*, hiding from vigilant brooms. No suspicious boxes, no hidden cache under floorboards; so I looked at the dresser again. Only this time I really looked at it, in a special way.

I'm a Shamus, not a mage. I don't cast spells, I don't brew potions, and I don't enchant items. But magic – like, say, a distraction spell – leaves tracks in the real world you can see, if you know how.

It works best if the spell is old. In fact, it mostly *only* works if the spell is old; new magic just clouds up everything in the area, which is why I couldn't do it at the crime scene. But I could trace the outline of a teenager's old spell, especially since she wouldn't have known how to counteract the effect, and I felt bad about how nobody would ever be able to tell Elizabeth that as I opened the bottom dresser drawer that the spell had led me to.

Inside was Elizabeth's childhood mage gear. Robe, wand, wooden athame, all sized for a child and probably kept only for sentimental reasons. Half-filled bags of chalk and sand; the throw rug in the study looked like it could both be drawn on for a protective circle and be easily shaken out afterward. A bunch of things that I assumed were spell components. A collection of Elizabeth's real textbooks. Again, I'm no mage, but these were serious texts, full of charts and diagrams and explanations of weather spells. A set of diaries that I contemplated for a moment, then decided weren't actually my business – and a bag that gave off a faint glow from inside.

I opened up the bag and shook out the contents; a half dozen or so lightstones fell into my hands. I whistled, low. Lightstones are a hot item in Cin City; seems like every month somebody's 'bringing in' a shipment that some adventurers 'found' in a ruin somewhere. These were obviously homemade, and they flickered and flashed a little — but if Elizabeth was making them as a teenager, then she had talent. I had the mental image of a young girl, studying during the day for as long as the sun and chores would let her; then, when it got too dark to read, going to her wizardly cache and carefully extracting a lightstone, hiding its brightness until it couldn't be seen from the outside. Just to get a few more hours of learning in.

This is why I had asked to look at the room. I mean, I knew Elizabeth was a mage. I knew that her parents also knew, and that they supported her. But that could have meant anything. But, seeing this, I now knew that Elizabeth kept long hours learning, and that her parents did everything they could to keep her safe while she did it. That told me a lot about her motivations. Elizabeth was used to being determined to do something.

She was also used to hating the Universal Dominion. I mean, you could tell that right off. This room was a refuge, with a bunch of subtle protections; but if a Dominion snatch squad had ever tracked her down, they'd have just burned through the roof, grabbed her away, and then burned the farm down to the bedrock as a warning to the next ten generations about the price of not giving up a mage-child to the Dominion.

That particular atrocity hasn't happened here in three hundred years. Because New California doesn't have any mages. Just ask anybody in Cin City, from the King on down; they'll all tell you. The Dominion knows it's a lie, but we're far away, and they're still trying to keep down all those hunks of Deseret that they ripped away and ate a few generations ago. And maybe because the Dominion doesn't understand why a girl like Elizabeth won't come to them on her own. A lot of mages do, I hear. Guess there are places where being a slave with a full belly and a whip to use on "mundanes" doesn't sound like a bad deal.

I looked around the room again. How many times in here did she stop and start at a sudden sound, or even a sudden silence? Some kids would think of it like a game, but I knew that Elizabeth wouldn't. You can't make a kid have this much discipline. And she'd be scared for her family, not just for her. And that would make her afraid and angry. And that made me angry, too. I felt myself getting hot under the collar, which is a bad thing for a Shamus to feel. But somebody had murdered a smart and skilled mage, and then turned her into a thing for some sick display. You'd have to be made of rock to not be upset about it.

And, dammit, this was another clue that Elizabeth's murderer wasn't from the Dominion. If Wolfie really had killed Elizabeth in the process of 'subduing' a renegade mage or whatever, this farm would've been a burned-out cinder by now. It wouldn't have mattered that Elizabeth was dead; he would have killed her family, too, almost as a reflex. In fact, it was odd that he hadn't tried it anyway.

That suggested to me... maybe Wolfie didn't know who killed Elizabeth, or even who Elizabeth was. That sand-devil implied there was another player out there, and until Wolfie could figure out who it was, he was maybe being cautious? And maybe that caution was now keeping Elizabeth's parents alive. That also gave me another time limit; eventually that bastard would get bored of waiting for me to solve the case and start amusing himself.

So, hey, nothing to worry about.

With the Gonzalez's permission, I took one of Elizabeth's lightstones. I told them that it was for having a sample of her 'special' work, which was true (I also told them that they might want to think about visiting their families for a couple of weeks, which I knew that they'd refuse to do). But I also wanted something of hers. Call it an instinct; I was sure that I'd find a use for it, somehow. If nothing else, I could shove it down the murderer's throat.

And yeah, before I left I did get visits by every relative within fast walking distance of the Gonzalez farm. They were eager, and angry, and very lucky that they could trust me not to throw their lives away. The last one to approach me was Elizabeth's mother, which maybe surprised me a little. I had assumed that she had already worked out that I was taking nobody with me on what the Lore calls a roaring rampage of revenge.

But Diane didn't hiss a rash promise in my ear, like the rest. Instead, she looked out at the lengthening shadows of afternoon, and said, "You ever hear of a woman called Leila Cordova Parsons?" When I carefully replied that, yes, I had heard of the most notorious 'cleaning lady' in Cin City, Diane looked at me with those pitiless eyes and said, "When you need to, you go to her and you tell her that you now hold the debt that she owes me. You will know when to do this, Shamus."

I must have flicked my eyes towards the house, because Diane shook his head. "George does not know. He is too good a man to know – and you will not bring him with you when you make an end of this, either."

"He told me the same thing about you, ma'am." I might have been startled that this respectable farm wife was on calling-in-a-marker terms with Cin City's foremost witch, but the Case is the Case. Diane smiled, bleakly.

"He would. Did I not say he was a good man? Too good for me. So he cannot understand this."

As I said: this happens.

CHAPTER EIGHT
Spoiled Wonder

The next day, I checked out Freddy's warehouse. Without Freddy, and I tried to feel bad about it. But it just ain't always safe to get mixed up in a Shamus's Case.

The place did look promising: it was a two-story building, padlocked shut on the ground floor, and what looked like apartments above. I could get up to the second story by an outside stairway, and although the doors were locked there too, one of Elizabeth's keys opened the door. I like it when I get lucky.

And that's where I stopped getting lucky. Somebody had knocked down inside walls until there were only three rooms upstairs: living area, kitchen, and either storage or work space. And all of them were as empty as a verbal agreement, because somebody had cleaned the place out. And I mean cleaned. Suspiciously cleaned, too. All that was left was the wood and metal furniture, and they almost sparkled. No dust or grime or even the smell of somebody living here, and that felt unnatural.

Which was good news, right?

I looked around a bit, but there's a limit to how much you can hide when there's nothing really to hide it in. But the same key that opened the door to the apartment unlocked the inner door down to the warehouse, and as I came down the stairwell I got a whiff of something that made try to decide whether I was lucky again, or still unlucky.

Icemold. Damned icemold. Worst drug Cin City's ever seen, and she's seen them all.

The Shamus who was my mentor told me once that icemold was the price we paid for the Mountain, and I couldn't argue with that. The cool, moist air that comes off of Her brings with it what my mentor called 'schmaltz'; kind of a living razzle-dazzle. Part of the Cin City charm, just like the good weather and food.

Only sometimes the schmaltz curdles, out in the bad

places where it ain't all a bed of roses. Places like Redtown, which lays in its own stink because it enjoys the smell. There they collect the schmaltz, let it rot, do a little fermenting, and hey presto! Icemold. There are words for how nasty it is, but none that I'd say in public.

Somebody had spilled a bit of icemold; I whipped out a bandanna and wrapped it around my mouth, because I didn't feel like losing my lunch. If I had walked in there when it happened I'd have thrown up, bandanna or not. And if somebody who wasn't me had done it, they might've walked out an addict. That didn't jibe with Elizabeth's working group being a bunch of innocents, did it?

Still, somebody might have been shipping or storing icemold here once, but right now the place was empty. From the faint stains and scuffs on the floor, I guessed that somebody had recently dumped a barrel of the filthy stuff, and then tried to mask the stench. Not a bad cover-up job. Most people wouldn't have been able to smell the remains. Most people aren't me.

I was really tempted to just burn down the whole site, but I remembered in time that the firemen aren't too thrilled to work in this part of town. So I found a mop and a bucket, then started muttering as I tackled all the places where the icemold stench was strongest. I don't like work but this was a duty.

And it was a ground-in duty, let me tell you. I had to really put in the old elbow grease before the icemold started to break up under the force of the mop and the water that I had muttered over. But that was the best I could do, with the current state of the Case. Oh, and I mumbled a quick something about how somebody should do something more permanent with the place.

The rest of the first floor was nothing special, just shelves and dusty crates. I gave it all the look-over, but nothing sung out to me. At least the place didn't stink of icemold anymore, just soap, water, and a little bit of schmaltz. Come to think of it, neither had Elizabeth's body or her apartment. If she had been a moldie, I would have picked up on it right away. So maybe there had been just the one barrel? But what was the point of that?

Going outside to canvass the neighborhood let me breathe easier, but that was all it did. The neighbors weren't what you'd call helpful, about anything. Shockingly, none of the other warehouse workers or street vendors had seen anybody clean out the top floor of the warehouse. And nobody had seen anything 'funny.' I didn't expect anything else, but if you don't ask, you don't get told.

#

It always worries me when icemold shows up in a Case. That drug sucks in the absolute worst kind of pusher and user, and moldies take a lot of people with them when they finally go belly-up. So I hit the streets to get the low-down. And in this town, when you want the low-down, you go talk to the dwarves. Or dwarfs. Some of them get mad if you pronounce it the wrong way. But not as mad as either will get if you call them 'little people.'

The dwarf-with-a-v that I looked up (down?) went by the name of Weedy Randy. Weedy had come down south from the Dwarvenwood after one too many run-ins with what passes for the law up there. I never got straight whether it was the weed, or just the old-style tobacco that got him more in trouble with the 'Wood. Now Weedy ran an 'herbal shop' off of the northern docks, which meant just what you think it means. He didn't look thrilled to see me, neither.

"I didn't sell it, Shamus!" Every time he saw me, Weedy immediately swore up and down that he doesn't deal in ice-mold. I just assumed that was just Weedy's way of saying 'Hi' until I saw him greet somebody else differently.

"Cool off, Weedy. I just want to know who does sell it right now."

Weedy peered at me, furrowed brow above an elaborately-beaded graying beard. He looked suspicious, but that's what happens in herbal shops, right? "What makes you think I would know, Shamus?"

I shrugged, and pulled out my pouch. I took out a grant

and tossed it on the counter. Weedy smiled at that. "Must be nice to have an expense account, brother," he said, then loudly continued. "So, you'll be taking a quarter-ounce of Virginia Steam, then? Guaranteed legit, and right off of the boat."

In a much lower tone Weedy went on, "Yeah, the answer's 'nobody': the supply's all dried up over the last few months. Ain't that a shame? Nobody's got any to sell. I had one moldie come in, desperate for a fix, and he told me that he heard from his old dealer that somebody's diverting the stuff before it can even hit the streets." He shrugged. "But I don't sell icemold, you know that. I tried to sell him something that would take the edge off until the convulsions stopped, but you know how moldies are."

He was practically whispering at that point; I suddenly straightened and shook my head. "We're the only people in the shop, Weedy. Use your normal voice."

"Good habits keep me alive."

"This isn't the Dwarvenwood. All of your stock's legal here. And you don't deal in icemold, remember?" I put a monroe on the grant, because he looked lonely and she's always happy to keep him company. Weedy looked mulish, so I relented. "Fine, get me some rolling papers, too. And while you're doing that, tell me where the moldie is."

Weedy looked stricken. "Put her back, Shamus: I gotta give that one to you for free. The stonefaces have probably sent him to Tourista Landfill by now."

"Crap. Do the cops know who killed him?"

"Yeah, sure. Whoever it was that sold him his first hit of icemold. But what did it now was that he tried to rob a Bee moms-and-pop a few weekends ago. The stonefaces" – cops, to you and me – "decided to call it a suicide."

I smiled, if a bit crookedly. It's always nice to see New Californian officials respect the Lore. And you could see the cops' point; trying to rob a Mormon-run convenience store is a great way to get your throat slit with a Deseret toothpick. Those refugees from the Dominion invasion are nice folks, right up to the point when it looks like you're about to show steel. Then they like to start in with the stabbing, and they don't wait for you to finish your thought first.

"I'll leave her where she is, Weedy. How about in exchange you send word if you hear any more about icemold coming through, all right?" Weedy doesn't like to get involved in his civic duty, but that was enough for a fancy dinner for two on the table, there. He nodded and made the bills disappear.

"You want me to bag those up?" he asked, pointing to the baggie and papers.

"Nah, I like my cigarettes better when they don't tell jokes. Nothing personal. Feel free, though. Later, Weedy." I tipped my hat and headed for the door. As I reached for it I heard the cough of somebody trying to get my attention; I looked back. Weedy looked resigned to saying something.

"I've maybe heard something about how one of the Redtown gangs might be mixed up in this."

"That's pretty vague, Weedy."

"That's why I didn't want to tell you. That, and the fact that it's Redtown. I hate those bastards, and they hate it when people get into their business. So you didn't hear that from me, get it?"

"Hear what? I was blinking so fast that I missed it." And I walked out the door at that. I thought about telling Weedy where I was going, but I decided to be nice. His herbs might be legal, but the guy was just a little too far foreign to be cool with talking to the cops.

Good thing I was, hey? I had better be. They were my next stop.

#

Joe Gannon Lacy may have started out as a Castle Flatfoot, and officially he still is, but these days he's happily settled into being a precinct captain. Not that he'll ever admit the 'happy' part. I was professionally impressed by the magnificence of the fish-eye he gave me when I breezed into his office. "How did you get past my adjutant? She has a list, and you're on it. Underlined."

"Hey, somebody got you one of those word-a-day calendars! Good for you for using it. I didn't see any adjutant. I did see your secretary. She rolled her eyes, just like she always does; so I came on through, just like I always do."

"She should know better. Why do I keep her around, again?"

"Hey, copper, your marriage ain't *my* business."

"Damned straight it's not. Want a drink?"

"Damned straight I do."

"Good, you know where the bar is. I'll have one finger of the scotch, Tom. Since you're up and everything."

As I poured, I said, "You may want two, Joe. We got a killer this time. It's bad, and maybe organized."

I handed him his drink; we clinked glasses and murmured, "*Lakiam.*" I sat, in the nice visitor chair. Gannon started to frown at me, but I could see the word 'killer' blinking in his head. "So, Shamus, how bad is it? Is it the Puma murder-suicide business?"

"Good guess," I said, and tipped my glass in his direction. "But more than just one couple. How did you know?"

"It just didn't sound right. Sure, sometimes a guy will snap. Or a girl. But nobody – and I mean nobody – in that apartment building thinks Estaban Puma killed his wife and then himself. My detectives told me that all of their neighbors made sure to take 'em aside and insist the couple had been murdered, probably by wicked Dominion mages because the Pumas were 'that way'." Gannon ain't one to laugh at murders, but if he *was* the kind to joke about it, the look on my face would've tipped him off anyway. "Oh, Christ on His Throne – ah, sorry. But don't tell me it's true?"

"It may be, Joe. I got a list." I handed it over. "Never mind who gave it to me, but all of them had little accidents in the last few weeks. And the one that isn't on that list is a Case from the Castle. I need them checked out. They were all in the same 'study group,' and I don't know if it was one the ATSE knew about."

"Really?" replied Gannon. "The ATSE's usually watching for that like a hawk. You talk to them yet?"

"I was expecting they'd come and find me, like they do. But I'll get to them. The Syndicate, too: I heard some stuff from the parents of the last victim. This Case the Castle hired me to Clear *ain't* real clear, yet, and I don't want to go into it blind."

"That sounds like cheating," observed Gannon. "It's more interesting when you don't know what's going on, because then people have to guess what you do know and don't know. You can shake out more that way."

"Sure. You can also get punched in the face a lot."

"That's in your job description, Shamus. Anyway, the group: what were they doing? Anything hinky?"

"Not according to my source. Just stuff about Mount Jeannie. Nothing alarming." And nothing worth being murdered over, I didn't have to say. But... "The place they were using got cleaned out. And there was icemold on the ground floor."

Gannon cursed. "That damned stuff. How much?"

"I don't know," I admitted. "Enough to spill, and give a burglar a really bad time. Anything like that in the Puma case?"

"Oh *Hell* no," said Gannon. "Nothing like that in their history, and it's not like a moldie can hide it, right? Can't believe they were peddling the stuff, either. That's just a slower way to become a moldie."

"Yeah," I said. "But it's still a thing that I need to figure out. I think you should just keep an eye out for anything along those angles for right now."

Gannon nodded. "All right, I'll tell the detectives to mind their mouths and not go drinking in mage bars afterward. Hell, I'll even remind them not to blab to the papers. Will that do?"

"You're a credit to the Force, Captain." I heard a distant bellow, which sounded different than the usual busy police station background noise. "Hey, what's going on there?" I said.

A second bellow from down the hall made me lean back my chair so I could get a good look out the door. A couple of cops were manhandling a bum who was giving them a decent fight all the way down to the cells. He looked familiar, for some reason, but damned if I could remember why.

I pointed a thumb at the scene. "Since when do you guys care about the *vagabundos*?" I asked Gannon.

He rolled his eyes. "Since they started drawing green crap on the walls and windows. Bad enough when the punks do it, but at least they were just writing normal crap. Dirty words and pictures. We've had some weird junk show up, though."

"Weird junk? Like, you know," and I wiggled my fingers. Gannon shook his head.

"Nah. At least, I showed it to a couple of people I know, and they said it wasn't anything real. But it was freaking out the shopkeepers, so we had to look into it. Anyway, a couple of kids came in, told us this guy was the one doing it. A patrol checked it out, and caught him in the act. I figure a couple days in the dungeons should dry him out, persuade him to stop defacing private property."

"Letting him off with a warning? You're getting soft, Captain."

"More like just too damned old for this job." Gannon got up this time to pour us both another drink. "Filling out reports and running over rooftops and busting perps and fighting the King's Guard for the honor of the Queen is a young mug's game. Especially since Himself and Herself actually get along pretty good." He carefully didn't mention any future, post-Guard plans, and I carefully didn't ask him about them. If the Lore tells us anything, it's that a cop talking about retirement is a walking dead man. Hell, I was surprised he was talking about being too old for the job.

It was starting to get dark when I stepped out of the precinct station. Cin City sleeps in shifts. All around me, the part of the city that was full of fussy people doing fussy jobs keeping the capital and the kingdom running were all heading home to their dinners and their families and their early bedtimes. As they went to bed, the part of the city that was full of fun and sin and bad decisions was stretching itself awake, wondering who was sleeping next to it, and whether there was going to be a scene soon.

I looked east. You can just see Mount Jeannie, off in the Gulf. The stars always hovering above her flashed brighter and brighter as the sun went down. When they were bright, pulsating pinpricks it was official. Night had come to Cin City, so watch the shadows and your back.

CHAPTER NINE
Million to One Chance

There was a light on in my office when I got back, politely letting me know that my day wasn't done yet. It also promised no funny business. If somebody wanted to ambush me, they'd do it in the dark. So I even whistled as I opened the door – only to see Dory sitting at my desk, with a resolutely unopened bottle and two glasses waiting for me.

My whistle died. There's more than one kind of ambush. I figured this wasn't likely to be the quick kind, either. And, hooboy, but it wasn't. Dory knew just what she wanted from me, and she wasn't going to take no for an answer.

But I still tried my best. "Look, Producer," I said as I poured our second drinks out. I let her keep my chair because I'm a gentleman. "I don't know a damned thing military about Sonora, their garrison up at Old Tucson, our militia, or what the blazes we should do about any of this." I tossed my drink back. "Ask a general what the king should do, why don't you?"

"I've tried that, Shamus. Tom." I get more formal when I drink, she gets less. It should even out, but maybe it doesn't. "I don't trust them."

"But you trust me?"

"Sure," Dory said. She tried to make it sound breezy, but she couldn't quite bring it off. "You keep your heart on your sleeve, where everybody can see it. I never have to guess what you want. Even when I'd want you to lie to me," she said with a snort.

Dory went on, "But the generals? They keep giving me the runaround. None of the *cobardes* want to be the ones who told the Castle to do the wrong thing. Dammit, some of them don't want to be the ones who told the Castle to do the 'right' thing. How many kings down south started out as lucky generals? How many kings remember that?" She looked at her glass, shook her head at the way it betrayed her by being empty, and forgave it with a refill.

I gently tried to slosh my drink. "You'd think some of them would want to fight. The Navy doesn't have this problem." The New Californian Navy, in fact, looks for excuses to go swashbuckling. They've been a lot more smug about it since some of the orc tribes started trying to put ships out into the Gulf, too.

"Oh, I got fire-eaters," said Dory. "Excuse me: the king has fire-eaters. But how do I know if they're right? Even the ones who seem to know their ass from their elbow haven't had that much experience. What if they get their troops killed? Then where will we be?"

"But if you don't send them, and if Old Tucson falls, the orcs will be here next." This sounded very wise to me, at the time. But that might have been because we were starting to make a real dent in the bottle.

"When Old Tucson falls. It's gonna take time for the orcs to pull themselves together after sacking Hermosillo and march up that far, they tell me, but it will happen. But we might hurt the orcs more if we're there with Sonora to fight. I don't know. Maybe. I don't really do war."

I contemplated that. It was true. But: "Okay, Dory. You aren't good at war. What are you good at?" She thought for a moment, and started to giggle. "Get your mind out of the gutter, Producer."

"Fine, Shamus," said Dory. "I'm good at trouble. Getting somebody into it, and others out of it."

"And what does your gut say? If we send troops, will it get the orcs in trouble?"

"Yeah, sure. But those kids will get slaughtered." Dory is sentimental that way. And, okay, so am I.

"So don't send kids, Dory. Send everybody who knows how to fight north. Man the forts with the recruits still learning how to march in order without falling down."

"Usually it's done the other way around, Shamus." But she didn't say no right away, though. I could see her thinking about it. I could also see her try really hard to come up with a 'no,' but in the end Dory simply couldn't. It's amazing, how deeply the hooks of duty bite the flanks of New California's ruling class these days. It's almost like it's a disease.

"Okay. Hrm. Yeah. The kids would be behind walls and in forts, at least. Even I know it's easier to soldier that way. And if we send good troops, they'd have a better chance of getting out of Tucson when it all goes bad. That could work. Yeah. The officers who really do want to march north will go along with this, too. They'd help."

"It's gonna be a risk," I said. Not to dissuade Dory, but to keep her thinking.

She shrugged it off. "You gotta bet big to win big. Or at least lose less. If we can just bloody their nose enough, the orcs will decide to keep away from us until they're done eating Sonora. And then I can think of something else."

I raised my latest glass. "To thinking of something else, then." We clinked glasses, and drank.

Dory contemplated the now largely empty bottle. After a moment, she started to laugh, softly. At my look, she explained. "I was just thinking that at least this plan will make Sonora grateful for a little while, and feeling a little better about it. And then I remembered there won't be a Sonora after this, either way. Still, at least we're not making things worse for them, huh?"

"Yeah. And who knows? Maybe they'll win."

Dory's voice was what you get when you're so drunkenly cynical you come out the other end. "Sure, Shamus, sure. Maybe they will."

#

It's none of your damned business whether Dory was there the next morning, or when she left.

#

I don't like reading the papers, but Dory had made a not-subtle hint that maybe I should start. So I shocked my local newspaper guy by grabbing the morning load. He didn't quite check to see if I was a *nagual*, but you could tell that he wanted to. I let it slide as I maneuvered my papers around the more usual coffee and pancakes at my favorite greasy spoon.

I eat at Garapenna's most mornings. Shoot, sometimes I leave and come back so soon the seat's still warm. The bird-headed guy who runs it showed up thirty, forty years ago on the run from the Dominion: the *bastardos* were trying to breed them some beast-men back then, until they got bored and decided to use the beast-men as mobile target practice. Tolva here was one of the few that got away.

Joke's on the Dominion: bird-man or not, Tolva's almost a wizard when it comes to breakfasts. And foreigner or not, the guy knows how a greasy spoon is supposed to look. He ain't hurting for business, but there was still a free table for me and the papers.

The war in Sonora wasn't front-page news in *Variety*, but you could see it poking in through the Court ads and Royal pronouncements. The Crown Princess was going to an awful lot of Navy dances lately; I decided that my guess why was beneath me. The *Union-Tribune* was acting a little panicky, underneath all the think pieces and op-eds. Mind you, wars cost money; and the editorial board had been beating a pretty solid drum against spending any simoleons on expanding the military. Not now, though. Fancy that.

El Vigia and *La Cronica* were where the action was. The two papers were sniping at each other, as usual; *Vigia* had apparently decided that the war was bad and we should stay out of it (while still supporting our Sonoran cousins), while *Cronica* was all about intervening on the side of our Sonoran cousins (just not in a way that would make the orcish invaders mad at us). Next month's annual baseball game between the two rags was going to be epic; the umpires might even have to restrict the number of bats and balls again.

So far, so business as usual. I went in a little deeper. Once I thought about it, there *were* a lot more refugees from Sonora lately. They were easy to miss on the streets, since the Sonorans mostly speak either English or Spanish and can get by in either of our dialects. But crime was up in the Tourista slums; and those new refugee camps, up in the Hawaii flatlands to the north of the city, were almost becoming neighborhoods themselves. *Vigia* was all over that, mostly by yelling at the Castle about how nothing was being done. One thing did leap out: there were a hell of a lot more ads for blacksmiths and armorers. If you made head-knockers and chain-mail vests, times were apparently booming.

And one thing definitely was missing from all the papers: all the wink-and-a-nod stuff. No coy little pieces about how something "miraculously" appeared or how a disaster was "luckily" avoided; the gossip sections now avoided mentioning certain prominent figures and groups. They weren't even trying to deny the existence of New Californian mages; the papers skipped over them entirely.

This didn't sound like something done on orders from the Castle; the Crown would love to have a veto over what gets published, but New Californian newspapers would love to tell them off just as much. No, this looked more like collusion, not coercion. Which worried me, whether or not it was justified. It might even be more a problem if it *was* justified; what was going on that I wasn't being told?

#

I also saw, tucked away under local news, a little bit about how a certain warehouse was now being looked at for a combination refugee center and breakfast bar. Apparently my prayers had been answered. Always nice when it's so prompt.

And, now that I had been reminded of it, I realized I had maybe seen some of the graffiti that the captain had mentioned, usually in the rougher parts of town, and back before this Case started. And yeah, it was weird. Too weird. I wasn't shocked that the cops or the local 'experts' hadn't picked up how weird it was, though. Some things you just don't expect to have show up on the damned wall. At least, not in real life.

It still wasn't exactly magic. I, for real, don't do magic. Still, there's a thing out there that people can tap into; magic is just how *most* people tap into it. But there are other ways. That graffiti might not have been in any language that I understood, but I could see that it *was* a language. And it wasn't a nice one.

Which didn't mean that it was insane crazy dangerous, though. Crazy only equals powerful in the Lore. But I decided I needed to go back to the police station. If the bum was still there, I had some questions to ask of him. And if he was gone, I'd probably have to ask some questions of the cops who let him go. Very, very subtle ones.

Only, when I got there, the cops wanted to see me. Well, Remy did. Still counts. And that turned out to be enough of a distraction to put the graffiti and its maker out of my mind. Again.

Remy pulled back the sheet to show me the corpse's face, but she didn't have to. From the smell alone, I knew: "Yeah, that's Weedy," I said. "Dammit, he was alive just yesterday. How did he die?" The face looked unmarked, and I didn't feel like peeking further under the sheet.

"Drowning," said Remy crisply. "Somebody strapped him to a chair, put a leather bag over his head, tied it tight around his neck, then filled it with water. Without using a hose. Then they must have taken away the bag. The local cops took one look and sent for me. It's obvious why, right?"

"Yeah." Magic-related murders don't happen often in this town; when they do, nine times out of ten the murderer uses a found or stolen magic item. Actual death-by-spell murders are rare enough to be officially nonexistent. Remy's trickiest job here was going to be finding a good mundane reason for Weedy's death.

"I'm going to go with 'held face-down in a tub of water' for the autopsy report," Remy went on. "You got anything to tell me, before I have to start lying on paper?" The hell of it was, she didn't even seem mad. Just kind of resigned.

"Like what?" I asked.

"Well, for one thing: they found a packet of icemold in the victim's pocket." Remy looked at me. "You knew him; he ever show any of the signs?"

"Oh *Hell* no," I said. Remy knows how Shamuses feel about icemold. "He didn't use it, wouldn't sell it, was scared of it. I'd have smelled it on him if he had. That had to have been planted on him."

"I thought so," said Remy. "But it was hard to confirm, given how disarrayed the corpse was."

"He put up a struggle?" I asked.

"Oh, yeah. Big time. Here." She showed me an envelope full of smaller envelopes. "Samples of blood and skin from what was under his fingernails. If we had magic in New California, which we don't, somebody might be able to trace the assailants with that. If we had magic. Which we don't."

"Nope, not us." I looked around. "This place is a real mess sometimes, Remy. Why don't you get a cleaning lady?"

"I'd love to, but we don't have much of a budget. Why, you know somebody willing to work cheap?"

I thought about the conversation I had with Elizabeth's mother. "Yeah. Yeah, I just might."

CHAPTER TEN

Character in an Alley

The most dangerous 'cleaning lady' in Cin City poured her own tea. This seemed nice and welcoming of her, except 'no servants' meant 'no witnesses.' Not that I thought she was going to brain me with the teapot and then dump me down a hidden trap door, but it was always smart to remember she could.

It wouldn't have been too hard to set up a meeting. I had just resolved to drop a note to Rose, back at the Castle, when she'd shown up with a note of her own. A response to a request for a meeting which I hadn't actually made yet, but witches have their little ways. Or so I'm told, because we don't have witches in New California.

I've had dealings with Leila Cordova Parsons before, now and then. Everybody has. On paper, for the last thirty years she's run the *Sindicato Nacional de Trabajadoras del Hogar*, which people publicly called 'the cleaning ladies' union' and privately called 'The Syndicate,' usually in as low a mutter as possible. In reality, she's head *bruja* of a vast array of hedge-witches and folk-magicians. Depending on what day of the week it is, the Syndicate's either a rival to the book-magicians over at the ATSE, or united with them against the Castle, or they're trying to keep the Castle and ATSE from getting too chummy.

So, you know something's going on when all three *aren't* squabbling with each other. Leila stirred a bit more sugar into her tea (clearly the Syndicate was having no trouble getting shipments of either up from Grand Panama), and gave me a friendly smile. It might even have been honest. "I was so pleased to hear that you were looking into what happened to poor Elizabeth on your own, Mr. Vargas. I was debating making arrangements myself to solicit your services. Diane was always very dear to me; I can only imagine how heartbroken she must be."

"The last I saw of Mrs. Gonzales, she looked ready to carve out the murderer's liver and feed it to him," I replied.

Leila delicately sipped her tea. "We all process grief in our own way, Mr. Vargas." She didn't seem distressed by the general idea, I noticed.

"Was Elizabeth working on anything with your group, then?" I asked. I was sure the answer was no, so I was not surprised to see Leila shake her head.

"No, Shamus," she said. "She was with ATSE, and I do not think that any of her colleagues were affiliated with us. We do not involve ourselves with weather, really. No, to her I was simply an honorary aunt and dear friend of her mother. I suppose that Diane mentioned something about a debt of hers?"

"Just that it existed, and that you owed it to her. She didn't say why and I didn't ask." I'm dumb sometimes, but I'm not that dumb.

"Oh? It's not really any sort of mystery. Well, I could surely tell *you*, at least. Diane did some security work for me, when we were both much younger and more hands-on when it came to business. We found ourselves in quite a few 'scrapes' back then!" Her laugh was accompanied by the gentle smile you might expect from the more delicate, but kindly, sort of grandmother.

My smile may have been a bit more fixed. Back when I was a kid, Leila Parsons had put a crew together and taken over the Syndicate in a single weekend. Some of the bodies never got found, although the flat-out worst of the old Syndicate leadership at least had their heads pop up eventually. Just so you'd know they were dead, I guess.

Leila then purged every witch in New California who even looked like they mucked about with black magic, starting with the ones in the Syndicate itself and working her way inexorably outward. By the time she was done, the Syndicate had its hooks in magical crime throughout all of New California.

People adjusted real quick to things. 'Course, it's said that Leila had personally executed enough magic users to impress even the most fanatical witch-hunter – only all of her victims deserved it. Even thirty years later you'll be hard pressed to find a black necromancer or diabolist in New California. Well, one that's still alive.

Now, as criminal bosses go, Leila's almost respectable. Nobody wants magic or mages underground, so we're flexible about the rules. Hell, most of the things that the Syndicate offers would be legit, if only we didn't have the Universal Dominion breathing down our necks. But when you're a criminal, you end up hanging out with other criminals. And it gets hard to keep saying that you're not that sort of criminal, but someone else entirely different. And better. So Leila and the Syndicate had an interesting working relationship with some genuinely unsavory crews.

And you never know when somebody who's fallen in with evil companions is going to decide that maybe a little evil, now and then, is kind of fun after all. You don't poke that particular bear with a stick, in other words. So I contented myself by saying, "I didn't realize Diane was, ah, well."

Leila looked at me. Not angrily, but steadily. "If the Universal Dominion is listening to us, Shamus, it is because I am letting them. And they will not hear a single word I do not want them to. I do not need music boxes."

"Fair enough, ma'am. Diane didn't seem like she was a Syndicate mage." You heard stories about the Syndicate's private magical enforcer squad, and it was hard to imagine Mrs. Gonzalez being one of them. Hard-eyed or not.

"That's because she was not." Leila settled back in her chair. "Diane was a *pistolero*."

It took me a moment to recognize the word. We don't use it much, after all. "Wait. She was a gunman?" I was as astounded as I sounded. The absolute one thing that the Universal Dominion makes sure of is that every mage in the Americas knows the area-effect spell that explodes gunpowder. The magical diagram that describes that spell is on their flag; it's also permanently burned onto the Dominion embassy's outer walls, written in living flame. And even the illegal mages learn that spell. "So how do you kill a mage with a gun, anyway?" I asked.

"Very, very carefully, Mr. Vargas." Leila's smile at the memories was genuinely nostalgic and possibly even wistful, and that was a little disturbing. "It was always the look of *surprise* on their faces that interested me. It's horrible for a mage to be shot with a gun, Shamus. Embarrassing. The kind of embarrassing that slops onto their allies, too, which is why we did it. Diane was a natural. I suspect that at her best, she could have even beaten a Dominion mage 'to the draw,' as it were, not that I would have ever let her try.

"But everyone eventually gets tired of doing the same thing every day," Leila went on, still giving off that haze of murderous nostalgia, "and finishing up the original Cinderella phase of the reorganization was very, well, fatiguing for her. And there was a man. There usually is, but hers was a good one, who I liked and approved of. So, Diane retired, and moved out to, Mother Mary help her, farm."

I shrugged in honest agreement with her mild distaste. "I'm a cobblestones sort of guy myself."

"Exactly! We sniff the fresh air, and we ask ourselves if it is supposed to smell that way. I am convinced it is unhealthy." Leila put down her cup. "But she was happy. And then she had a daughter who was a mage, and Diane was happier. And I was happy, too: both for her sake, and because I could see the advantages in being 'Tia Leila' to a mage of the ATSE. Certainly the ATSE did."

"And now the apple cart's upset?" That remark of mine made Leila's mouth set a little, but she got over it. Which was a point in her favor.

"My apologies, Shamus. You are right; this is about a murdered woman, not plans and understandings and connections. I assure you, I can be just as furious that this was done at all as I am furious that it was done to someone I knew, and had affection for, and was ready to help guide. I will have my vengeance for this; so what we can give, we will give." She looked at me steadily. "What do you need?"

I thought about it. "First off: you need somebody to get

over to Remy in the coroner's office. Somebody who can do the v-word thing." I don't care how good Leila's spells might be; smart guys don't say the word 'vudu' where the Dominion might hear.

Leila nodded. "Good thought. I can send Rose over; she is already caught up in this. But you need more, yes?"

"As much as I can get, ma'am. But, more than anything else? Obfuscation. I can't let the ambassador know where I'm poking my nose. If he can track me, he can track down the people I talk to. I don't want people in danger who can't handle it."

"You cannot protect everybody, Shamus."

"Which doesn't mean I can't try'n make it hard for that son of a bitch. Can you maybe work it so he can't track me down, no matter what? Mages here obviously have a trick or two for that."

Leila poured herself another cup of tea, but didn't drink from it while she looked off into the other side of the room for a moment. "We can, but in your case there would be drawbacks."

"I'm listening."

"We have an enchantment that will make you appear to be not worth scrying, or viewing. We use it to keep casual scans from the Dominion from alighting on any of us; it works perfectly well, as long as you do not actively use magic. Since you are not a spell-caster, that will not affect you."

"That sounds great," I replied. "Now tell me the catch."

"The catch is, since you are not a mage, you will not be able to 'peek out' from under the enchantment. We will not be able to track you, either. If you get into trouble, no mage will know to provide assistance. And this enchantment will do nothing to protect you against a direct magical assault."

"But I'll be able to investigate normally."

"But you will be able to investigate normally."

"Good," I said. "That's all I've ever needed."

"I hope that will be enough, Mr. Vargas." She stood, and so did I. "I would like to give you a half dozen apprentices and a crate of 'healing potions' to help in the investigation, but if we could hand out those sorts of resources openly, then Elizabeth would probably still be alive. But we can hide you from prying eyes." Her smile then dropped sixty degrees. "And if you should happen to then scoop out those prying eyes yourself, why, so much the better."

I somehow managed to smile at that, because I knew damned well that she meant that 'joke' literally. I also knew that, 'Aunt Tia' or not, this help was coming with a price tag: "So what do *you* want, ma'am?"

"Nothing you can't give, Shamus. First: somebody ordered Elizabeth to be killed. One way or the other, that person must pay for that."

I stiffened a little. "It's a Case, ma'am. I'm not going to just forget to Clear it."

"No offense was intended, Shamus." I think she meant it, too. "But some things you must say aloud. The second thing is, somebody actually murdered Elizabeth. I want that person's name, and I do not care who it is."

"Why?" I asked.

Leila put down the silver bell she had just rung to summon a servant, or apprentice, or whoever it was she had running errands. "Do you really want to know?" she asked. Her tone suggested that I didn't.

I thought about it, and decided she was right. I put on my hat. "I can't make any guarantees, ma'am," I said as I stood. "But I can make a promise. I won't stop digging until either the Case breaks, or I do. And if I get names, you'll hear them." She nodded to me in understanding as I was escorted out.

I'm not going to tell how they warded me. I might need them to do it again, someday. Also, the Syndicate might not take it well if I started blabbing secrets everywhere. Let's just say that an hour later I was hitting the streets again, with a song on my lips and nothing at all on my shoulder.

#

That good mood lasted just long enough for the Flatfoots to find me – although I wasn't hard to find. They just didn't want to go into Leila's place to fetch me. The Castle likes 'em smart like that.

I knew these two. Hell, so do you. Al and Sancho: Al was the tall skinny one, and Sancho was the short fat one – see what I mean? You already know that Sancho likes to talk, and Al seems to mope all the time, and that Sancho's got a full head of hair while Al's fighting to keep the ones that he has left, and everything else. The Lore's the Lore for a reason, my friends. It's all in there, somewhere.

"Afternoon, Shamus," said Sancho, somehow making it sound like 'Hey, it's the *gilipollas!*' Flatfoots are traditionally kinda adversarial to Shamuses, but Sancho really *respects* the tradition, y'know what I mean? Al just looked at me like somebody had killed his dog and he was trying to be brave about it in front of his mama. I'd call his face 'lugubrious,' only I'm pretty sure that I'd spell it wrong.

"Howdy, Flatfoots," I said just as politely. "You slumming on the streets?" I tapped the cobblestones with my foot. "Don't worry, nobody's stolen 'em. Yet."

"Shut your yap before I shut it for ya, peeper," said Sancho; I was pleased to see that he hadn't been neglecting the Lore after passing the Flatfoot exam. "You got business with the Lieutenant, so let's get going."

"Sancho, Sancho," I said. "You gotta give me more than that. How can I start sweating from a guilty conscience if I don't even know which lieutenant I'm seeing?"

"Fine," said Sancho. "It's Foster. She wants to talk to you. Now. Happy?" He glared at me. "Please tell me you're not happy."

"Sorry, Flatfoot, when it comes to Foster I got a light heart and a smooth brow. Lead the way." As we started going to the paddy wagon, I said, "Oh, by the way, *why* does she want to see me?"

Al spoke up. "There's been a murder, Shamus." His voice was like the rest of him: glum, and maybe just a bit smug about that. "Some noble's kid. She wants you to tell her why it happened."

I gave Sancho a dirty look: the Lore needs to be honored, sure, but I don't like to crack wise around dead people unless they deserve it. Yeah, I'm such a swell guy that way, sure. "Somebody I know?" I asked.

Sancho pulled out a piece of paper. "Says his name was Frederico Baldwin-Cuaron." He looked up. "You ready to sweat, now?"

"Nah," I said. "But I can manage some swears, if you like." I *wanted* to swear. Dammit, Freddie was a good kid. It'd be nice if it wasn't him that turned up dead – but with my luck, it would be.

#

One look at the alley convinced me that it wasn't my day. It sure hadn't been a good one for any of the three dead people in it. The cops and Flatfoots didn't look real thrilled to be there, either. The whole scene smelled like death and paperwork, and a lot of cops don't know which smell they hate worse.

I looked down at the corpse I cared most about. "Dammit, Freddie," I said. "I *told* you that this was none of your business." Because it wasn't. Shamuses get bashed around a lot, but that's okay. It's part of the life. Your average José doesn't have my kind of crazy-stupid luck. Freddie certainly hadn't, although at least his parents would be able to have an open-casket funeral.

Lt. Foster coughed. "Part of your Case, then?" she said, as if the two other dead bodies weren't a clue. They were all getting the full chalk-outline treatment, too. You know, just in case a random illegal mage was to drop by later and needed to know where the bodies were before she started casting information spells.

"The way things are going? Yeah, probably." It sure hadn't worked out for Freddie that I had gone so long without getting something to keep me from being spied on. "Who were the other two?" I asked, mostly since I was already brooding about the rising body count in this Case.

"Redtown scum," said Foster without a trace of hate or even disgust, like there was literally no other word to call those people. I'm hard on Redtowners but not that hard. "It looks like a robbery gone bad."

"Looks like, huh?" I lit a smoke. "What does it feel like?"

"Like they were here to do a murder and make it look like an icemold deal gone bad," said Foster promptly.

"Icemold?" I said, just as promptly. "That's crazy. Freddie was the kind of guy who kept water in his hip flask."

"Sure," said Foster, "but you never know with moldies, right? The family would be the first to want to keep it quiet that one of their kids was molding out. But yeah, they were here to murder. If you take a whiff of them – don't take a whiff, just take my word for it – you'll smell oil of epazote." I nodded. According to folklore (but not *the* Lore), epazote's good for fogging up detection spells; if you find the right herbalist, it even is. But it's expensive to make, so nobody wears it to a regular drug deal, even when they're dealing with a rich guy.

"So what happened to them?" I asked.

"Sr. Baldwin-Cuaron," said Lt. Foster. "He had a switch-sword; it looks like he flicked it open after they stabbed him in the gut, then started doing some stabbing of his own." Foster waved at the alley. "It all got messy after that."

I crouched, to get a closer look at one of the Redtowners. Yeah, that looked like a switch-sword slice, all right: straight as a line, and still smelling a little of burnt meat. "He have a permit for it?"

Foster snorted. "Yeah, right."

"You never know," I said. "Every so often, somebody in the nobility decides the law on magic weapons applies to them, too." Not that regular New Californians fall over themselves to obey those laws, either. And as long as the cops never have to *see* the weapons, nobody's going to make a point to enforce those laws. Everybody's got better things to do, right?

Lt. Foster stood over me, probably deliberately. "You want to give me a hint here, Shamus?" she asked. "The family's gonna want to know right away why one of their sprigs got trimmed down, and it'd be real nice if I didn't have to check and get back to them on that."

I conceded that Foster had a point. "It's to do with the Case, yeah," I said. "Kid had some information for me about it. I took the info, thanked him, and told him to keep his nose out of the rest of it. Guess he didn't listen to me."

"So you didn't tell him to keep digging?" asked Lt. Foster.

"Would I really do that, Lieutenant? Come on, you know me better than that. I wouldn't want Freddie here on my conscience." I stood up. "Guess I should have told him harder."

"So I can tell his family that at least he was doing the right thing?" asked Lt. Foster.

"Sure," I said. "For whatever good *that'll* do. You should also point out that he took two bad guys with him." The living call that sort of thing 'dying well'; the dead never say if they agree.

CHAPTER ELEVEN
Connections and Warnings

"A word, Shamus?" Foster said as they started loading corpses on the coroner's wagon.

"Sure," I said as we moved to a corner. I offered her a smoke; she took it. "And I'm guessing that the word ain't 'Nebraska'."

"First off, I'm just passing this on," Foster said, and I almost groaned. When somebody says that, it never ends well for your digestion. "But the word from around the Castle is, you don't like the Ambassador for the murder?"

"I ain't cleared him completely yet," I admitted, "but unless he's suddenly allowed to just throw demons around, then yeah."

"What does that mean for the Case, Shamus?"

I looked at her. "It means I probably won't end up pinning the crime on the Ambassador. But it's still a Case, Lieutenant. It ends when it ends."

"Well," Foster said, "some people might want to tell you to take it a little easy, now that the prime suspect ain't one anymore. And some people might even suggest that this Case of yours might be better off going Cold." She ground out her cigarette with one sensible boot. "But me?" she went on, "I'm not dumb enough to tell a Shamus what to do with his Case, especially when it's just some Castle flunky who wants me to do the chiming in. You have a good evening, Tom."

After she left, I looked at the crime scene again. Part of me hated doing it, because part of me loved doing it, too. Murder! Mystery! And now the Castle sticking its nose in! This was what Shamuses were for.

If only three more people weren't dead.

#

It was getting towards evening, so I decided to get in some background research about Wolfie before I grabbed a little shut-eye. And I *really* needed a distraction. Which is why I naturally and inevitably found myself at the *Puerta Verde*. The bouncer raised an eyebrow – but my Shamus suit got me in, and a suitable amount of the King's retainer even got me a respectful nod as I entered one of the five best modeling agencies in Cin City.

What? If you want to know a man, or even a Dominion mage, you go talk to his regular hookers. And if he doesn't have any, or doesn't care, that tells you something, too.

Trixie and Slye were starting to get a bit old for the Life; old enough by now to own their own shares in the *Puerta Verde*. But they knew what they had, and they still knew how to make it move. I was flattered that they even went to the trouble to try and vamp me after I sat down at their table. They were just being polite, but politeness counts for a lot.

"Buy us a drink, sailor?" said Trixie. She was the brunette.

"It's me, Trixie. I bought the whole bottle. The real stuff, so don't splutter when you drink it." The girls usually just drink colored water; they're not there to get drunk with the johns.

"Big spender," purred Slye from behind me. She was the redhead. "Who's signing off on the expense account?"

"The Castle, girls, and they paid in advance." That got their attention, and made them all business. Well, all another business. Not the one they were actually in. And I noted they weren't real surprised to be suddenly talking politics, either.

Trixie said, "All right, Shamus. You have our attention. What do you need?"

"Nothing much, just some information. You two have the Dominion embassy contract, right?" The look of disgust flitting through both confirmed that, sure enough. "Yeah, thought so. The things we all do for the realm, huh?"

"Hey, you're welcome to switch jobs with us and see if you can still say that," said Slye, and fairly waspishly.

I put up my hands. "Ladies, you don't want to see some of the crap still stuck in my head, either. Trust me. I gather the Ambassadors were both monstrous?"

That got a shrug from Slye. "Kind of. Cackle was an old fart, and that's usually not too bad. A lot of 'em are just happy to be there and able to contribute, you know what I mean?"

"Not quite at that stage yet, Slye." I responded, almost cheerfully.

"Stop it, Shamus. But Cackle just didn't like girls." Slye frowned. "Okay, he liked to screw girls. He'd have us both, once a week, regular as clockwork, but it was all real mechanical. He enjoyed it, but he didn't even care if we were awake for most of it."

"And he barely talked to us at all," Trixie chimed in. "We had his contract for five years, and in all that time he'd never even call us names. It was weird. He'd been paying out a lot of money for that servicing contract; a lot of guys like to get their money's worth by chattering on about their day or whatever. Not old Cackle, though."

"Dominion mages aren't exactly what you'd call raised right," I said. "Speaking of which: you two are talking pretty openly about him. The geas put on you by Cackle break?" Technically, that's not supposed to happen at all to a New Californian. In practical terms: the Castle would do something if the Dominion ambassador suddenly had a dead hooker to deal with, but if it's just a *spell* keeping the hooker from gossiping on the Ambassador? Well, that's not a fight the Castle wants to have. It's all part of the balancing act.

Trixie was shaking her head, though. "He never geased us at all. Cackle never seemed to care about what we'd say about him." She frowned. "But the new ambassador didn't care, either."

"So the new guy did keep up the contract?" That was what I had figured, coming into this conversation. But the two of them were now talking like it was all over and done with.

"Yup," said Slye. "We went in the week after the switch-over, same as always. And I mean just the same as always. Okay, the new Ambassador was younger, so he managed to get going a little more often. But he didn't give a damn about us, either. Didn't bother to try and geas us, didn't make any kind of blood-curdling threats, didn't even try to stiff us of our fees. Just paid out the money and said he'd let us know if our services were required in the future."

"But the retainer's still getting paid out," interjected Trixie.

"Yeah. We're on call, in case the new guy wants us. But I don't think that he does, really." Slye shrugged. "One session was enough, I guess. It was enough for us, that's for sure."

"Huh." I knew better than to ask a Cin City hooker why a john would bother with sex at all, under those conditions. She'd gleefully go ahead and tell you, and sometimes use little diagrams or marionettes, just to really ram her points home. But I was getting a feel for both Cackle and Wolfie here, and there was something off about them both. "How did either Ambassador treat you two? Were they ever nasty when they felt like it, held a grudge over little things, stuff like that?"

Trixie and Slye looked at each other, then started to shake their heads no. "No, not really," said Trixie. "Cackle would be rude, sometimes, but it was never personal. He didn't care enough about us to be nasty."

Slye jumped in. "But the weird thing was, he didn't care about himself, either. He'd always have a scrape or burn somewhere that he'd just shrug off until it hurt too much or got inflamed, then he'd just magic it away. Did he act like we were meat? Sure – but sometimes it was like he was just screwing us because he was meat, too."

And that wasn't just unusual. It was worryingly bizarre, coming from a Dominion mage. Those guys are all convinced that the universe exists to please them. Plus, Dominion mages more or less hate everybody else, including their countrymen. But it's a personalized, cultivated kind of hate. You'd think that either one of these guys would have loved to let a couple of Cin City hookers know their place in the world (at least, compared to a Dominion ambassador's), but apparently they had other things to do.

I was starting to wonder what was so messed up about these two ambassadors that the Dominion was willing to pack them off to foreign lands, hopefully forever. I somehow doubted it was because either was full of the milk of human kindness. The Dominion would've just squeezed out all the milk and used it to make cheese.

I put some simoleons on the table. "For your time, gals. And a bit extra to not talk about this." Slye looked affronted, but I stopped her before she could talk. "I know, you two are just doing your patriotic duty by talking to the Shamus about a Castle Case. But don't talk about it even after all of this hits the papers. Hell, you two go to the Syndicate and tell them I sent you to get your nails done." If anybody found out that Trixie and Slye hadn't actually been geased, they might be tempted to snatch 'em and grab 'em for info. The Syndicate would probably also try to get dirt on a couple of Dominion ambassadors, but they'd pay well for the privilege.

"Sure, Shamus," Trixie said as she made the bills disappear. "Tomorrow fine?"

"Tonight would be better. Don't run, but–" This time, Slye interrupted me.

"Relax, Shamus. Trixie and me, we got signed up by Castle Security when we took the servicing contract. I'll get our handler to run us over to the right people after our shift's done."

"Nice of him to be on call like this."

"You mean, nice of us," giggled Trixie.

#

Later that night, while I was in the middle of staring at things and trying to make them into clues, there came a knocking, knocking on my office door. I looked up, and blinked at the shadow; it wasn't a raven. In fact, whoever was out there blocked most of the light from the hallway. Before I could tell him that the door was open, he figured it out for himself.

The lummox lumbered into the room, practically sideways, and everything about him screamed *sicario*, foreign edition. This one was a ken barbie, so freshly down from Old California that his tan was noticeably lighter where his old tribe's zinc-oxide face-paint used to be. Even with the pattern, I couldn't tell what tribe he was from (barbies all look alike to

New Californians), but it favored two-handed mauls. The one strapped on his back would wreck the room just from being drawn. Whoever the ken worked for had managed to get him to shave, wear a shirt and jacket, and put his blond-at-the-roots hair in a scalp-lock; but from the waist down he was pure Old Californian loincloth and heavy-boot barbie.

"You Tom Shamus?" he asked. Hick-thick accent and I got the feeling his conversation couldn't fly too much higher above the ground than this. I sighed, but inside where he couldn't see. There were expectations on how a Shamus was supposed to crack wise in this kind of scene, and I didn't much want him cracking me afterward.

"That's my name on the door, *vecino*. Shelled out for the extra glitter, too." For a wonder, it didn't set him off. Guess they still teach people to read, up there.

But they'd lost the idea of charm schools, looks like. "You come with me," he said. "Now."

"What, at this time of night? The horsebusses don't run no more, and my feet are tired. Come back tomorrow and we'll go in style."

One of the ken's fists came down and broke a coffee mug. He had tough hands, I noted unhappily; at least, there was no blood. "No. Now, Tom Shamus." Well, it was going to be like that, then? I stood up.

"I said tomorrow. You can wait in the lobby. Or go find a bridge to hide under and jump out at travelers. Amscray, ken." That got his attention. You have be a very stupid barbie to not hear what a New Californian puts into the word 'ken.' Or 'barbie.' And the barbies don't really love us, either. So I wasn't really surprised when he started bellowing like a bull and tried to rush me.

How do you fight a guy bigger and stronger than you? It helps if you have a weapon. It helps a lot more if you keep your stupid Shamus mouth shut and don't start the fight. But if you're on the short end of that, it helps to be faster. I was maybe a little faster. Fast enough to move out of his way and let him smack into the desk, at least.

That jacket probably had a kidney belt underneath it and that loincloth definitely hid a cup, so I settled for a quick one-two behind the ear. By the time he blinked that off, I had pulled the crossbow from the place I stashed it and had the quarrel aimed right at his gut. The ken froze. Guess they still have those up there, too.

"What part of 'amscray' didn't you hear, *amigo*? Get out of here, and come back in the morning. Say 'please' and 'thank you.' Then I'll think about coming along like a good boy."

A voice from behind me cleared his throat; I carefully did not jump at the sound. I'm kind of proud of that. "Regretfully, Shamus, it simply cannot wait."

#

I turned my head just enough to see who was leaning in the doorway, exhaled angrily when I saw who it was, and took the quarrel out of the groove. "What the hell, Sam! Did you want me to shoot him?"

Big-Eye Sam benignly looked over the scene. Behind him in the hallway were two more kens, only dressed more civilized and maybe even owning something like a sense of humor. "No, I just wanted to see what you'd do. And what our new associate here would do, given his head."

"A test, huh? Guess he failed?" I said.

"Not yet," Sam smiled past me. I turned to look, to see the ken standing there. He was carefully not making any movements, even though nobody was actually aiming anything pointy at him.

"You a boxer?" the ken rumbled. He made little fist motions, to show what he meant.

I nodded. "Used to be. Years ago."

He smiled at that. "No hard feelings, then." The ken offered a hand; I took it. It was civil enough.

"Jimmy," said Sam, "Why don't you go downstairs and check on the carriage? This ain't the best neighborhood." My ken – I guess his name was Jimmy – went down, readily enough.

Sam turned to me after the ken lumbered down the stairs. "Hey! He passed. Send me a bill for the desk."

"And an hour of my time. And the coffee mug. And that's going to be on top of paying for whatever the Frog wants from me."

"Oh, so you *are* coming, Shamus? I was about to say 'please' and 'thank you'."

"Yeah, yeah, lemme get my hat. If Kermie the Frog wants to see me, I guess I had better be seen."

#

Everybody knows where Kermie the Frog hangs his slicker: down underneath the Elhai docks, for the sake of his delicate complexion. And by 'everyone,' I include especially our loyal and hard-working constabulary. Knowing makes it so much easier for them to get their weekly payoffs.

Kermie first showed up about twenty, twenty-five years ago. He was just one more moth, attracted to the bright lights of Cin City; only this moth came ready to carve out a giant hunk out of the underworld, so that he and his new 'Adventurers' Guild' could burrow inside. I was just getting to be a grown-up at that point (hah!), so like Leila and the Syndicate, I just heard all the stories afterward. The kind that are too crazy not to be true.

But I wasn't worried, even as Sam and his brute squad brought me down to meet their boss. For one thing, I had no current beef with the Guild and they didn't have one with me. They did their business outside of Cin City, and little of it had to do with me anyway.

Hell, the Adventurers' Guild only stayed in the shadows here to keep their own magic-users safe. And to avoid paying taxes, past the usual bribes to everybody from the king on down. And to *not* answer questions about whether all the stuff they acquired was gotten legally, or peacefully, or safely. And to not have to explain why all those deaths out in the countryside actually *weren't* murders – fine, they were criminals. Just very specialized criminals who left innocent people alone. Since my conscience was clear, that was one reason for me not to be nervous. And there was another, too.

As was his wont, I found Kermie the Frog stretched out in a steaming mud bath while various nubile maidens of assorted species poured water over him. His batrachian eyes focused on me and blinked once, slowly, as we made our way over the catwalk. By now I was familiar enough with him not to shudder at the two saws that made up his smile.

"Glad you could drop in, ayuh." Kermie's accent wasn't like the Yankee ones in the Lore; but then, the Lore often exaggerates. "Take a chair and stay a bit."

I sat. Kermie's people are the last remnants of the Old Americans, over on the East Coast, and they got pretty thoroughly cursed by the Universal Dominion a few centuries back. As I heard it, there had been a few wars, and the Dominion was not *quite* sure that they could conquer the Atlantic Coast, so they expanded west, instead. Lucky us, hey? But the Dominion never forgets a grudge, and if they weren't powerful enough to conquer the Old Americans the Dominion was willing to settle for being utter bastards.

In this case, the idea behind the curse was to turn half of the East Coasters into ravenous carrion-eaters, and half into rutting frog-man hybrids, but apparently the spells didn't take quite right. Kermie, for example, was a vaguely frog-like humanoid with functioning gills, a taste for high humidity, and a rather larger taste for female company. Compared to some of the highlights of Cin City's lowlifes, he was pretty damned tame. And he hated the Universal Dominion. Which the rest of us all did, too; but Kermie was so reliable about it you could use him to reset your clocks.

None of this meant that Kermie the Frog wouldn't have his men take me out and beat me to a pulp, if he thought it had to be done. But since I was a Shamus, he'd have to have a good reason for it, and my conscience was as clean as it ever was. Nothing worth dragging me down here just to get a good look at me first, at least.

Kermie leaned back in his bath; at his muttered "All right,

ladies," the maidens started traipsing out, presumably to the showers. No giggling, though. I was mildly disappointed; they're supposed to giggle. The Guild boss shrugged. "They're tired. The girls were up past their bedtimes." He added. "You're late."

"Sorry, Mr. Kermie," I replied. As usual, Kermie's chairs were almost indecently comfortable. "My invitation must have gotten lost in the mail."

Sam spoke up; he was sitting, and fiddling with a carafe of what smelled, wonderfully, of coffee. He passed me a cup and went on, "My fault, Boss. I was going to bring him around directly last night, but the Producer was there and we had to dance around her guards." We all chuckled at the thought of two sets of mooks trying to not officially notice the other, and I sipped my coffee. I was not shocked that it was just the way I like it, and it was perfect. The Adventurers' Guild acquires a lot for resale, but it keeps the best for itself.

Like a good host, Kermie waited until I was outside my first cup before he started the talky-talk. "Let's just get down to it, Shamus. I called you in about the girl's murder. A bad business, that. Very bad. And very bad *for* business."

I carefully put the cup down, and turned up the Shamus accent because Kermie was an immigrant and they like that. "Look, Kermie. Lemme lay this out for you. I already got the Castle yapping at me that they're *very concerned* about the case, and tomorrow I figure I'm gonna get waylaid again and told the same thing by the ATSE. I mean nothing but respect, but whaddya going to tell me that's gonna get me more on the Case?"

Kermie coughed a chuckle. "Heh! You get that many people sticking their spoon in your stewpot, Shamus?"

"Assuming that's not some Yankee dirty talk? Yeah. Everybody always wants to tell me how important a Case is. Just before they tell me how they can't help any. I could put it to music and sing it in bars."

"Fair enough, Shamus. Fair enough. Although Leila helped you out, hey?" I smiled and raised the mug at him in respect for his spies. Assuming Leila Parson didn't just tell him all the latest news, over crab cakes or something. Kermie went on, "Turns out, though, I do have something for you. Got a kid just off of the boat, knows a thing or two about getting into and out of places he shouldn't. Should be right helpful to you."

"Just off the boat, huh? From where? And does he have any papers out on him?"

Kermie waved a webbed hand. "He's from east of here. Pretty damn far east. And if there are papers, they're not in Spanglish or Court English. But aren't you going to ask me why I'm giving you a thief?"

I was honestly chagrined. "Sorry, dammit. I hate missing the straight line. Okay, I'll bite: why do I need a spy from the Adventurers' Guild? Sorry – a 'partner'."

That got another wet chuckle. "Why, for when you break into the Dominion embassy." Kermie made it sound like the most natural response in the world, too. It almost convinced me.

But not quite. "Kermie. Do I look like a suicide? Or somebody who would let somebody else jump into a watermill? The Dominion has traps! Good traps. The kind that make people forget you ever existed. Besides, what would I even want in there?"

"The evidence that the ambassador killed that girl."

"I ain't sure that he did, Kermie."

"Really? He confessed it to you in public." Idly, I wondered who Kermie's source was. But it could be anybody: the guards, the doc, Dory via one of her spies, a spirit in the room. People like to talk to Kermie, and not just because he pays well for the privilege of listening. It's a knack that most Adventurers have, and Kermie has more of it than anybody else. One reason why nobody minds that the Guild's run by, honestly, a frog-man with razor-sharp teeth.

"Yeah, he did," I said. "But then I got hit with a sand-devil later on. You know what that means, right?"

Kermie indeed did, and he didn't like it. He absently gestured with his cup; Sam moved pretty quickly to fill it up. Kermie sipped, and said, "He still confessed, though."

"He's got an angle about that, I figure. Everybody always does." *Including you,* I thought. There had to be a reason why Kermie was palming off a spy on me. "Maybe he's trying to make a splash with the Castle, taking advantage of the murder to scare them into giving him stuff. I'm still working that part out," I confessed, both to him and myself. There was something there that I was missing. "But even if Wolfie did do it, I don't know why Eliz– Ms. Hernandez got killed. If I know why, I'll know how, and then I'll know who. But I don't see how risking deathtraps in a wizard's lair is gonna get me to 'why'."

"Fair enough, Shamus. You're still getting the kid, though. Sneaking and picking locks just ain't your style."

I decided to let that slide. I was having trouble deciding if I liked all the cooperation I was getting in this Case so far; it was a refreshing change, but nothing comes for free and I figured that Kermie wanted something. On the other hand, Kermie was telling the stone-cold truth about this, at least: I don't pick locks. Maybe having a spy along might be handy.

CHAPTER TWELVE
Smooth Operator

The next morning, I bit back a snarl as I met my pet spy. Or thief. Hell, call Lucas B. Coltrane a 'rogue.' Kermie had forgotten to mention a crucial detail about the kid. Specifically, his ears.

If Lucas had just gotten off the boat, it had sailed through Grand Panama first – and how an elf managed to sail all the way from the Atlantic Coast to here without getting hanged as a pirate was probably a great story, assuming I could believe a word of it. Lucas had the friendly smile of somebody who would steal your back teeth and then put them back, just to show you he could, and if I had a daughter I would have forbidden him to stay in the same town with her. Which wouldn't have made a difference anyway. Kid had that look.

We don't get many elves in Cin City. The ones who do show up find a disguise, real quick. The Dominion thinks they're all magical enough to be worth enslaving, which is why most elves still live in the swamps east of the Mississippi, where at least they know all the good hiding spots. On the other hand, elves have a longstanding contest with Yankees like Kermie over who hates the Dominion more. So does what's left of Deseret. And what's left of Sonora. And, hell, New California. For the Universal Dominion, making friends is what other people do.

The kid looked skinny, so we retreated to Garapenna's where I interrogated him between bites. I had to admit, Kermie had found me a live one. I know enough of the patter to tell a real rogue from a fake, and this kid had the knowledge and the reflexes. And not just mentally. Lucas had steady hands, and fast; I wouldn't let him dip a pouch or two to demonstrate, so he just grabbed a fly out of the air instead. Sure, Lucas was never going to look or sound like a native, but with something to disguise his features, he'd be able to fake being a refugee from Sonora, or maybe one of the clans from Old California. You get a lot of weird accents in Cin City, these days. And closed mouths about why they came here.

I just didn't know what to do with him. I wasn't gonna break into Wolfie's house, that was for sure. Lucas didn't have any ideas on the Case, either. Although he knew more of the Lore than I'd thought.

"Don't you pee-eyes do disguises? I could do disguises." I was starting to think elves had hollow legs; he had already put away two *chilaquiles* and was on his third plate. "Spy on the crooks that way! Just like Batman!"

That got me blinking. Guess Lucas's swamps weren't completely barbarian after all. But: "Nah, we don't do disguises," I said. "Shamuses can't use 'em; we ain't lucky that way."

"Lucky?"

"Best word I got for it. Bottom line is, a Shamus tries to dress up like somebody else, it always gets figured out. And then things get complicated."

"Okay. Guess it's a hoodoo thing." I figured 'hoodoo' meant magic, but didn't feel like straightening him out about that. "So, you don't need a sneak, don't need a dipper, don't need a locksmith; what do you need?"

"Damned if I know, Lucas. I got a full day of walking around ahead of me – hey, you paying attention?" Lucas was kind of staring into space at that point; I wondered if he was thinking, or just about to burp. Guess it was the first one, because he snapped out of it.

"Yeah. Sorry, what?"

"I said I got a full day of walking around. I don't know how you're supposed to help with that either, kid." I made sure not to say 'You'll get underfoot.' Wasn't Lucas's fault: he had skills, just not ones to bring to this Case. No need to rub his face in it.

"Yeah," Lucas said. "Tell you what, Shamus: lemme give you my address. I'll swing by the office every morning, and if you need me for something, I'll do it. And if you need me other times, have somebody get me. That work for you?"

"For me? Sure. What about Kermie?" I had gotten the feeling that Lucas was paying off a marker by helping me. But Lucas just shook his head.

"Nah, the Frog won't croak over this. You'll see." Lucas got up, actually dropped a couple of simoleons on the table to cover his breakfast, and left. I was touched – and wondered whose pouch he'd dipped them out of.

#

I finished my own breakfast and started running down addresses. I'm not gonna lie: legwork is the biggest part of being a Shamus, and the part of the job nobody wants to hear about. Hell, I don't want to do it, either. But it's got to be done, because Cases don't clear themselves. You just gotta get used to the idea that mostly, legwork doesn't pan out.

Like that morning. I had gotten ten, maybe fifteen names and addresses off of Elizabeth's correspondence, and struck out at every one. At least, none of them were secret mages, or started babbling about cults and conspiracies while I was there. Most of 'em didn't even really know the victim; Cin City is a town where you can shop at the same store all your life and never connect with the other shoppers. Or even want to. I had high hopes for the bookseller that had made up a lot of her correspondence, but it turned out Elizabeth just ordered from their annual catalog and paid by mail. Nobody even recognized her last name.

I was puzzling over that when I suddenly felt someone far too close behind me, a whispered "keep walking!" hissed in my ear – and, most importantly, the prick of a knife-tip somewhere dangerous on my back. So I kept walking; the hand now on my shoulder gave a heavy hint that I should duck into an alleyway, once one came up, and when I started moving there the hint became a shove clearly meant to knock me around a little.

I did box, back in the day. I know how to stay on my feet. And I also know a knife don't make you brave, but it can make you and the other guy dead. So I decided to not do anything stupid, at least until the guy was done talking. I figured that there'd be talking, first. It's a thing, with thugs that get sent to 'give you a message.' Kind of like a ritual, but with not so much incense.

So, yeah, me making assumptions meant that I almost died right there. Because this guy, he didn't bother jawing; once we were out of sight of the public he went right in for the kill. But he wasn't really good with that knife, so we were even on the first dance. I got a slice on the arm for my troubles; he got a trashcan in the face.

Didn't stop him, though. Oh, I bet it hurt. For damned sure the slice was painful, in a way that it shouldn't have been. But this mook didn't care about the pain. He got up *way* too fast for my liking.

The guy lunged again, clumsy enough for me to try shoving him into the wall, face first. It didn't quite work; the bastard didn't even lose his knife. But I got so close I could smell the icemold on his breath. Guess that's why he wasn't feeling the pain; you need to do a lot to make a moldie say ouch. But I was willing to try: I hate icemold. I don't feel too friendly about anybody who licks it, either.

At this point we were grappling for the knife, and I almost thought I heard a giggle as the two of us bounced around the alleyway like the pinball machine at the Royal Museum. I was mad and he was crazy; I don't know who would have won that fight. But I didn't have to, because all of a sudden the moldie's face went slack as a bag of alchemist's goop smacked him in the temple. Based on the sudden numbness from the drops that hit my hand, it was one of the knockout goops. Not even icemold can fight those; the mook dropped like a stone.

A second later, Lucas descended from the top of the roof, half-leaping, half-bouncing off various fire escapes and pipes and whatnot. His landing was as graceful as the fall, damn the show-off. And from his grin, the elf knew it. "Guess I know what you need me for after all, Shamus," he said.

"Yeah, yeah, don't rub it in." I was already going through the moldie's pouches and pockets, looking for clues. And wincing a little. "How did you figure I needed another angel?"

Lucas had retrieved the knife, and was treating it surprisingly gingerly. Or maybe not too surprising; that thing didn't look too healthy. Neither did my arm, where it had sliced me. "This is a rough city, I hear," said Lucas. "I figured somebody might try to mug you."

I stopped what I was doing, looked at him, then reminded myself that Lucas was a foreigner. "Kid. I'm a Shamus. We don't get mugged."

"Yeah, right. Nobody's that loved."

"Who said I was loved? I stick my nose into a lot of places, find out things people don't want found out. A lot of them take issue with that. I've had fists, knives, axes, bows, and one time the bitey end of a dog pointed in my face, and more fights than I can remember. But I don't get mugged. Not in Cin City."

"But people will try to knife you?"

"What? Oh, yeah, sure. That's normal. It just means that I'm on the right track in a Case."

"This town is weird," Lucas muttered. He finished wrapping the knife in a cloth, being careful not to touch it with his bare hands. "You got a priest handy that can bless stuff, Shamus?"

"What? That knife hot?"

"Not as bad as it could be, but if you got stuck with it, we shouldn't mess around with just bandages."

I closed my eyes, put my hand on the butt of my gun, and poked around a little inside my head, trying to figure out if I could ride out the spiritual infection on my own. Didn't like the answer. "Yeah," I said aloud, opening my eyes. "We're gonna have to get a specialist for this. I know a priest, though. He'll work it out."

"Great. So what's with *this* guy?" asked Lucas, prodding the passed-out moldie. "You know him? He on something?" Great, aside from everything else, Lucas had 'Adventurer' written all over him. They just love the thrill.

"Never saw him before in his life, and yeah, he's on something. Icemold." I waved around a small vial of the stuff I had found on the goon; it was well-sealed or I wouldn't have touched it. "A drop of it, you think you're immortal. Ten drops, your heart explodes." I looked at Lucas. "The cops in this town, they don't play nice with anybody caught with it." I didn't say that went double for foreigners, but I figured Lucas could work that out on his own. "Other than that, he's got nothing on him. No papers, no cash, not even a nichols for the horsebus."

"Guess we wait for him to wake up, then ask him?" Lucas's thought was a good one, if only we weren't in the middle of an alley in the less nice part of town. Despite what I said before, if a local lowlife decided that I was running a Case on him, he might start something. I didn't feel like having to waste time straightening it out. Besides, I had an excuse.

"Not with that knife still ticking." Don't ask me why it's supposed to tick. Ask the Lore. "We'll just go see that priest I know."

"What about the crazy guy?" Lucas asked. "He evil enough?" The tone in Lucas's voice settled it: kid was a paid-up Adventurer. If I said 'yes,' he'd slit the guy's throat with his own knife and sleep like a baby afterward. Adventurers weren't *psycho*. Just really, really us-and-them.

So I was firm. "No. I don't have time for the paperwork. But give me your knife." When he gave me one, I used it to hack a lock of hair off the mook. "Just in case he decides on a rematch. Now let's get to Father Mike's." I was looking forward to that, actually.

CHAPTER THIRTEEN
Evil Is Bad, Okay?

Funny thing; months can go by without me seeing Father Mike, and here I was, twice in two days. Maybe I should leave a toothbrush here. Or just make him give me receipts; in the end, the Castle pays up pretty good – for royalty – but only if you remind them. They're always happy to take your taxes, though.

Mike was doing something fiddly with a tent pole when we showed up at St. Phil's. Probably for the soup kitchen. Mike's feeding enough people these days, on what little he can find, to impress even his own God.

I wondered if Mike would probably smell the knife on us, and it turned out he did; the way he squeezed a bend in the pole with his bare hand was a surprise, though. Him swinging around looking for something to hit wasn't a surprise at all. That's apparently an orc reflex. They're not real big on evil magic. Go figure, huh?

"Hey, hey!" I yelled, gingerly waving my hands around. "It's fine, Mike. It's fine! We just need this thing made safe, all right?" Damn, this knife was worse than no-fooling demon sand? Maybe I should just run in and get my holy-water shower out of the way.

Mike was already relaxing. He looked down at the pole he'd just squeezed into something like a bat. Mike sighed. "It's only going to be safe when it's destroyed, Tom. And what is it?"

"It's a knife. Well, it looks like a knife. I'm great with you taking it apart, Mike. I get queasy just looking at it, too." Mike frowned, looking at my sleeve. "Yeah," I went on, "and it got a slice in. Not real bad, but I want to know what cut me. And I figure you'll be able to get more out of where it came from than I can." I ain't much for modesty, but I don't know more than a specialist. Mike was a specialist.

"All right, then." Mike looked at Lucas. "Afternoon, Mister?"

"Lucas Coltrane, Father. Pleased to meet you. I'm here to

bail him out" – he aimed a thumb and a grin my way – "when he starts getting stabbed with evil hell-knives."

"What? Why? You lose a bet, Mr. Coltrane?"

"Nope. And 'Mr. Coltrane' is my uncle. I'm just Lucas."

I looked at the two of them, being all perfectly friendly. I wasn't expecting a no-fooling fight to break out, but – "What's with you two?"

They both stopped moving towards the church to look at me. "Not sure what you mean, Shamus," responded Mike. "Something I missed?"

"I guess. You know. Elf? Orc?" I gestured, helplessly. "The Lore?"

"What is the Lore, anyway?" asked Lucas – of Mike, I saw. "I keep hearing about it from people here."

"Long story, Lucas. Literally. Some places have libraries. Cinderella has the Lore." Mike turned to me. "Only the Lore isn't always right, Tom."

"Okay, okay." I didn't feel like arguing with him over that. The Lore is always right – just sometimes it's just written down wrong. "So, I guess then that orcs and elves aren't at each other's throats on sight?"

That got a harsh laugh from Lucas. "Hell, no. He ain't no Dominion mage, right?"

"Likewise. And don't swear. This is a church."

"Sorry, Father."

#

Fifteen minutes later, and the embarrassment over my assumptions about elves and orcs was already starting to fade. That's the thing about being a Shamus; you're always wrong, until you're suddenly right. You get used to it.

The slice on my arm didn't need more than a stitch or two, physically. The praying was a bit more involved this time, and included a couple in Latin that felt extra tingly on my skin. That wasn't fun, but it was better than the incense-and-chanting that I was expecting but knew better than to ask for – and sure did a business on the nastiness in my arm, which was a relief.

So now the three of us were around Mike's working table, the one he wouldn't feel bad about losing if a spell of his went wrong. Not that Mike used magic, either. Nah, he just called upon his god to help out with things, and his god is a soft touch about that. Well, every faith tradition's different, hey?

From the way he was looking at the knife – now safely suspended over a pot of steaming holy water – I still had Lucas pegged for being a mage himself, only he wasn't all that trained in it. I'd heard that most elves were like that; they *could* be mages, but a lot of them didn't want to do it, thanks to the damned Universal Dominion. I swear, everybody on the continent has a grudge against those guys. If we could only get everybody to swing at them at the same time, the Dominion would go down, hard. Good luck having that happen this century, though. Or the next.

Mike's way of examining the knife was interesting: some book-searching, a little use of incense (Ha! Finally), and a whole lot of praying out loud and muttering what I assumed were more prayers, only ones that the heathens in the room shouldn't be hearing. As if I could use them anyway. But whatever he was doing, the knife didn't like it. Every time he chanted something in what I guess was Ancient Latin, the knife would jerk on its string, just like it was trying to get away.

It was also getting a certain amount of rust on its blade from the steaming holy water, even as I watched. "What's going on there?" I asked. "Is that normal?"

"Sort of," said Mike. "The evil in the blade's been spelled to obscure itself. But it doesn't have enough to do that and also reverse the rust from the holy water." I opened my mouth to ask Mike whether that meant he was torturing the evil knife, but I didn't follow through. I mean, what was I going to do if he said that yes, he was?

After a few minutes of the inquisition, Mike finally stopped. "Well," he said, "it's not a Dominion blade." I was both disappointed and unsurprised as he said, "Too much Infernalism in it."

"Infernalism?" asked Lucas. "That what you call Satanspawn here?"

"Probably," said Mike. "Your folk Christians, Lucas?"

"Well," Lucas said, and nothing else.

"If I was going to have a problem about you being a pagan," said Mike, "you wouldn't be in here."

"Fair enough, Father. Fair enough. Nah, my own folks aren't Christians, but we know plenty who are. And for sure there's a Devil." Lucas kind of shuddered. "You learn that fast, out in the swamps. You learn that real fast."

I was taking notes. "So, demonic blade? That fits with the sand-devil." I swallowed the swear I was going to use and came out with a tepid, "Gee, I really want Wolfie to be guilty."

"He's guilty of something, Tom."

"It's not the same, Mike. And aren't we all supposed to be guilty of something?"

"Some work at it more than others."

True, that. I looked more closely at the knife. It was bad steel, double-edged, with grooves down the middle. The hilt was wrapped in some kind of leather that I really didn't want to touch, and there was a hooked pommel of either wood or bone, worn smooth and shapeless – and the whole thing made my eyes itch if I looked at it for too long.

I couldn't tell if the scratchings on the blade meant anything, since people write using the goofiest alphabets these days. It was funny: the knife looked cheap, like it was made some primitive smith who didn't even have a drop forge. And it wasn't really that powerful. But the damned thing made up for it by being pure meanness and spite.

I figured that I knew, but I asked anyway. This is why I had gotten an expert. "What were the spells on this, Mike?"

"The usual. Bleeding, blood poisoning, lasting pain; after getting stabbed with this you should have been knocked out from all the yelling and throwing up by now. But the knife is weak."

"Drained recently?" For a moment, I thought that we had the murder weapon – only, no, we had found the knife that had killed Elizabeth on the scene. Mike was shaking his head anyway.

"No, it's just not that powerful. Normally, something with these spells would be so nasty that I'd have to break out the consecrated oil and do a full exorcism, and I might even have had to call in the bishop if you hadn't gotten here soon enough. But this thing? It's such a paltry little piece of evil." Mike looked at it. "In fact, do you have everything you need from it?"

"I dunno. Do I, Father?"

"I can't get more off of it, and I can't trace it back to the diabolist who made it. More bad enchanting; a better artifact would hold an impression better." Mike looked offended at that, like it was an attack on the art of enchanting itself to make a weapon too crappy to be tracked.

But I didn't have anything more, and Lucas made an expressive shrug when I looked at him. So I just said, "Wreck it then, Mike."

"With pleasure." Mike untied the cord holding the knife over the pot and carefully lowered the knife into the holy water. The sound we all heard only confirmed what Mike'd said: it just should have been *louder* as the evil was overwhelmed once and for all. 'Paltry little piece,' yeah.

"Well, that's the knife." Mike's voice grew a little harder. "What about the hair, Shamus?"

"What about it?" I won't say that I was defensive. Much.

"The hair you took off of the guy, instead of having him arrested."

"Or killed," Lucas said helpfully. Mike gave him an epic orcish side-eye; Lucas looked aggrieved. "What? Fella had an evil demonic knife. You can absolutely kill those on sight."

"He was unconscious!" I said.

"What, you're not as evil when you're asleep?"

I decided to change the subject at that point. "I just grabbed it to clear the Case, Mike. When I need to track this goon again, the hair can lead me right to him. And if he comes after me, well, I have a bit of his hair, taken in a fight. That'll make it harder for him. But no black magic, no curses. I swear it, Father."

Mike knows that I don't swear lightly (I *profane* a lot, mind you). So he let it go. Reluctantly. So I pointed to the knife in the pot, before he started up again. "That good to go?"

"What, that? Sure. The holy water's killed all the spells by now. What do you need it for?"

I shrugged. "It's still a clue. I figured that I'd take it over to the University, see what the smart girls think of it. Maybe they can tell me where it's from."

Mike fished the knife out of the water. "Yes, it's dead. So, yes, that's a good idea. I wouldn't bother with the theology department, though. They'll just tell you what I did."

"Figured, Mike. I was going to go hit up Research Archeology. The tomb-looters know where all the weird stuff comes from."

"And sometimes they even know how to turn them off before things go boom," muttered Lucas. He saw us looking at him. "Oh, I could tell you stories."

I put on my hat. "Pick out the best ones. You can tell them on our way to the University."

#

Nothing tried to kill Lucas and me on our trip to midtown, which was nice. The farther north we went, the snazzier the view unscrolling past the horsebus windows got. Well, once we got past the docks, at least. I wouldn't say that Fond is a bad neighborhood. It's not like Hawaii is now, or Tourista's always been. But once we started to move through Vertigo and further uptown, things start getting flashier.

I wouldn't say prettier. In Vertigo, you pay your taxes, you don't cause trouble, you keep up with the Garcias, and you display your lack of taste whenever you can – because if you don't, your neighbors will. There's more 'salvaged' magic glow tubes and gaudy outdoor crap in Vertigo than anywhere in Galivant; the fad this year was for authentic Old American artificial

Christmas trees, and every damned yard had one. Complete with what their owners fondly thought were historically accurate Christmas tree ornaments.

Oh, well, antique dealers need to eat, too.

Hi ho, hi ho, back to school I go; I should buy a mug for my office, call myself an alumnus. On the other hand, the University of New California (Cinderella) is pretty nice. Peaceful, even. Brick and stone buildings, lots of lawns, architects who weren't drunk; if you squinted a little and tried not to hear what people were saying, you could even tell yourself that you were surrounded by sages and scholars, instead of old cranks and young wild-eyes. For a little while, at least.

The School for Research Archeology had an interesting place in the University hierarchy. Up until now, I had just assumed they were fronts for the Adventurers' Guild, but Lucas had set me a bit straight on that during the horsebus rides. "It's not that the Guild doesn't like their style, or so I'm told, but it's that, well, they get enthusiastic."

We were in the snazzy main foyer (Research Archeology may not be popular at faculty parties, but it's definitely rolling in cash) and walking to the stairs at that point, but I had to stop. "Enthusiastic," I deadpanned. "Really. Do tell."

Lucas snorted. "Yeah, yeah, laugh it up. But there's maximizing return from a dungeon extraction, and then there's zapping an Old American device with a lightning spell to see whether it'll turn on again. As we say back home, you know how to tell which guy's the RA?" At the shake of my head, he said, "He's the one whose last words were 'Hey, y'all, watch this!'" The elf looked happy that I laughed. Probably didn't expect me to get the joke. Which I didn't, really; but the way he told it was still funny.

"So," Lucas went on, "you think this professor of yours will give a line on the weapon?"

I waved it away. "Who, Sofie? Sure she will! She's top in her field. She'll take one look at it, maybe turn it over a couple of times, then tell us where it comes from, who made it, what's it used for, and whether the guy who made it is left-handed. She's just that good."

CHAPTER FOURTEEN
The Museum Things Belong In

Sofie looked at the blade, turned it over a couple times, shrugged a little and tossed it back on the table. "Well," she said, "it's a knife."

"No kidding?" I said as Lucas manfully tried to smother a laugh. "And here I was thinking that it was a scale model of Excalibur."

That earned me a chuckle from her, at least. Sofie – "Benefactor Sofia Huston Redgrave" to the Castle – may have been 100% New Californian high nobility to the bone, and particularly the blood, but she had her job despite her lofty status, not because of it. New Californians prefer it when the top-shelf nobles stick to being decorative; that way at least we know where they are, and what kind of trouble they'll be getting into.

I had gotten Sofie out of a little unofficial trouble a few years back; a little matter of a friend of hers getting caught up with a flimflam man who had a sideline in the illegal, but lucrative, trade of foreign slave exports. In between all the yelling and the ambushes in alleys and people being thrown through doors, the two of us discovered that we had hit it off. Since then, we had a deal: I would come by and tell Sofie non-boring things, in exchange for letting her buy the drinks and not have it mean anything.

We were in Sofie's combination study/artifact workspace, which was a nice combination of wood paneling, airy windows, and a tastefully boastful collection of certain items that she had personally looted from her expeditions. There were the obligatory crossed leaf-spring swords underneath an Old American stop-sign shield – I swear, somebody's churning them out in a shop somewhere – but the rest of it was more interesting. Shrunken-head, big-hair fetishes from the barbie tribes up in Old California, woven blankets showing feral chupacabras and odd saucer-like vehicles from what used to be Sonora, a collection of crumbling boards of Old American circuitry from the one military base dig Sofie managed to do up in the Cold-Lands; she had packed a lot of field work into only a couple of years. I wondered whether she missed the adventuring life. It seemed rude to ask, though.

I went on, "Seriously, Sofie. What can you tell us about the knife?"

"Well, it's obviously new. Not local, but you knew that. You said it was magical?" I nodded. "And vicious? Well, then. It's Haida."

I groaned; Lucas looked confused. I asked, "Are you sure, Sofie?"

"Well, if you like, I could go into the Adventurer's Stacks and search through forty shelves full of books of badly-drawn pictures of artifacts to confirm it," she said. Rather dryly. "Half of the pictures were drawn after the fact, and probably copied from some other Adventurer. Just be aware that the other half of the remainder will be hard to see through all the dried blood on the pages. Or you could take my word for it, Shamus. The design is obviously from the Pacific Northwest, and there's only one group up there that's cranking out evil knives and summoning demons."

"And that's the Haidan, right?" Lucas asked, too brightly.

Sofia gave him one look, then another, considerably more considering look, and responded a bit more warmly than I expected. "Haida, Mr. Coltrane. They're called the Haida."

Lucas gave her a charming smile. "My apologies, Professor. Clearly I have neglected to... **join the party**" – even I could hear the emphasis on what was clearly an Adventurer's Guild recognition signal – "and get up to speed on this."

"That's all right; that is why we have specialists in every field. I **like your shirt**, by the way. I have **one just like it**."

"**Close cover before striking!**" I muttered. When the two looked at me, I waved it away. "Sorry, literary reference. I was feeling left out of all the secret society stuff. Lucas, the Haida are those Commie lunatics up the Pacific. Way up the Pacific. The ones fighting the Canadians."

"Wait, what?" said Lucas. "The Canadians are fighting *kami*? Is 'kami' what you guys call the Universal Dominion?"

I had to think about it for a second. "No, you're thinking of the *east* Canadians. The Haida are fighting the *west* Canadians. And it's 'Commies,' not whatever 'kami' are."

"I'll– you know, I'll just take your word for it," said Lucas. "So the Haida are bad guys, then?"

"You could say that," replied Sofie. "The Haida are raiders and pirates and slavers. They're nastier about it than they have to be, too. Their magical practices can be best described as a cesspool. About the only nice thing about them is that there aren't many Haida, and Free Canada does its best to keep it that way."

Lucas picked up the knife. "Feels like a blade for murder, even without the spells. Their mages are also assassins?"

"Yeah," I replied. "And spies and demon-lovers. They don't call them demons, though. It's a religion thing for them, apparently. And, before you ask: they're not allies with the Dominion."

Sofie jumped in. "More like the Dominion won't even admit the Haida exist, really. Dominion mages can't just get their heads around the idea of demon-summoning. It implies there's something out there more powerful than the Universal Dominion."

"Sure, maybe," I said. "But I don't think the Haida want allies."

"So why is a Haida knife down here, then?" asked Lucas. Sofie and I gave each other an uncomfortable look.

"It's a long story," Sofia said.

"Nah, it's a short one," I replied. "You get idiots everywhere."

"Tom..." said Sofie.

"I'll be good," I said. She pouted, and I sighed. "Fine. I'll be good, dollface." Sofie likes it when I do the Shamus patter. "We used to have some members of their religion around, out in the open and everything. Not for a while, though."

"Really?" said Lucas. "What happened to them?"

"Pretty much everybody," said Sofie. "About thirty years ago the, ah, cleaning ladies went loco on the cult, and what they missed, the Castle swept up. There may be a couple of the old-time true believers over in Redtown, but if they are, they're elderly."

"And hopefully about to croak," I said, and then continued, "Unless this is their work. So, Sofie: is the knife local, or an import?"

"Oh, it's definitely an import," Sofie said. She used a wooden pointer to show three identical spots on the blade. "See here, here, and here?" I opened my mouth, and she hastened to add, "Don't just say 'yes'."

"Yes," I said, and got the stick wagged in my direction in reproof. Sofie went on, "What those spots mean, Shamus, is that the knife was beaten out by hand. This absolutely was not stamped by a mill here; the metal's too poor and uneven. And the knife was enchanted, right?"

"Right," I said. "Nasty enchantments, too. Nastier if they had worked right."

Sofie chuckled a little. "More proof that they were foreign. If we had any mages, not that we do, the enchantments would be better than this. In every possible way. No, somebody brought it down from the North. Unfortunately, that means you can't trace it back to the original makers."

"That's what Mike said."

"Father Miguel would know," said Sofie. "From the other side of it, you could say. You were hoping that my scholarship would help where his god couldn't?"

"Something like that," I allowed. "Still, now we know who we're looking for," I said. "And where we can go around here to track them down and start asking questions. That's great, Sofie. That's perfect. I owe you one."

"Hooray, finally! I'll start running a tab. Good to meet you, Lucas." Sofie's smile was a bit dazzling, and the elf blinked at it a little. Guess he wasn't used to being on the receiving end of a charm offensive. "*Do* come by afterward and tell me how it all worked out, gentlemen."

"I'm sure he will," I said as we got up to leave. Sofie flashed me an ever-so-slightly dirty look. "What? I'm suddenly supposed to be blind and deaf? Some Shamus I'd be, then. Take care, Sofie."

"You too, Shamus. And watch your back."

"Only where there's a mirror."

As we hurried down the front steps, Lucas looked sidelong at me. "You and her?"

I laughed. "Nope. Knock yourself out."

"No warnings?"

"About what? Sofie's a nice lady. You should be aware, though: she's one of the richest people in New California. Her family's money is so old some of the gold's from Fort Knox."

Lucas stopped dead in his tracks. "They know the location of the storied secret vaults of Fort Knox, long lost to the sight of man and reputedly guarded by all the fiendish devices and dread beasts that the Old Americans could design and spawn?" There was a definite gleam in his eye. I wondered if he was quoting from an Adventurer's Guild prospectus, too.

"Well. No. They've just got a lot of money, and they're bad at wasting it. And Sofie's a Green. From one of *the* Green families." At his look of confusion, I explained. "Okay. The nobles around here, they're either Greens, or Greeks. Greens are mostly descended from the ones that came down from the north, when Ronnie the Great founded New California; the Greeks are descended from the bigwigs already living here that managed to survive the founding. These days, it's just mostly politics. Greens marry into Greek families, it's no big deal. But some of Sofie's extended family think it'd be beneath the family for one of them to marry the Crown Princess."

Okay, sure, that was one way of putting it. Another was that after my ancestors invaded my other ancestors, there was about a century or so where it was worth your life to be in the wrong part of town. And that 'Greek' was the polite form of 'greaser,' just like 'Green' was the word used when it wasn't wise to snarl out '*¡Gringo!*' But, hell, it really did get all sorted out, years ago. Just one more flavor in the Cin City soup.

Lucas nodded. "Got it. So, no luck for me there?"

"Depends on what you mean by luck. Go ahead and take her dancing; Sofie ain't a snob. You want to pitch some woo, go ahead. Our nobility doesn't fuss over that too bad." Which was a nice way of saying that, when it comes to the New California upper class, adultery is when you don't tell your spouse which bed you're sleeping in tonight. "You can even get Sofie to treat you serious, but don't ever expect the rest of them to do it. Starting with her husband."

Lucas, bless him, actually looked mortified at that last bit. "She's married? When was she going to mention that?"

I answered, seriously, "She must have thought you'd already know. But you'd have to meet the husband before things got too hot and heavy, so it'd be no big deal anyway." Lucas looked almost pop-eyed. Damn, but were all elves this straight-laced? "What? It's only common politeness. She'd need to know how well you two would get along before she started planning out her social calendar. Oh, hey! *Tortas*! I'm starving."

Cin City street vendors serve the best *tortas* in New California. The other towns say that this is a filthy lie, but they would, wouldn't they? Lucas seemed still a bit boggled, so I ordered pork for him and lamb for me. As we chomped down, I continued explaining around a mouth of sandwich, "If it makes you feel any better, this is all just the rich being rich. Commoners get married, have kids, and go nuts when their spouses go stepping out on them.

"But when it comes to the upper crust?" I shrugged. "It's a lot of fun, reading and watching them hop in out of each other's beds and having big scenes at parties and keeping the gossip mags full of content. And it keeps them out of everybody else's hair, too. If you don't want to be in on that, don't be. If you do, expect a lot of drama to come along with the fun. And if you want to change the whole system, well – it's good to want, kid."

That made Lucas thoughtful and quiet. Which was good. That way at least we had enough time to eat our lunches before we heard the first booms in the distance.

CHAPTER FIFTEEN
Nobody Throws A Fireball In MY Town!

Lucas jumped faster, I jumped smarter. He didn't seem to care about the garbage can he knocked over on his way to a wall; I just found a handy stoop and crouched behind it. "You part jackrabbit, kid?" I called.

"You know the best way to block a fireball, old man? Be somewhere else when it goes off!" came Lucas's reply. No fear. Maybe even a little excitement. And I admitted that he had a point as I joined him, with me closer to the corner. I was probably gonna be scout.

"Then why are we planning to check it out?" I asked, rhetorically, as the Cin City populace started realizing that, hey, that was a fireball, and it was probably thrown by a mage. As we both turned the corner and started heading in the direction of the sound, people were starting to move. But the panic would be going the other way if we were lucky.

"Because I'm crazy and you're dumb?" grinned Lucas. Yeah, he was excited. And fiddling with various pieces of lethal-looking gear. "This happen often?" he asked.

"Nah. This doesn't happen at all. We don't have any mages, remember?" By then I was leading him through what was now a milling crowd and would soon be a nervous mob. I needed alleyways. Hell, roofs would be better, but we were on the edge of the government district. They don't let roof-runners do their thing in this part of town. "And even if we did, they'd be quiet about it." Another couple of booms. "This ain't quiet."

"You think this is loud?" Lucas laughed once. "Try doing this underground. There ain't no boom like a dungeon boom."

It's easier than you think to get through a crowd. You just got to give them a chance to see you first. Hugging the walls helps. And look like you know what the hell's going on. It was still about a mile, through streets first filled with panicky clerks and then worried guards, and it was a good thing I didn't lose my hat, because they wouldn't have let me get on through without it. Even then, one guard with more swagger than sense tried to argue, until Lucas tripped him with his own scabbard and pointed to me when the guard's sergeant came running up to inquire as to what all the commotion was about. Good thing that I knew him.

"Clancy! What the hell's going on?" That stopped him long enough to recognize me, and to start swearing at his luckless minion. After a little bit Clancy wound down enough to answer my question.

"It's looking bad, Tommie. Begorrah." He pronounced it 'baygrah,' and as an afterthought: Clancy was aiming to get Castle duty, but he was still learning the Lore for the Flatfoot exam. "We just got the first reports in. Spell-throwing, bold as a brass band and twice as loud."

"Nice one, Clancy. Good patter. You got a name?"

"We're lucky to get reports, Shamus. Besides, they're wearing masks."

"They? There's more than one?" That was bad, bad, bad.

"Two, and they're having themselves a proper donnybrook, Tommie. Up on the roofs, at least."

Could be worse. Could be a *little* worse. "Any idea who they are, Clancy?"

"We both know one of the two boyos is the Ambassador, for sure and certain. I mean, who else could it be?"

"Right. And the other's probably just some foreign wizard, too," I muttered. "Because..."

"...New California doesn't have any mages," we both said in unison. I went on, "Can you spare anybody?"

"Not even a horse, Tommie. Not that you could get one too close to a fireball fight."

"Horses are smarter than us."

"You see me saying you're wrong?" said Clancy. "These boyos need to take their business out into the hills, at least. I'll not be letting the fire brigade go in there just to be burned alive, but it's just a matter of time before the fires spread."

I can hear a hint, especially when it's made in that bad an

accent. "You wanna ask for anything else, Clancy? Since I'm here, and everything?"

Clancy looked affronted. "Sure and I haven't asked you for a thing, Shamus! What with me being just a humble sergeant of the guard, and all." Another, much larger boom rattled the windows around us; when we straightened from ducking, Clancy's voice was rougher, more honest. "But if you see anyone, tell 'em to run this way. Safer here."

"Got it. Good luck, Clancy." And we were off again. Got to admit, I could have used another minute or so to completely catch my breath, but we were almost there.

"You got a plan?" asked Lucas as government offices started giving way to workshops and warehouses. I shook my head.

"Why? Do you?"

"We don't do plans," Lucas replied as we picked our way through a couple of overturned carts (no dead people or horses, at least). "Plans pop like blisters when you put any weight on 'em. So what do you want to do, Tom?"

"You heard the guard, Lucas: we gotta get them moving out of the streets and into the hills. Let 'em fight there. Or at least we should latch onto the one who isn't Wolfie and find out what's going on?"

"We assuming this is about the case?"

"Yeah. Either that, or we pissed off a luck god somewhere."

#

Ever see a wizard's duel? No? Well, you didn't miss much. Unless something thrown around doesn't miss *you*, and that's when things get exciting. These two seemed to be sticking to fire, which meant that we were mostly going to be okay. Acid's bad, ice is worse than you think, and rocks on your head will wreck your day, but fireballs mostly go out after they hit. Maybe because mages like fireballs, so they work on the spells more.

Or something. The point is, Lucas and I could keep low and watch the skies. We were in the right area – we just needed to see where the fireballs were coming from. Damned if I knew what we could do once we found the idiots, but one step at a time.

"Hey, Lucas! You got anything that tells you about spells?" The two of us were in an alley, intelligently avoiding barrels like the plague. A fireball hits one of those, you're either covered in burning splinters (bad) or boiling liquid (worse).

Lucas said, too brightly, "Sure!" He pulled a small stick out from his coat pocket. "See this? If it's burning, we just got hit with a fire spell. If it's wet, it was a water spell. Covered in ice? Cold spell."

"Funny guy."

"That's what everybody says, Shamus. You know what we have to do, right?"

"You're gonna say 'roof,' aren't you." I didn't make it a question.

"I'm gonna say 'roof'."

"Which will let them see us, Lucas."

"Yeah, but we'll see them, too. Or have you gotten one of your plans working yet?"

"I've got one going right now. I call it 'let the Adventurer try to get us both killed.' It's doing great!"

"Good for you!" Lucas turned serious, looked up, then pointed to one building. "I think that warehouse is our best bet. Shall we go?"

It turned out to be a good bet. Anybody who worked there was long gone, leaving behind only the smell of sudden fear and a look of disarray. We were close enough that the booms from the fireballs were cracking window glass, and the lock on the hatch to the roof was so old even I could have picked it. Lucas didn't even slow down. Up on top, it was, well, a roof. It had a good view of the other buildings around it, and enough crates and chimneys scattered around that we had something like cover.

Which was good, because the two maniacs tossing fireballs at each other were up among the roof-tops, too. Both were wearing hooded cloaks and masks covering their faces; at this range, it was hard to tell anything else about them. They were half-running, half-gliding along the roofs; when one of them jumped, they spent far too long in the air before gravity decided to object.

There was a lot of damn magic going off and all at once, and I wasn't happy about that at all. This close to the fight, the air was dry and unsatisfying, like the life in it had been scooped out. It's not necromancy, not really, but it made me want to cough. Especially since the stink of burned sweat was pretty damned thick up here.

"So, Lucas. You ever deal with rogue mages before?" I asked, as we huddled out of sight of the duelists. Lucas was taking the time to assemble an absurdly small-looking crossbow. He shrugged as he worked.

"Kind of. You can get some crazy hermit types in the swamps and the sewers." Lucas stopped, considered, and went on, "Well, they're all crazy, but some of them are also mean. Usually we have, heh, our own specialists to deal with that. You armed?"

"Nothing with range. How far does that thing shoot?" It didn't look real deadly. Hell, the bolt on it was blunt and wide-tipped.

"Maybe twenty feet. Bright side is, if it touches bare skin, it doesn't matter how much arcane energy you throw around; you're off to sleepy-time. But I gotta get close enough to fire. Also, small question: who am I aiming it at?"

"Only got time for one shot?"

"Only got the one bolt. This stuff ain't cheap."

"Well, one of them is Wolfie, so him. We just have to figure out which one." At that point, one of the mages noticed someone below. He(?) threw the half-grown fireball in his hand in that general direction, and was rewarded with a small boom and a couple screams of fear. At least they weren't screams of pain, but still... "Yeah, screw it, aim for that *cabron*." Even if it wasn't Wolfie.

Lucas was already calculating angles. "Hell and damnation," he said mildly, "but he's a little too far away. I'm going to need to get over to the building across the side street."

I looked. It was a jump, but I decided not to insult the elf by suggesting he couldn't make it. "All right. Wait until I get his attention, then sidle over there."

Lucas really was a pro; he didn't argue. He did give me the stick he pulled out earlier. "Throw it at something hard if you need a distraction. Try not to breathe the smoke." At my look, he shrugged. "I didn't say that it wasn't useful for *something*."

I got about as close to Nasty Mage as I could without falling off the roof; at this point, he and the other one were playing pop-up-and-shoot at each other. I looked at the stick, looked at the back of the mage's head, decided that it was probably hard enough, and flung it right at his skull.

Yeah, I forgot that Dominion mages have spells against missile weapons. The damn thing bounced off his shield. Or tried to; turns out the shield was hard enough to break the stick, too. The smoke cloud was gratifying. Well, what I saw of it; I was already diving down the fire escape. Just in time, too: Dominion mages tend to react badly to surprise, which is why the space where I had been suddenly filled up with lightning bolts.

If this had been a fire escape out of the Lore, I'd have been zapped by the metal in it. Fortunately, this was real life, which meant that it was made out of wood. But this was Cin City, so it was also rickety enough that all it took was a couple of metal screws melting to have the whole thing start to collapse.

And it was Cin City, so at least there was another dumpster of garbage to break my fall. This and the fire escape collapse was becoming a theme. I hate themes.

I kept quiet. It felt like everything else in the area had the same idea, including the cobblestones in the street. After a few seconds, Lucas's voice called down.

"You still alive?"

"Yeah," I said as I clambered out of the trash. And was pleasantly surprised to see the dirt and gunk shake itself off of my suit. Guess Mike had splurged when he had gotten my clothes fixed. "How is that son of a bitch?"

"Out like a light. Good job on the distraction; he got a face full of goop when the shield shredded the bolt. Tell me again why no throat-slitting?"

"Is he five-nine, two hundred pounds, left-handed, black hair, red eyes, and has a bloodline that puts all of us mongrels to shame?" I started looking for a way up as I bantered.

"Kind of?"

"Then the bastard probably has diplomatic immunity. And bosses with mass curse spells. Where's the other one?"

"Ran off as quick as she could."

By then I had climbed up the equally rickety fire escape of the other building. "She?"

"Trust me."

"Great. Now we have to go after her." At least she was headed into a more crowded part of the city now. The buildings would be close enough for even me to jump from roof to roof.

"Any reason besides the obvious, Tom?" asked Lucas.

"Ain't the obvious enough? She'd rather explain this to me than anybody else in Cin City, about why there was a magical duel in the factory district. I'm a sucker for a sob story sung by a sincere sister. Just ask anybody."

"All right, then." Lucas pulled out a little glass vial, and before I could react he smashed it down by Wolfie's head. "Let's go."

"What was that?" I asked as we started moving across the rooftops. We could still barely see little Miss Wizard Duel ahead of us. "Nothing fatal, I hate to hope."

"Nope. Just a little something for nosy mages. Safe as houses normally, but if you cast a scrying spell in the area, well, oof." Lucas grinned. "You'd throw up so much you'll see somebody else's shoes come out."

"Ain't that a shame."

"Yup. Best of all, it's originally from Quebec. Maybe the Dominion will think the Imperials are getting frisky again." Lucas spat. "'Course, *somebody* should."

#

We were lucky: the mage we were chasing was tired enough that she slowed down after the first panicked flight, and she was smart enough *not* to look back to check for pursuit. Sometimes you need to just clear the area and try to blend in; not the best thing to do here, but who expects a Shamus to be tailing you? Anyway, as long as we didn't make too much noise, we were able to keep moving and jumping fast enough to keep her in sight. I swear, though, they make the gaps between the buildings wider every year.

She was definitely heading back to the City's center, which made sense; it was getting towards dark, and with the hooded cloak she wore it'd be real easy for her to get lost in the crowd. We needed an angle. "Hey, Lucas."

"Yeah, Tom?"

"You want high, or low?"

Lucas responded instantly. "Low. I can get to the street faster, and I'm better at running through them."

"You know these city streets?"

"You mean, your really boring and predictable city streets? Gee, Shamus, I guess I'll just have to hope for the best." He didn't wait for more banter; Lucas more less grabbed the next drainpipe and half-slid, half-fell down the building. I shook my head. And there I was, ready to bullshit him all about the architecture of planned cities. Oh, well, I was on the job anyway.

It was harder with one above doing the chasing than it was with two, and it took me a moment to figure out why: Lucas was just better at finding places to jump and dive. I could do it, sure. I'm no tumbler but I did this growing up and I wasn't fat. I was just a little stocky and out of practice. It was a good thing that she wasn't trying any more big magical jumps, either. Just little ones, while she kept looking at the street and not backwards.

It was coming back to me, I told myself as I almost got it wrong on one jump and nearly caught the roof with my teeth. Sure, this was great exercise. Can't imagine why I ever gave it up and just moved around on the ground. And then, thankfully, the mage decided that she was safe enough to go to the streets. She didn't even bother with stairs, instead drifting down fast enough to be useful but slow enough that the landing didn't hurt. Guess her lack of fireballs after the fight was her own choice, then.

Following her was gonna be tricky. I could keep my distance while up top, but if I followed her down the fire escape there was no way she'd miss *that.* But if I went down another way I might miss her. I must have thought about it for a good two seconds before I checked a roof access door for the building I was on, found it unlocked, and started jumping down the stairs two and three at a time once I figured she couldn't hear me. You can do the wrong thing in this business, but the worst thing that you can do is dither.

And, wouldn't you know it, as I burst through the door at the bottom of the stairs I came upon a tender scene between a few men, and a few crates of spirits missing the proper tax stamps. I assume, at least. Usually you don't unload legal whiskey from a milk delivery carriage.

I didn't want to linger: still, the traditions of the Lore must be upheld. We all stopped dead in our tracks, I counted a four-beat, then grinned and said over one shoulder, "Don't have time today, boys. Didn't see nothing, was never near the place, just stick it on my tab at Rick's."

And then I was out the door. I was on the street for at least three seconds before I heard the careful thwack of a crossbow bolt deliberately hitting the doorframe, by now well behind me; they had seen my Shamus suit, which was good, but there was still the look of the thing and their own pride to consider. Good lads.

(And, do you know? They actually did put a bottle of whiskey on my tab at Rick's. Which ended up being the start of an entirely different Case.)

When I turned the corner... well. It was in fact darker, down here in the streets. The lamps in this part of Cin City were lightstones, because only the rich and the poor want to see at night; here in the middle, being cheaper in the long run was more important than getting a good, bright flame going. Besides, a lot of people in this part of town liked being able to see where they were going (barely), without other people seeing what they were doing when they got there.

So. Dark, and most of the people there were wearing hooded cloaks. I was starting to see the flaw in this plan.

Fortunately, Lucas took this opportunity to hiss at me from an alley – well, no, he didn't. He walked right up to me, slapped my shoulder in greeting, and then said, "Right over there. Black cloak, gold trim, pretending to look at that bookseller's cart," in a perfectly reasonable, conversational voice. It's nice to work with pros.

I'm one, too, so I got her fixed in my head with no more than a casual look. "Now, or later?"

"Lots of people on the street here, Shamus. I figure not all of them are guilty of something anyway?"

"Oh, sure. At least half have a conscience so clean, they don't even bother to sit with their back to the walls."

"Truly, this is the Earthly paradise," murmured Lucas. He had his own hood up, presumably because of the ears. New Californian commoners honestly don't care too much about elves (or even orcs, as long as they have money, shoes, and haircuts), but he'd stand out here. "Wait until she gets going, give the crowd a chance to clear out, and then do *what*, exactly?"

"We do our damnedest to not look like a kidnap team. If she doesn't want to talk, I give her my business card and tell her to give it to whoever does end up grabbing her. That might give her a clue that she's going to end up talking to me anyway, so it might as well be now."

"Makes sense. What's a business card?"

I opened my mouth, and closed my mouth. Eventually I said, "It's a Shamus thing."

"All right. And there she goes. Let's start the tail."

The basic mistake goons and mooks make when they're

tailing somebody is this: your average mook wasn't hired to skulk. He was hired to intimidate. So if you tell him to be subtle, he'll think that you're telling him to not visibly growl and point at whoever he's shadowing. But Lucas and me, we *were* subtle, and we weren't trying to put the scare into her. We just wanted a quiet word or two. So, hey, we managed to last a whole ten minutes longer than your average knuckleheads would before she noticed us following her.

She ran. Wouldn't you? But down here we were faster, and she was finally low on oomph from all that magic she was tossing around earlier. She ducked into an alleyway that turned out to be a cul-de-sac, and that's when I got nervous. Bad idea to corner a mage, right?

I looked at Lucas; he backed off. I walked into the alley, hands where she could see them, my card between my fingers. "Hey. This ain't no kidnapping, lady. No robbery, no funny business. Just want to talk to you out under the streetlights, where everybody can see you walk away nice and safe afterward. Say yes and I'll back out and then you can follow."

"Who are you?" Young voice. New Californian accent. Sounded intelligent, if a little tense. Well, to be expected.

"Name's Tom Vargas, lady. I'm a Shamus. I'm just here clearing a Case."

"Shamus? That's like a detective. Yes, a detective." I raised an eyebrow, but only inside, where nobody could see. She went on, "You're investigating something?"

"Yeah, that's right. I'm trying to solve a murder. I think that you may know something about it, so I just need to ask you a few questions. If you don't want to do it here, you can come to my office later. Here's my card. Has my address on it, and everything." At her silence, I went on, "Can I come closer, and give it to you?"

She hesitated for a long moment. "Put it on the crate there. Then move back." So I did. She carefully moved forward, grabbed the card, then stepped back. She tried to look at both it and me at the same time, which was a bad idea normally but I wasn't actually trying to subdue her, and then put it away.

"I'll decide later if I want to come by, Shamus Vargas." Damned if there was something weird about the way she was talking. The way she pronounced my title, for example; like she knew how to say it right but never had to before. "But how do you know I can help you? Whose Case are you trying to Clear?"

"A local woman's. She's dead now. Her name was Elizabeth Gonzalez-Hernandez."

Her head snapped back at that. I've seen it described in the Lore, sure, but I've never actually had it happen before. And her hood must have been bunched up, because the sudden movement caused it to fall back, exposing her face.

I stared at her. She stared at me. And I guess that she had a little magical oomph after all, because she raised one hand and suddenly the entire alley was filled with dazzling, overwhelming light.

The next thing, a rapidly-blinking Lucas was shaking me out of my daze. "The hell, Shamus? What did you say to her?"

I looked at him. In my mind's eye, I saw her face as the dazzler spell illuminated it perfectly. Dark hair, dark eyes, pale complexion; I'd recognize her anywhere. And the last time I saw her, she was lying dead on the ground with the blood spreading on the Castle's floor.

"I told her I was investigating her murder," I explained.

CHAPTER SIXTEEN
Fer Sure

The two of us had hightailed it on over to the city morgue, as soon as my eyes recovered; I knew Remy liked to work late. And early. True, she did that because it meant nobody would bother her, and we were bothering her. And she wasn't shy about saying so as I wasted five minutes going through drawers in the morgue before I calmed up enough to ask her where Elizabeth's corpse was.

Remy didn't like that question. Go figure. "I'd notice if one of the bodies got up and walked away, Shamus," she said. Remy was just grousing, though. She *had* let me and Lucas come in, although how much of that was because of Lucas's rakish good looks I didn't know and decided not to guess.

But I ignored that for now as the three of us stood over the icebox that had Elizabeth's body. I'm not sure why the Ancient Americans used that word. I mean, they never actually used ice to make things cold, right?

The slab room is awful, for a Shamus. It's not the dead people. Everybody goes, eventually, and the world keeps on spinning. What's rough about the slab room is that everybody in there's probably got a Case that could be cleared. How did they go? Might have been murder; might have been something legal that still kills a man as sure as a knife across the throat. But they all had something in their lives that still shouted out for justice. I imagined their ghosts, hovering above their corpses, turning silently to see the Shamus come in. Except that I can't clear every Case in the world. I can't even know about all the Cases.

They'd turn away when they saw I'm not there for them, I think. They'd probably tell themselves that it figured. Nobody cares about what happened to them. And, hell, they're not even that wrong, sometimes.

Elizabeth was in the icebox, just like Remy had said. Had I hoped that she wasn't? Maybe. Remy cocked an eyebrow at me, as if she was too polite to say 'I told you so' out loud. "I saw her walking around, clear as day," I growled.

"No," snapped Remy, "you saw somebody who looked like her walking around. She hasn't moved since the orderlies brought her in here. Believe me, if she could have moved she would have when I did the autopsy."

At 'autopsy,' Lucas (who had been looking faintly green) forthrightly turned around, headed for Remy's office, and sat down. Me and Remy looked at each other; she shrugged. "You need to check anything else on the corpse, Shamus?"

I shook my head. "Then maybe get it together, Tommie?" she said, a little lower, and my mouth tensed for a moment until I decided she was right. "Good," Remy said. "Come on, and let a girl get you a drink for a change."

As we went into her office, Lucas might have looked a little defensive. "Sorry," he said. "I see them when they die, and I see them after they've been dead for a few decades. But any time I see a body in that condition, it's usually about to open its eyes and start shambling."

"Maybe that's it," I mused, getting myself back on track for the Case. "She went zombie? No, she could talk and do things on her own."

"Damned right it's 'No'," agreed Remy as she rummaged in her filing cabinet for a bottle and three mismatched glasses. "This office doesn't let corpses reanimate. Not while I'm running it. No zombies, revenants, liches, and especially and particularly no God-damned vampires. *Absolutely* no vampires, which is the only way that your scenario could work." She touched the discreet square-and-compass medallion that hung around her neck. "I did the tests myself. Not only is that corpse not Undead, it can't be."

Lucas noticed the ashtray, looked permission at Remy to smoke, then pulled out a cigarette pack. As he lit up, he said, "I'm going to say illusion magic of some kind. I can think of five or six spells – not that I know any magic myself – that could make anybody or anything look like your victim. Two or three of those spells, her own mother couldn't tell the difference."

"I've met her mother," I said as I grabbed the glass of rum Remy handed me. "Don't be so sure. And how hard to cast are the really good spells?"

Lucas shrugged and sipped his own drink. "It's not the casting; it's the strain of keeping it up. She'd have to– okay, right, I see your point."

I explained to Remy, "Lucas pegged her as being female during the fight she had with Wolfie, and she didn't change her size or weight afterward. She was throwing a lot of magic around then, too. No way she was keeping a useless illusion spell in the air then. Especially when she dropped that dazzler on me during her getaway."

"Well, that eliminates the two usual wheezes," said Remy. "Not undead, not an illusion. Maybe she has a twin sister? Or just somebody with the same build?"

I shook my head. "I went out to see the parents. There was no sign of a twin. Besides, why hide it? Elizabeth wasn't a fugitive. The powers-that-be would have loved to hear that she had a sister that shared her talents." I sighed. "And maybe somebody we don't even know of yet was impersonating a dead woman, sure, but that won't tell us *why*."

"Then I leave figuring it out to you, Shamus. You want to hear the preliminary autopsy report?"

I grimaced. "No, but tell it to me anyway."

"All right. Ah, excuse me, Mr. Coltrane?"

"Please, Doctor, call me Lucas." Apparently, Lucas was feeling recovered enough to turn on the charm again.

Remy pointed to the cigarettes. "Those smell remarkably good. May I?"

"Be my guest! They're from back home. The best tobacco the Old Americans could genie; we found some surviving strains when folks resettled the coast." Lucas blew a perfect smoke ring. "They even whiten teeth!" He jerked his head towards the pack. "How about you, Shamus?"

"Shamuses have their own brand," I explained patiently to the foreigner. "So, the autopsy report?"

Remy took a drag, which I swear took six months' worth of ground-in fatigue off of her face, and pulled out a folder. "A few things. First off, the death was what I thought: a thin blade that sliced up under the ribcage. It was fast; a little *too* fast, if we're talking mundane means. She was dead a second after the knife went in."

I frowned. "No signs of torment? Any kind of abuse?"

"No and no. No abrasions, her hands were relaxed, nothing that suggests a struggle or an outrage. One other thing, though, and this is going back to your who's-the-murderer question: if the Dominion ambassador killed the victim, he did it on his knees. The angle of the blade suggests the murderer was somebody shorter than five-nine."

"Dammit," I said. "I really want Wolfie to be guilty of this. Anything in her stomach?"

"Sure, Shamus. Partially digested food. Look around, would you?" Her wave showed a dingy office with no windows, city-purchased lightstones to more or less light the place, and stains so old they were probably historically significant by now. "Does this look like an Old American forensics lab? I got a cleaning lady suddenly coming in tomorrow to clean up the place; while she's here she can maybe, you know, check things."

"Trust me, she will. She may even come early." I rose. "Thanks for your help, Doc."

Remy rose too. "Any time, Shamus. Thanks for the smoke, Lucas."

Lucas looked perilously close to winking. "Any time, Doctor. Feel free to stop by the docks if you ever want to get a pack or two. I'll let them know to give you the discount."

Judging from Remy's half-smile, she might take him up on that offer. As we left behind the morgue (and the rest of the police station) behind, Lucas looked sidelong at me. "Are you aware that the good doctor there is a Freemason?"

I stopped short, looked at him with pure shock on my face, and clutched at my heart. "*No*! It all makes sense, now!" Then I stopped mugging around. "I've known for years. It's not illegal to be one in New California. It's not even all that secret."

"And the Dominion doesn't care?" Lucas asked.

"The Dominion doesn't rule here." *Yet*, the always-worried part of my brain said. "Remy grew up in Tourista, and the Masons are big down there. They're open about it, too. Given how many Touristas are descended from people fleeing the Dominion, the Masons can get away with it. Hell, some of Remy's own ancestors were on the Last Flight from Chicago before the Dominion shattered the city."

"Really?"

"Really. They all even salvaged their airplane seats after the plane was scavenged for parts; their descendants call themselves the Five Hundred, and by now they run Tourista." I left out the bits about how Lucas should not trifle overmuch with Remy accordingly. He was a smart boy who'd figure that out on his own.

#

Being back at the station reminded me again that I needed to tell somebody about that damned graffiti. If I didn't have Leila's charm on me, I'd be worried somebody'd put a forget-about-it whammy on me. Or maybe they had: I gave Lucas a look. "Do you remember about the graffiti?" I asked.

He gave me a look back. "No?" Lucas said. I felt worried and vindicated for a moment, until I remembered he'd joined up after I discovered the graffiti. So maybe I was just getting old, after all. Hey, it beats the alternative.

"Right, never mind," I said. "I should go talk to whoever arrested a bum who was drawing some weird crap on the walls, let the cops know that something may be up. Civic duty, and all that."

"Oh, you have that here?" Lucas said. "Nice. I like places where the people are civilized enough to stay bought."

"You don't know the half of it, friend," I said. "In Cin City, the guards even tip you the nod when your bribe's about to expire."

#

Turned out 'him' was a 'her.' From the name, Sgt. Shauni Buchannon Quinn's family was originally from one of the barbie clans, and she had the blond hair and looks to match. Within a minute, I found myself wishing that I had made her acquaintance a bit earlier.

By that, I mean before the bum got released. "Like, gimme a break, Shamus," she said. Her accent was pure New Californian. Those ancestors of hers must have come south a couple of generations ago. But they must have also kept up talking barbie among themselves. "We totally picked that bum up for vagrancy, and he stewed in the cell overnight, but then he got bailed out in the morning."

"Bailed out?" I said, all cleverly and stuff. "I thought the Captain said you were gonna keep him in the cells for a couple days."

Sgt. Shauni's shrug (heh) was perfectly New Californian, too. "Well, fer sure, I guess the Captain figured that nobody would make bail for the guy. What was I supposed to do, say that we didn't want the money?"

"Alright, alright," I said. "I get it. Refusing bail money's a bad habit for the cops to get into. Just tell me about the guy, then."

"Which one?" she asked. "Like, the bum, or the guy who bailed him out?"

"Both," I said. "Dealer's choice which one you start with."

"Okay." Sgt. Shauni thought about it. "The bum was, you know, a bum, okay? Didn't smell too bad; he knew what soap was, even if it wasn't, like, always his best dude or whatever. Pretty tall, really old, didn't talk at all. He just lay there on the bed all night. It was all just so *totally* creepy."

"Which cell was he in?" I asked. Sgt. Shauni pointed to the reinforced cage that they use to store mages.

I blinked. "Wait. This guy was a mage, Sergeant?"

"Hah! As if," she said. "But it was, like, we never have mages staying over and it was easier just to, y'know, stash him in that one for the night. Less crowded, and the other prisoners thought he was totally gross anyway."

"Gotcha. No name?" I asked. Sgt. Shauni looked at me. "Right, you wrote down 'Juan Doe.' Any items on him?"

"Just, like, bum stuff. String and bits of wood and what-*ever*. I totally made sure he took it all with him when he got bailed out and everything." Sgt. Shauni found the paperwork and handed it over. "Like, see for yourself, Shamus."

"What about the guy who bailed him out?" asked Lucas, his tone somewhere between fascinated and slightly appalled. Sgt. Shauni squinted at him.

"I'm sorry, sir; like, who *are* you, again?"

I looked up from the paperwork; luckily for me, Sgt. Shauni wrote a lot more formally than she talked. The release all looked in order, dammit. "He's with me on the Case, Sergeant," I said. "And it's a good question. This form just says 'P. Cash'."

"That's, like, the name he gave me, Shamus," Sgt. Shauni replied. "And, *yes*, I know that the 'P' stands for 'Paid.' Duh! Like, where would we be if people had to give their own names when paying bail?"

"Having to feed more prisoners?" I said.

"Exactly! You've been in the canteen. That'd be, like, police brutality, fer sure."

"Anyway," said Lucas, "since I *am* with the Shamus: what about the guy the bailed the bum out?"

"Oh, he was like totally *grody*." I blinked at the swear. "Short, dirty brown hair, only one grey eye – he didn't have an eyepatch, which was *so* gross – and he had breath that would, like, gag a smurf. The dweeb *smelled*, and barf me out, his bail money totally smelled too. And he had a tattoo on his neck that was, like, they tried to do a bear but it totally looked like a hamster, y'know? He tried to talk me up, too. As if!"

I looked down at the paperwork. There was an X where 'P. Cash' was supposed to sign his name, which was a surprise. Most people in New California can read, write, and do sums; they need the first for the Lore, and the other two for tax evasion.

"Some guys like to live risky. All right, Sergeant: if your would-be boyfriend ever comes back to get his money, stall him and get your captain. You gotta wonder why somebody's bailing out a bum."

"Like, whatever, Shamus," said Sgt. Shauni. "Hey, don't you have somewhere else to be right now?"

I gave her a smile and a wink at the traditional Flatfoot send-off to a Shamus and left the cellblock, Lucas in tow.

Lucas looked sidelong at me as we walked to the door. "What the hell is a smurf?" he asked.

"Damned if I know."

#

"So what now?" said Lucas as we left the police station.

"I don't know. Go get some sleep?"

Lucas looked at me as if I had started speaking Old American at him. And not the liturgical kind, either. But he took pity on the old, decrepit Shamus, and waved two fingers at me in farewell.

Which was the idea. I gave the elf a couple of minutes to clear the area, and turned to look at one particular shadow. "You can come out now, Elizabeth."

And she did. Smart kid; Elizabeth didn't waste time asking how I knew. She just said, "So, Shamus. Why did I die?"

"I'm working on it, ma'am. I'm working on it."

CHAPTER SEVENTEEN

This Feels A Bit Like Cheating

"So what am I, Shamus?" asked Elizabeth. She toyed with her pie, sadly. The taste apparently wasn't the same for her, somehow.

I considered her over the battered, yet certified genuine Formica table. I had decided that she would probably be happier with people around. And if she wouldn't, I would be, so we had retired to Garapenna's. They don't do much at night, but you can at least get pie and coffee. The interview was going all right. All things considered.

"Don't you mean, who are you?" I asked her. She shook her head, with a surprising lack of water drops. Elizabeth and I had both gotten caught in the post-dusk quick storm, but if she showed any sign of being half-soaked by the rain, it wasn't obvious.

"I don't know if I know that, either. I remember being Elizabeth. I remember Elizabeth's parents, first crush, best day, worst day. Well, second-worst day." She looked at me, very calmly. "What happened that actual night eludes me, and I am not going to try to grab hold of it. But I guess you can't expect a copy to be perfect, can you?"

"Doesn't make you a 'what,' though. You got free will, right?" I raised a fork to forestall her. "Let's assume you have as much free will as I do. If you've got that, you're a person."

"You don't know that I have free will, though."

"I don't know that *I* have free will, either."

"My body is on a slab at the morgue, Shamus."

"Really? And here I am, seeing you sitting there, and everything." Elizabeth scowled at me; I swallowed my grin and went on. "Then there's the tapping."

"The tapping?"

"Yeah, the tapping. You're doing it now with your fork. Badadda badadda badadda ting! Badadda badadda badadda ting! Badadda badadda badadda ting! How is it your mother never threw a roll at you when it got too bad?"

"Excuse me," Elizabeth snapped. "What does my mother have to do with it? And I'll have you know that she would never, ever throw a roll at me!" She stuttered to a stop after that. I finally let the grin out.

"So, you have bad habits, you get pissed off when they get pointed out to you, and you defend your mother when strangers mouth off about her at you. Sure, you're just a thing. A copy. No free will there, huh." I shook my head. "Kid, if you're not a real person there's no damned way to tell. Sorry about that." Then I reached out, stabbed a forkful of her dessert, and took a bite. "And that pie? That pie just sucks. Try some of mine."

She did, and her eyebrows lifted up. "Okay. Okay, sure, that tastes normal."

I spread my hands, grandly. "Behold, my child, the Way of the Shamus: when in doubt, make it simpler. You're a person, all right? You're a who, not a what."

"Yes." She did look happier at that. "But that doesn't make me Elizabeth. Even if I'm a copy with free will, I'm not really the original one."

"Fine."

"Fine?"

"Well, not fine from her point of view, but clearing her Case is my job, not yours. You want to help, though?"

"Of course I do!"

"Good. You can start by stop saying 'copy.' I need you to identify with her, because right now nobody knows her better than you do." I thought about how to say this right. "Call yourself an 'edition' of Elizabeth. We don't have a first edition Elizabeth, and that's a crime and a tragedy – but we haven't really lost Elizabeth, because the important parts are still around and kicking."

She smiled at that. "I thought Shamuses hated books."

"Nah, we just fight with them too much to stay together long."

She took a deep breath. "All right. I'm Elizabeth, Second

Edition. What do you need to read up on?"

"We'll start with your friends," I said. "The ones who got killed."

She took a breath. I did wonder, idly, if she *needed* to breathe. Or eat. "They were a good bunch. *Companeros de estudio*, you know? We were all weather-watchers together, took the same classes, did the same 'special sessions,' that sort of thing. One of them, Billy, he was kind of sweet on me, but he got over it."

"You said 'were.' So when did that change?" I asked.

"I don't really know, Shamus," said Elizabeth. "I came back from visiting my family last Christmas, and they were all doing something private. They weren't mean about it, and they didn't shut me out of everything, but one day a week was for whatever they were doing and they didn't invite me along. I felt a little bad, but I just chalked it up to Cin Citiers being Cin Citiers. I was the only country mouse in that bunch, so I thought it was probably due to that."

"And then they all started having accidents." I said. "When did you confront them about it? Before the Pumas died?"

Well, Elizabeth could certainly tear up, at least. "Yeah. One was awful, two and three were numbing, four finally made me admit it wasn't a coincidence, and when I asked Estaban and Diane about what was going on they wouldn't talk to me. They told me to stay out of it. I pushed it, and they pushed me away. Two days later they were dead."

"Did you talk to the ATSE at all?"

"I would have, except that after the Pumas died I bluffed my way into their apartment. You know how it is: 'do not meddle in the affairs of wizards,' right? The cops assumed that I was there for ATSE, so they let me 'clean up' the awkward stuff. And I did, like a good little artisan. But I found some of their correspondence.

"The Pumas, the whole group, were involved with underground researchers. Really underground researchers. Ones that weren't with ATSE or the Syndicate. It all had to do with questions about weather-working, pretty esoteric stuff, and the other researchers were looking for something. I guess they found it." Elizabeth shivered, although it wasn't cold in the diner. "I didn't want to go to the ATSE with it, because my friends had been murdered, damn it, and – look, I'm a card-carrying member of the Guild, all right? But I'm also a New Californian. What if the ATSE decided that everything needed to be swept under the rug?"

I nodded. The ATSE likes to handle things quietly, when they can. They can get away with it because nobody likes to see a convicted mage get handed over to the Dominion, but it doesn't give 'em many options between 'Well, don't do it again' and 'Sorry, but you have to die now.' And if the ATSE found a bunch of unsanctioned weather-workers? Well, that's a valuable skill set to have in New California. The ATSE might be tempted to ignore past sins.

"Okay," I said. "But what about Tia Leila? She doesn't sweep things under the rug. She shoves them there, and beats them with a stick."

Elizabeth seemed slightly surprised I knew about her connection with the Syndicate. "I thought about it," she eventually said, "but I wasn't sure what her reaction was going to be. The Syndicate and the ATSE, they don't always get along, and if Tia Leila thought that the ATSE was going to cover up dead weather-workers?" Elizabeth shuddered. "I didn't want to start a war."

"So you went to the Castle," I said, "because 'for all their faults'."

"Yeah. 'For all their faults'." Elizabeth smiled, wanly. "At least, I assume that I did. That's the one spot where the second edition's lost some pages."

"All right," I said, pulling out Elizabeth's keys. "Let's concentrate on what you do remember. Any of these to your secret lair?"

Elizabeth looked over the set, pointing to each one. "That's to my apartment. Which was... full of sand, I think?"

"Yeah, sorry about that."

"That was you?"

"Sand-devil."

"Nasty. This one is to my parents' house."

"You gonna talk to them?"

"God, no. What can I say to them, Shamus? 'Hey, your daughter came back from the grave as a solid ghost? I don't even know if I'm going to last past the week."

"Fair enough. If it helps, they both want revenge. Papa wants his hot."

"And Mama?"

"She'd rather it was cold enough to ice your drink."

"That's my parents. You're keeping them out of this?"

"I plan to. Although your mother apparently knows her way around a pistol."

"...You're joking."

"Heard it from 'Tia Leila' herself."

"Yeah, I guess you would have actually talked to her."

"This a Case, Elizabeth. I'm going to talk to everybody who might know who murdered you."

"Okay. So, this one is to my locker at the University. Nothing's there. And this one was to a... guy. Nothing's there, too. That was over a year ago. This last one? That's for the place where me and the other mages would work. All of my stuff's there."

"Not any more, it's not. It got cleaned out real good. As in, right down to the floorboards."

"Was there anything left?"

"Just the remains of a barrel of icemold." I was interested in Elizabeth's immediate reaction: disgust and anger, but not complete surprise. "I was assuming that you weren't caught up in that sort of thing."

"You assumed right."

"What about your friends?"

"None of them touched the stuff. Although Billy, well, he grew up in a hard part of town." Elizabeth looked a little pained about that. "He didn't use icemold himself, but he knew some people who maybe weren't the best people, you know?"

"Any Reds?" I asked, not quite idly.

Elizabeth shook her head, but not strongly. "Nobody from Redtown itself. But maybe somebody who had Red friends."

"So are you going to go after Wolfie again?" I asked Elizabeth. She looked down at her mug of tea like she had stashed an answer there, then shook her head.

"He's too powerful. I don't know what he did to me, when I died. I don't even know if first-edition Elizabeth really knew what he did. But, ha, Wolfie is *strong*. Too strong for me to beat him in a straight-up wizard's duel."

"Yeah," I said. "You know, you shouldn't have done that. At least, not in the middle of the city!"

Elizabeth looked contrite and defiant at the same time, like she agreed with me and wanted to do it again anyway. "I'm less than a week old. That count for anything?"

"Sure, but don't go too many times to that well. So, he's powerful. You think you can take Wolfie down if somebody takes a little of the shine off him first?" I wouldn't mind if somebody else did the heavy lifting for a change. And if anybody deserved last dibs on Wolfie, it'd be Elizabeth.

"Maybe? It's weird to talk about." Good thing Elizabeth liked talking about weird things. "It's like there's a link, from him to me? I can feel things that he's feeling; wind on the face, itchy socks, when he's about to burp. I also can keep track of him. Like, now he's way over there." Elizabeth waved to the right, vaguely. I'm the same way with Mount Jeannie, so I could tell she was pointing in the general direction of the Dominion embassy. Which would make sense, sure.

"And maybe I could do something with that," Elizabeth said. "It feels like I could, you know? But it'd be hard. Pushing too much on the link makes me kind of tired, and I don't snap out of it quickly. It sometimes makes it a little tougher for me to stay completely solid, too."

"Okay," I said. "So if we do something with that, we gotta

make it count. Hey, can he track you, too?" That'd be a problem – but Elizabeth was shaking her head.

"It's just the one way. When we were fighting, I could feel it on both ends when I hit him with something, but if he felt the same thing, he didn't show it." Now Elizabeth was looking mad. "And he didn't recognize me at all, I'm sure of it. I knew him the second I saw him, and he didn't know me at all."

I patted her hand; her fingers gratefully clutched mine. Alive, dead, or in-between, Elizabeth had a strong and steady grip. "Don't worry," I said. "Before this is all over, he'll know who you are."

#

The Lore has a bit about how you shouldn't say some names too often, because then their owners come looking for you. I should pay more attention to the Lore.

I hadn't exactly dropped Elizabeth off. She didn't want to tell me how she spent her nights and I didn't want to push it. Instead, I showed her where my office was, gave her a hint about where the spare key was stowed, and watched her walk off into the darkness. I had offered her back her lightstone, both for light and for comfort; she took it – and then handed it back. "I think you should hold on for this for now," she said. I'd have argued, except for some reason I agreed with her.

Elizabeth then said that she'd keep in touch, and I believed her. Why not? Who else could Elizabeth even talk to, at this point?

I sighed heavily after she was gone. Elizabeth was a tough kid in a tough spot, and I'm not used to having the murder victim look over my shoulder during the Case. Well, that's a lie. I am used to it, but they usually don't say anything that other people can hear.

But despite what I told Lucas earlier, my night wasn't even close to over yet. Plus, despite what I had told *Kermie* earlier, I was running out of alternatives to shaking down the Ambassador's house to see if any clues fell out. Trouble was, going in on the ground level wasn't really the best option, either. That all added up to me needing to see a man about a magic carpet, and if I hurried I could catch him before the races really started, so it was time to go.

I got delayed.

There were three of 'em; that old Redtown troika wheeze, and they got their shots in real fast and clean. One big guy to bounce me off of the alley wall, one small guy to get the boot in, and the third to congratulate himself on how tough and bad they all were. And, Hell, three-against-one was pretty brave, for Redtowners. Those mugs ain't happy unless they've got ten times your number and all the weapons.

"The Hood says hi, lackey," said the leader, half-genially, as he stood over my groaning form. He had an eyepatch, which reminded me of Shauni's description. He also had the smell, but that's normal for Redtown. "He also says that you're done with your 'Case.' You hear me?" He waited a couple of seconds. "I dunno, 'rads. You think he heard me?"

"I don't think that he heard you, 'rad," said the Redtowner with the intrusive knee. The leader laughed. I admit it: he had a good nasty-laugh.

"Yeah, I don't think that he heard me, either. Lemme say it again, louder." He skipped forward, his foot blurring to aim itself right at my gut. Which meant that he was pretty surprised when his foot met my hands, instead. I'm not an idiot: when you walk through the dirty streets of Cin City, you wear a damned cup. And you get your brass knuckles on while you're rolling on the ground.

I used his falling into a heap to yank myself up (hearing a rewarding pop from his ankle in the process), and got a couple of real good shots in on the big guy's solar plexus. He should have worn a kidney belt, but I ain't his mother. He can make his own life choices; well, he was staying in Redtown, so maybe he couldn't.

The little guy thought that he was a knife artist. As I faced him, out came the switchblade, and he started up with the entire 'toss it from hand to hand' thing that the punks love.

He looked shocked for a second when I whirled and kicked the knife while it was in midair – but not as shocked when I grabbed him and introduced his chin to my knee.

I know, I know. Some argue that the Lore *clearly* shows that Shamuses are expected to know the manly art of fisticuffs, which doesn't mean feeticuffs. To which I say: tell it to Saint Jackie, chum. Besides, compared to a moldie with an evil knife, these mooks weren't much of a workout.

I got the leader's attention through the simple point of stepping on his ribs. Which creaked, even though I was stepping lightly; nobody eats all that well in Redtown, you understand. "Hey, 'rad," I said. "Tell the Hood I said 'Hi,' back. And that I am disinclined to acquiesce to his request." At the leader's blank expression, I sighed. "Heathens. Tell him I said 'No.' Now collect your buddies and amscray."

I turned, strode, then swung back suddenly to kick away whatever thing the leader had in his hand. Whatever it was, it sounded fragile, and smelled nasty for a second as it rolled further into the alley. Did I mess up his fingers in the process? Wasn't trying, wasn't feeling too bad if I had. "Naughty, naughty," I chided him as I yanked away the guy's shirt. Yup, there was the tattoo. And Shauni had been *nice* about how awful it was. "Do yourself a favor and wait until I'm gone before you pull yourselves together," I continued as I left for real, this time.

Got about two, three blocks before the shaky hands and stomach – and the bruises – set in, but that was okay. Dammit, I'm getting old. Course, when I was younger I would have stayed longer, and gotten more battered trying to pump those clowns for information. I already knew the most important thing: whatever was going on with the Case, it involved Redtown somehow.

And I still had to see a guy about a magic carpet.

#

"Nah, Shammie, nobody breezes the *casamoteo* when we're whizzing steeplechases," said the rune-monkey. That's what I heard, at least. Slang changes fast with Cin City kids; they think it's funny to confuse old guys like me.

But Carlos Reyes O'Malley was a good kid, for a half-wild scion of one of the most prominent Greek families in Cin City; he wasn't really trying to pull my chain. I could more or less tell from that line that the illegal carpet races didn't go anywhere near the Dominion embassy, which made sense. Although... "Whaddya mean, 'Shammie'?" I said.

Carlos looked slightly embarrassed. "Yeah, sorry. Look, if my dad hears that I called a Shamus by his first name or anything like that, he pulls the cork on all of this. I ain't no dummy."

That did sound like a threat that Papa Reyes might make. Or maybe an excuse; Carlos was getting a little long in the tooth for late-night wind-riding, even if the machismo of them was so strong you could see pieces of it collecting on the carpets' fringes. I knew him from a few years ago, when one Case had his brother about to take the fall for an alley murder he didn't do. Thanks to me finding the real killer, Carlos turned out to be happy to oblige when I needed a line on things like the carpet races.

Come to think of it, there were a lot of kids from the upper classes here tonight. These races were always a working-class thing; half sport, half middle finger to the Dominion (when they could get away with it). But the crews looked pretty mixed.

Not that any of them were doing magic, you see. Oh, no, not at all. They were just replacing runes in sockets, touching up the designs painted on the carpets, and praying really hard for specific advantages in the upcoming races. Nothing magical there. Fer sure, as my primitive ancestors might say.

"I don't snitch to the parentals just because I got some lip from a *salvaje* speedweaver still coming down after running a truly pestilent air-tube." When Carlos frowned at that, I went on, "See? We talked funny when I was your age, too. That was back when cavemen fought the dinosaurs."

"I hear ya, Shamus. I'll play nice. So, why do you wanna know about the races? You looking to do a run?"

"Yeah. I'll be here, just as soon as I get twenty years and my sense of invulnerability back." Carlos grinned at that, and why shouldn't he? He had both of those on me. "Let's just say that I wanted a way to get a look-see at the embassy that wouldn't stand out."

"Rug races ain't exactly what you'd call subtle," observed Carlos.

"Sure, but nobody looks too hard at 'em by now. They're too busy yelling at the cops because those loco teens are tearing up the airways again. And writing letters to the papers about how the younger generation's going to hell in a handbasket."

"Gotcha, Shamus. But the rest of us ain't dummies, either. We don't go near that place. The ambassador don't see nobody, so we don't give him a reason to start looking, see?" Carlos shrugged. "The old guys" – by which he meant those still racing, even into their early thirties – "say that the old ambassador used to be a real hard-ass about carpets. They used to hafta race down the coast and keep a lookout. It's better now, so why push it?"

"Huh," I said in my clever way. "Didn't you start racing here about four, five years ago?" At least, that's when people started complaining to the papers about the noise.

"Yeah," said Carlos. "The old ambassador just kinda gave up about the whole thing. Didn't even try to raid the old routes anymore. It took a couple of years, but people kind of drifted into using this spot more regular. I don't know; maybe the old asshole had the flu or something, and didn't feel like getting back into it."

"Yeah, maybe," I said. "What does the new ambassador think?"

Carlos shrugged. "Don't know, won't care until he does. We laid a little low when the new asshole showed up, but he ain't really done nothing before today. I got enough to worry about in the air without looking for more crap on the ground. Because, between you and me, Shamus?" He leaned forward. "That thing in the east going on with Sonora is getting pretty scary. We had a couple people from the militia talking to some of us about the carpets. And the people to fly them."

He looked around at the cheerfully chaotic night scene. "This may be all gone in two weeks. May not come back, either. Not easy to armor a carpet."

I looked at Carlos. On a guess I said, "Got a commission, did you?" He shrugged.

"Yeah, but they did that for all the flyers. Historical, or something like that. Hey, you want to hear something funny?" Carlos laughed, with even some real humor attached. "You think Papa wasn't wild about me flying? You should have seen his face when I told him that I was putting on the uniform. Couldn't even try to argue me down, either. Best he could do was ask me what I was rebelling against."

Carlos offered his flask; I took a swig, winced, and offered him my own. As he drank, I said, "And you said?"

"Please, Shamus. I'm educated. I stared at him, right in the eye, gave him the Look, and said 'I dunno. Whaddya got?'"

As I said, he's a good kid. I let him get back to watching the other races as I walked off. There was something that was bugging me about all of this, and I needed to think about it a bit.

I didn't get it, until suddenly I almost did: why did old Cackle stop caring about illegal carpet races? And why didn't Wolfie start? Sure, the racers will solemnly insist that they're importing the carpets and just 'black boxing' it, whatever that means; but even for New California, that's a pretty threadbare excuse.

And the Universal Dominion hungers for mages. It always has. Word on the street is, the parts of Deseret that the Dominion gnawed off in the last war still haven't been digested properly, and that kind of stomach trouble requires a constant supply of fresh mages to soak up the bile. And it wouldn't matter how powerful the mages were, either. Just enough to use cantrips would be fine.

You'd think that they'd at least look into raiding the rug races that were going on practically underneath their noses. But they hadn't. Why? I got the feeling that if I could ever figure out why the Dominion's ambassadors were acting so weird, I'd get everything there was to get about this case. I probably still wouldn't like the answers, though. I ain't that lucky.

CHAPTER EIGHTEEN
Culture and Stuff

There was a white envelope in the mail. The kind that makes you feel kind of grubby for just looking at it, then mad because what gives a piece of paper the right to look down on you? I knew what it was, but I opened it anyway. Yeah. An invite from the International Film Preservation Foundation (modernly known as the Lorekeepers) to tonight's Double Feature at the opera house. Me and an 'associate' – I wondered if that meant personal or professional. Then I wondered whether the difference even meant anything in my case.

I didn't actually need an invite to go; it is the privilege of a Shamus to be allowed to spend at least ten minutes at any location in New California before he may be lawfully thrown out. But this hinted that the Lorekeepers thought I should actually go to one of their soirees, for once. And that I should bring a buddy. Even if it was just for swank.

I brought it up with Lucas after another long day walking from interview to interview, trying to find somebody who might have seen Elizabeth arrive at the Palace. No luck in those, by the way. But Lucas begged off; he figured that putting an Adventurer into a room with that much wealth in it was simply asking for trouble. Plus all the people wanting to take a look at the elf.

"Isn't that your thing?" I asked.

Lucas shrugged. "Doesn't feel right. Call it a hunch." Adventurers and their hunches. "You could bring Elizabeth."

"No. Too confusing," I said, and then peered at him. "I don't remember telling you about my meet-up with her."

"You didn't have to," said Lucas. "If you hadn't met with her, we'd have spent today looking for her; if she had told you anything I needed to know, you'd have told me." Lucas looked smug. "That's logic, that is."

"Will wonders ever cease?" misquoted I – and I then tried to shove Lucas as hard as I could. I failed, but only because he was diving for cover himself. The crossbow bolts coming out of the lengthening shadows thus missed us both by a good three, four inches.

#

You can find alleys like this all over town. The alley's a little narrow for two but not sideways, there's room for an occasional dumpster like the one that I was now hiding behind, and there's always a lot of gloom. These places are dark even at noon, and it was a lot closer to night than noon right now. Not a bad place to try to get a shot off, especially since everybody besides me and Lucas had taken one look at those crossbow bolts in the wall behind us and went running. I decided it'd be nice if one of them ran into a cop; I wanted more backup than the pricking of my thumbs. Or even Lucas's.

There's a fun game to play at times like these: how fast can the shooters reload? If it's faster than how long it'd take you to get to the next bit of cover, then you duck and hope whatever you're hiding behind is thick enough. If it's not, then you go somewhere else where they can't draw a bead on you. Or, hey, you can do something stupid, like charge the dark alleyway where the bolts came from. Because nobody ever does that.

Except for lunatics from the Adventurer's Guild. Lucas turned his own dive into a roll that got him hugging the lip of the wall just outside the mouth of the alley, a few moments before two more bolts came firing out and clipping off the corners of a couple of bricks. That was my own hint to back off and around the opposite lip. This time, when the crossbows went off, we were both treated to a bolt apiece. Even more badly aimed this time.

I looked over at Lucas. "Two?" I mouthed. He thought, but shook his head no. I had to agree: the first shots weren't too bad, but the others were pretty awful. That probably meant somebody with a couple of Cin City Specials.

For this one I have to blame the Lore: people have been trying to turn crossbows into guns for centuries. The state of the art these days is a crossbow light enough to be fired in one hand, with an enchantment on the limb and string to have it re-cock itself. Not nearly as much stopping power as one of the old guns, but it'll kill somebody in street clothes and won't explode if a mage looks at it cross-eyed. But trying to *vaquero* it up by dual-wielding isn't smart, either. I mean, you still have to reload the damn quarrels. Not that one person shooting a crossbow in each hand was *much* safer than two shooters; it's hard to second-guess how an idiot will move.

That's why I'm so successful, I guess, because I left my office without anything of my own to fire back with. Which left me pressed flat against a building, and Lucas duplicating me on the other side of the alley mouth. He didn't have his crossbow out, either; guess he was out of special goop.

So, time to try thinking. We could run away, but I don't like people shooting at me. Bad habit to encourage. If we stuck around, the shooter would leave, which was also a bad habit to encourage. Can't go around without splitting up, can't go through, can't go under. But could we go high? I took a gander at the windowsills, and grinned. There was a flowerpot on one ledge, just where I needed it. And I always carry a stone. You never know when you'll need a stone.

I'm no mime but I can get stuff across; Lucas was ready when I threw the stone. As I hoped, the idiot *vaquero* in the alley shot one bolt at movement and another at the sudden crash. Lucas almost got *himself* shot at that point, the damned fool. As I did my own rush, I saw Lucas credibly slam our shooter back into the wall.

And then I saw the shooter get up, his eyes glowing green. When Lucas noticed that, a shudder went through the Adventurer's body, leaving behind someone with no sense of humor and a relaxed attitude about bloodshed. The elf shook twin daggers out of his sleeves and started moving and slashing, with none of the usual reluctance or self-doubt about stabbing other people.

I can't get into that state, and that's good. But it's great when somebody on your side *can*, because it's one hell of a distraction. In this case, the shooter was so busy shouting and growling and getting shallowly sliced and throwing Lucas around that I was able to get within truncheon range.

You know all those stories about berserkers ignoring deadly wounds and blood spurting from the stumps of their arms and the rest of it? Those are great stories, sure. And they're almost all true. Which is why I smacked the shooter's damned knees, then his elbows after he fell down. I don't care what you are, you can't walk on broken joints. Or at least not quickly. The shooter was giving crawling a game try, using his busted elbows, when Lucas picked himself out the garbage, scowled, and hit the shooter in the back of the head with a carefully-administered knife pommel. Said shooter shuddered, vomited once in a half-hearted way, and passed out.

"I assume you want him alive," Lucas growled.

"We don't have necromancers here."

"I know, I know. Bastard cracked a rib, though."

I didn't point out that Lucas had been trying to carve chunks off the other guy. Adventurers like to hold a grudge, but always think it's weird when somebody holds one against them right back. Then again, the rib-cracking bastard *did* shoot first.

The crossbows were junk by now, but I looked them over anyway. Like I thought, they were enchanted repeaters, but different. Usually there's a side-hopper to magically push the bolt into position while the cord's being re-cocked, but the magazine on these was underneath, and looked like it used a... spring? Hand-made, cheap, and even I could tell that the enchantments were cheaper. Pieces of the damned things were falling off, even as I watched.

So I started going through the shooter's pouch while Lucas pulled various odd-looking cords and charms out of his coat pockets ('restrainers,' he said tersely when I cocked an eyebrow at them). Not much cash, a few keys, and a college identification card. Our guy here was one Bernardo Campa Verdugo. I thought about it. When he wasn't leaking green light from his eyes, I could believe that Bernardo here could have been a student.

But he had been leaking green light, so it was time to call in the specialists. I'd let the cops do that, though. And man, but I couldn't wait for the mages of the ATSE to stick their fingers into this particular pie.

Speaking of the cops, a guard patrol came up running as we finished securing Verdugo. Guess somebody *had* run into one, after all. Getting the patrol's attention was the easy part; what was slightly harder was keeping them from knocking on the perp's head a few more times 'just to be sure.' New Californians can really get behind a 'no evil mage, no problem' strategy. But they're good lads and lasses on the Night Watch, always ready to listen to the kindly old Shamus. Especially when he reminds them that they can legitimately call a few ATSE 'artisans' away from their dinners, just to take care of the prisoner. Misery loves company, hey? But that wasn't going to be our problem. Once the wagon and the artisans came to collect Verdugo, I claimed Shamus privilege to have us stop by the next morning to give our statements, not to mention get full details on the interrogation and/or exorcism.

In the meantime: the opera house awaited. Lucas raised an eyebrow, in lieu of him asking me if that was a good idea, what with people shooting at me; I shrugged instead of explaining it was part of the job, and he dropped the subject. One of the nice things about Adventurers is that they take a lot of this stuff in stride.

#

I'm no leading man but I clean up all right, and I even keep a fancier version of my usual outfit around for special occasions like these. Oh, and as for who I was bringing? In the end, I'd sent a message to Father Mike. Less conspicuous that way.

Well, all right. A six-foot orc in a black cassock and clerical collar ain't really what you call inconspicuous. But Mike was just another spectacle on the runway as the two of us arrived at the John Williams Opera House. And he wouldn't fuss if I needed to go have a quiet word backstage.

Mike is supposed to hate the Billy. It's a church – but not his church, and his church can't do anything about it, either. Even the Catholics among the working class get mulish whenever somebody starts talking trash about the Lore, and the effect it has over everything in New California – and as for the nobility? Hoo-boy. One of 'em heard about indulgences, once, and thought that it was a good idea so he ran with it – and then so did the rest. You ain't seen nothing until you see a New Californian duke try to pay the Archbishop in advance for the former's upcoming adulteries. Especially when the duke asks if he can get a bulk rate.

Me, I like the Billy in spite of itself; it's got no taste worth mentioning, but the seats are comfortable and you can get a decent drink. The opera house is on two levels, so that regular people can do Saturday viewings without getting in the way of the muckety-mucks, and vice versa. The Lore's for everybody, right? It took the New California ruling class a while to learn that lesson, but now that they had, it seems to have stuck.

One of the other nice things about the Billy is that Shamuses these days have a dedicated box. Mike and I were escorted there, very nice, with bottles of soft drinks in a bed of crushed ice and a selection of popcorn for our pleasure. This went a long way to get Mike into the spirit of the thing; priest or not, he loves the Lore as much as anybody else in New California does. Well-educated in it, too.

"Ha! They put Carmalita Prinze Perroni in the Willow role tonight after all. I thought that having her understudy for Buffy was a ridiculous publicity stunt, direct descendant of the original actress or not. Still, this is very exciting! Whedon composed very little in the way of actual musical numbers during his life; I can't wait to see how this matches up with the Povenmire and Marsh *episodio* coming on after the intermission!" Mike looked over, and saw my eyes glazing over. "Philistine," he said with a smile.

"Hey, I like classical music," I said defensively. "I just don't think about it much. Besides, I'm not gonna be here long. No, you can stay," I continued hastily as Mike scowled and looked for his things. "Somebody's just going to fetch me so's I can have a quiet word with somebody else."

And, right on cue, there was a discreet knock on the door. I smiled. "And there we go. Don't worry about saving me any popcorn, Mike."

I was shown into the private viewing room that the Lorekeepers reserve for the muckety-mucks when they want to have a quiet chat with nobody listening in; somehow, it's more or less dead air when it comes to detection magic. I'd been in one of these rooms once, during one murder Case where the victim was found dead and locked inside, with no way to magically discover the murderer (even if we did have mages, which we don't). I solved that one pretty quick by just looking hard at everybody who had a grudge, and getting lucky right off. Some people just don't think real clear under stress.

Tomas Garcia Garcia – Mr. Gee-Gee in my youth, and 'Mr. Chairman of the IFPF' now that we're all supposed to be adults – was sitting at the table. When he saw me, he brightened up like I was a favorite student of his (he was always one of my favorite teachers), and levered himself up from the table so fast I couldn't get over there in time. His hand was still pretty steady in mine, but Mr. Gee-Gee was getting old. Well, we all are. Most of us get to, at least.

"Tommy!" he said. "Sit down, so that I can." I thought about offering to hold his chair, but a glare stopped that. So I compromised, and got him a coffee and the three snacks from the cart most likely to be forbidden him by his doctors. From the way Mr. Gee-Gee dug in, I had guessed right. I grabbed a cup myself.

"Always good to see you, sir," I said as I poured milk for both of us. "And how can I help the IFPF today?" A Shamus ain't a Lorekeeper, and Mr. Gee-Gee can't tell me what to do. But if he needs me for something, I'm going to be there to find out what. And to get it for him, if I can. And that's not just because he trained me, all too many years ago.

"I need to consult with you as a Shamus, Tommy." He sipped, added a bit more brown sugar, sipped again. "I understand that you are dealing with a Case that involves the ambassador, yes?"

"Yes, sir. At least, he's trying to get involved in it. Only the evidence keeps pointing away from him, and it's driving him nuts." I felt fine talking about the Case to him. I mean, if Mr. Gee-Gee were unreliable, I'd quit it all and move to Virginia, because at least there they're used to everything you see being crazy.

"That's what I thought. I should give you two warnings, Tommy: one from the Castle, and one from me."

"The Castle?" I said, innocently enough. "Couldn't they just send me a page?"

"They don't want this written down," said Mr. Gee-Gee. "Now that it doesn't look like the Ambassador did it, there are people who want you to take your time about catching the murderer. The longer, the better."

"It's good to want," I said flatly.

"I knew you'd say that."

"You should, Mr. Gee-Gee: you're the one who taught me the line. Okay, I heard what you told me." Mr. Gee-Gee flickered a smile at how I didn't actually agree with what he had told me. I was also wondering why they weren't listening to Dory about this. I had given her a good reason why it couldn't be Wolfie, hadn't I? "What's the warning that I'm gonna care about?"

"Just this: the Dominion's ambassadors have been acting odd, over time. Alarmingly so."

"Really? What have they been doing?"

"Skipping the shows here, mostly." I startled slightly at that news. "Exactly. They may hate everything else about us, but the Dominion embassy has always been a patron of the Billy, and by extension the IFPF. But for the last few years they've gotten less and less interested in our performance schedule. When it was the former ambassador, I just assumed that he was getting old. But the new one doesn't seem to care, either. I don't think that he's attended a single performance here, despite repeated invitations."

"Did either of them say why?" Mr. Gee-Gee shook his head, and that surprised me, too. The Dominion's never shy about saying why they're upset this week. And if they're not upset but they still want to be, they'll come up with a new reason on the fly.

"I do not care for pandering to those people," said Mr. Gee-Gee. "And I will do everything in my power to keep New California free of their rule. But I know how the Dominion acts, Tommie. So when I see one of them acting differently, I worry. When they're here and monopolizing the viewing rooms and making us beg for restoration cantrips, at least I understand what they're doing. I truly do not understand this."

"Neither do I, sir. Do you think that they're plotting something against the IFPF?"

"I don't think so. I think that the Dominion might be simply forgetting that the IFPF is worth plotting against. Which is even more alarming from my point of view, because if the Dominion is really losing interest in the thing that diverts them most about us, then we need to fix that. And quickly."

#

After I finished up with Mr. Gee-Gee, I caught the rest of the performance. Why not? I wasn't lying to Father Mike; I do like classical music. In manageable chunks.

It was swell. Povenmire and Marsh ain't always my favorite composers (too syrupy) but *¡Compórtate!* is one of their classics and the kid they had singing the female lead sang "*Lo Que Podría Haber Sido*" so clear you could almost see the notes. When they brought the cast out for their encores, the leads did the duet "*Ciudad del Amor*" – and then the *prima donna* belted out "*Pato Momo,*" which ended up having the whole theater up on its feet by the end.

And while we were all standing, the lights went down again and the orchestra started in with the Royal Anthem. That didn't always happen, at least for regular performances. I glanced at the Royal Booth, but the King and Queen weren't here tonight. It must have been because of all the soldiers down there in the main seats; only, when I looked around, there were just as many kids in uniforms singing about lemon drops and chimney tops in the upper section (I even saw Carlos, in fact). They had better uniforms, sure – and they had plenty of worried-looking mamas and papas wondering just where things had gotten so complicated.

I wondered, too. Sure, I'm a good New Californian, and I don't spit when I see Ronnie's mug on my pocket change. I wouldn't live anywhere else, even if I could. Most of the guys my age are the same way. We just don't wear it on our sleeves.

But the younger generation these days, they're running wild. Youths should be out lounging in parlors or hanging out on corners, smoking cigarettes and hassling the Man before having rumbles in the back alleys over their doomed love affairs. Instead, these kids, well-born ones, were off drilling with the city militia and organizing the refugees and envying the hell out of anybody who had actually gotten into the Sonoran Expedition. Which wasn't *bad*, right? Well, it wasn't. But it also wasn't what we were used to.

The Anthem ended; luckily, it was the version that didn't have all the extra lyrics tacked on later about how wonderful the world was. In the silence that followed, I saw Carlos pick his moment and shout out, "PLAY BALL!" As the theater broke out in slightly relieved laughter, I grinned.

Okay, so maybe the kids *were* still New Californians at heart.

CHAPTER NINETEEN

:Two musical notes, in rapid succession:

And wasn't thinking about the upcoming war a great thing to go to bed to?

But, for a wonder, nobody was lurking at my digs to try to fight, jabber at, or seduce me. I was starting to worry about this run of luck; when things finally balanced, it'd probably be spectacular.

I got the first installment on the payback the next morning, just as I expected, and before Lucas and I even walked into the police station. It turned out the ATSE had assigned Eddie Cazals to handle things on their end, and he did not like me at all. Partially because I kept calling him 'Eddie,' but mostly because...

"Oh, it's you, Shamus. Join the damned union." Which was actually polite of him; usually Eddie adds the word '*carnero*' at the end.

"We've been over this, Eddie. I ain't one of you guys. In any way."

"I don't care – hey, wait, who the Hell is that?" Lucas stopped, puzzled, and still drinking a cup of what a Cin City merchant will smilingly lie and call 'coffee.' It's not bad, actually. But it ain't coffee.

"You got a problem, friend?" the elf said, his accent noticeably getting a little thicker as the sentence went on.

"Maybe I do now. You sign up with the ATSE yet, redne – outlander?"

Lucas technically smiled away the half-uttered slur. "Is that what y'all call your local group? My crew goes to so many different places – some of 'em on the ass back of beyond – we just can't keep track."

You never can tell if Eddie's deliberately trying to be a jerk, or he's really just that talented at it. I figured his bosses had assigned him to me to get me to clear the Case faster, but this was out of hand, even for him. And if this kept up then there'd be a crowd to watch the street theater. "Gentlemen," I started.

"This is New California, not whatever steaming swamp you pulled yourself out of. You come here, you show solidarity with your brothers and sisters!"

"Sorry, but I don't see the family resemblance. Hey, you look pale. When's the last time you did any work outdoors?"

"Are you calling me a manager?"

"Why, does it come up often enough for you to need to check?"

"*Gentlemen*," I snapped. They both looked at me. "Thank you. Dead girl. One of your 'sisters,' Edward." This was not a good time to piss him off further. "Probably killed by somebody trying to kill both of *us*, Lucas. I need to clear this Case. *Capice*? Good." Then I went into the police station. I assumed that they'd either follow me, or go out of town and have a damned wizard's duel where nobody could see them. They chose to follow me.

Every police station in Cin City has a cell that's been worked on by an ATSE artisan, and the bigger ones have a room that's been carefully fixed up to make it easier for the people who we don't admit exist to do the stuff we don't talk about. This one was pretty standard. The carpet just happened to sport a design that could be converted into a pentacle with a little work, and there were plenty of threaded holes in the walls that could be fitted with hooks and incense pots. When the door was closed, I could 'hear' the protections that made it impossible to scry the room.

Eddie's not entirely wrong, you know. The rules for joining the ATSE could easily stretch to include Shamuses. They've let in more marginal cases. But I answer to a higher authority, and I don't do divided loyalties. The ATSE gets that; I just wish that they'd tell Eddie.

The table and chairs normally in the center of the room had been moved to one side to accommodate our Mr. Verdugo; he was spread-eagled on the ground, with chains at legs and arms and a sigil-inscribed hood covering his head. He had been changed into a loose shirt and pants; there was the faint aloe and ozone smell that gets associated with healing spells. Guess we had hit him pretty hard, at that.

There were two artisans working the scene: one was fiddling with the pentacle, while the other was touching up the designs drawn on Verdugo's clothes. I recognized the painter. "Hey, Daisy," I said – after getting into her line of sight, and letting her see me first. You don't disturb somebody drawing magical sigils. You just don't.

Daisy carefully finished the final brush-stroke, gingerly stepped back, wiped her brush, and conscientiously packed away the napkin she used to clean it. Only then did she smile back at me, and not a moment before. "Morning, Tommie," she said. "Bad one for this, ha?"

You'd never know Daisy Fukunaga Araujo for a mage. A kindly grey-haired *abuela*, tall and dignified edition? Sure. But she had the hands of a mage and the watchful eyes of one, too; and she drew the straightest runes in the city. I wondered if the ATSE sent her over because they were worried about the interrogation-slash-exorcism. Daisy looked calm enough, but she always did. I've seen her coolly draw containment wards faster than a fire elemental could blot them out, with no more reaction than a few loose strands of hair. The only reason she didn't scare me was because I had no reason to be afraid of her.

"Never a good day for this kind of thing," I agreed, and pointed a thumb at the other artisan, who was now going over the restraining and confinement gear that the ATSE uses to make the arrest of a mage stick. "He new?"

Daisy looked over. "Yes. At least, I've never met him before. His name is John Perez; the head office sent him over to learn the ropes." She leaned forward a little, to keep her voice low. "I think he's an orphan. Or maybe a natural child of somebody important. We were quietly told that the situation is difficult to explain."

That's the joy of living in a realm where every so often a noble is shocked to discover the bed he's sneaked into is actually his wife's; you always have a lot of upper class bastards around. And, sure, illegitimate children, too. Usually it all works out, but every so often somebody needs to be placed somewhere. Like this 'John Perez.'

"You carrying him?" I asked.

"What? Oh, no, he seems competent enough. John just doesn't seem to enjoy being here, poor child. I'm sure he'll adjust."

Well, never get in the way of the experts. They seemed to be setting up for the procedure, so I joined Lucas behind the yellow line marked into the carpet. He was taking what I assumed to be a professional look at the proceedings, which made sense. I didn't think that Lucas had more than the touch of magical talent that all elves supposedly had, but Adventurers tend to push any advantage to its limits. Besides, there was nothing else to do except watch the proceedings, and wait for the exciting parts.

Hoo-boy. Excitement. I had no idea.

Here's something that the Lore doesn't tell you. Interrogations are boring. Exorcisms are boring. Combinations of both are boring. That's because they're run by cops and lawyers, and that crowd just loves boring stories where they already know what the ending is. If something new comes up at one of these things, somebody's screwed up somewhere.

Almost everybody in that room was trying not to screw up anything. There were the three from the ATSE, me and Lucas, somebody from the DA's office and somebody from the public defender's, a couple of cops to ask the actual questions, a couple more with pikes, and let's not forget the perpetrator himself. The room was big, but it still felt crowded. And full of old sweat, some from times when the interrogations *weren't* boring. This kind of thing was no joke.

Demon possession is a little more common than other kinds of necromancy, because you can hide it better. But not much more common, because you can't hide for long that you're hosting a Hellspawn that doesn't even speak an Earthly language. There's always some idiot who thinks having a demon doing the crime will get him out of legal trouble, so interrogations like these require getting the demon to answer a few questions first. And since demons enjoy lying, things can get vigorous.

But for me? *Boring*. Most of an exorcism happens below the surface, where I can't see. From the outside it sounds like a mage (Eddie, as it happens) pronouncing a series of nonsense syllables until there's a response from the guy strapped to the pentacle. Somebody writes that down. The syllables continue until there's another response, and that gets written down, until eventually the guy starts shuddering and talking and then a few questions get asked until the host passes out. Then the exorcist banishes the demon, and the lawyers huddle together and decide whether to charge anybody with a crime. They usually do.

Like I said, real exciting. So I wasn't paying attention to the interrogation, like they say I'm supposed to; but I was paying attention to the people around me, like I really *am* supposed to. And that's why I saw John start to move back, very quietly, to the door. There were two guards standing there, just like *they* were supposed to. Nobody gets to leave until an exorcism's done (people either go before the exorcism starts or hold it in, if you're wondering), and it wouldn't be the first time that somebody's freaked out at a little anti-demonology demonology, but this guy had been sent over by ATSE, and by now I was getting up and intercepting him, as smoothly as I could manage.

My left hand clamped over his right wrist, stopping him from pulling something from his pocket. I could feel that whatever-it-was he was holding was hard and circular, like a ball. Before John could react, I slammed him against the wall, pinning his other arm against his side while I yanked his hand up as far as it could go. "Don't let go of that," I hissed. "I don't know where it's been."

In the sudden silence I could hear the swish of two pikes as their owners readied them, the tips aimed right at John's neck. Bless Cin City cops: none of 'em live on their salaries, but they don't mess around when it's important. I could also hear Eddie suddenly shift from boring nonsense syllables to ones with a lot more urgency and gutturals in them.

And that's when it all cut loose. John snarled and broke the ball in his hand – then yelled in pain, because that did nothing good to his palm. I had my head turned away, so I missed pretty much all of the light show that exploded out of the ball; the guards got a good enough taste of it to daze them hard, unfortunately. Even more unfortunately, our Mr. Verdugo treated it like the prearranged signal that it probably was and snapped the bonds on his pentacle with a titanic heave. He levered himself up using the closest table, then flipped it; papers and lawyers went flying, and the table itself went smack right into Eddie, who had ignored everything else so he could throw down binding spells.

This must have slowed Verdugo some, because he had only taken a couple of steps and ripped the hood off before a disc of glowing purple sigils went smashing into his head like a Virginian knight's shield. Daisy still looked perfectly cool as she swung the shield three, four more times before it spluttered and died. Which left her with no weapon or defense, and it didn't look like Verdugo was down for the count.

What was I doing during all of this? Tripping Perez. He hit the floor, but wasn't down for the count, either; instead, he rattled off a quick sentence in some language I didn't care for and suddenly my nose was bleeding. The rest of me wasn't too happy, either. You ever take a beating in the ring? Yeah, like that, only all at once.

Good thing I took all those beatings in the ring, then. I blinked, stepped forward, and punched the grin right off of Perez's face. Then I delivered a vicious kick to his tender regions while he was still on the ground. I don't care how good at magic you are, you don't shrug off a shot there unless you've already specially warded it. Or wore a cup... nope, looked like Perez hadn't. Such a shame.

Then, well, I pulled out my gun and went in to stop Verdugo from eviscerating an *abuela*. If it was just a rogue wizard I'd have gone for one of the mage-stickers now lying on the floor, but for a demon I figured I'd stick with something more spiritual. Even if I could've used the pike to help keep me on my feet.

I'd have done better if I wasn't still a little woozy, but I wasn't really trying to bash his head in. As long as I could wave the gun around, I could keep the monster in Verdugo's head on the back of its heels. And it did not like the gun; oh, no, it did *not*. Shamuses may not be good at healing the sick, but we're not bad at smacking around bad guys.

We're also not bad at distractions, because while I was doing all that, Lucas was blinking off the dazzler and throwing a knife that kind of hurt to look at for too long. His aim was off; he didn't do better than score Verdugo's side, but even that was enough to make the possessed human scream and hesitate. And then it was Eddie's turn again.

Eddie is, as I may have mentioned, an unpleasant man. That includes his exorcism techniques. Some mages persuade, others threaten, a few confuse. Eddie just beats the crap out of a demon until it leaves.

It's a hell of a thing to see, if you can manage it. Eddie somehow reached into Verdugo's head with one hand and yanked out the demon's ethereal head, which was just as ugly as you'd think. He then put that head in an elbow lock and proceeded to rhythmically smash his fist into the demon's noses and eye, yanking back a bit more each time to pull more of the demon out. The demon did try to fight back, of course, but since it was using its hands and feet to keep hold of Verdugo's body there wasn't much it could do.

Well, at one point it did try to use its tail to strike at Eddie's head, but it misjudged the strike; instead of whaling on Eddie's neck it swung by his teeth – and Eddie promptly lunged out and bit down on the tail. The responding scream of pain almost made me feel bad for the demon. But it was enough to pop the demon the rest of the way out of Verdugo.

I felt a tap on my shoulder. I turned, to see Daisy calmly

looking at me, pike in hand and looking perfectly composed. "Could you excuse me, please?" I reflexively stepped aside; she dimpled a smile. "Thank you, Tomas." She then looked for a moment, paused – and shoved the blade right through the demon's head, and about half an inch away from Eddie's.

"Everybody duck!" Daisy said cheerfully as purple-gold energy started flowing down the pike. As I did, I saw one of the lawyers start to stand, unsteadily. So I yanked her down, too.

I could describe what it sounds like when a demon implodes, but I won't. It sounds ridiculous when you put it on paper. But I'll tell you: the smell is something that'll make you get drunk before you can forget it properly.

I picked myself up, gingerly. Perez was on the ground, whimpering, while two blinking, scowling guardsmen looked ready to give him another kicking. Verdugo was stretched out; dead or knocked out, I didn't know. Everybody else seemed more or less all right, except for Eddie – who looked mostly disgusting, what with all the demon ectoplasm covering him. He started to speak, half-retched, wiped his face, and spat. Finally, Eddie scowled and said, "I need a goddamned towel."

Lucas promptly handed him one without saying a word.

CHAPTER TWENTY

But Wait. There's More!

The hell of it was, the cops still had to do the interrogation afterward. In fact, now they had to do two. But it all went a lot faster this time. When Verdugo woke up, he took one look at all the cops scowling at him and immediately started yelling for his lawyer. He even got one right away. It got him out of the room – and into somewhere that'd hold him until somebody needed him.

But 'John Perez'? Oh, but the wheels of justice spun extra-fast for this. Captain Gannon had come down himself to do the interrogation, freshly-signed warrant and all. The ink wasn't even completely dry yet.

"Hey, you see this paper, asshole?" The funny thing about Gannon is, he's a calm guy. Even the swear words come out conversational. "This warrant is for multiple counts of attempted murder by magic. I have witnesses who saw you try to bust out of here after you sabotaged a demon cleansing. I have two *expert witnesses* from the ATSE who'll swear to the original sabotage." That should have worried Perez more, I thought. The Dominion has a self-imposed blind spot when it comes to demons; since demons don't exist, anybody who can get rid of them has to be a con-man of some kind. It all makes it easier to openly try somebody for something involving demonology without having to worry that the trial ends with a Dominion smash-and-grab.

Gannon went on, "I even got somebody who can testify to the whammy that you tried to put on him. What I *don't* have is any evidence that you're who you say you are. Not that I care. I'm happy with what I have."

"Give me a lawyer," said Perez. His accent was not even remotely New Californian, although he was fluent enough. Gannon looked at him in what looked like honest confusion, then tapped the papers in his hand to straighten them out – and to get Perez's attention.

"What part of 'attempted murder via magic' was unclear,

you would-be cop-killing piece of shit?" replied Gannon, evenly. "That's a High Justice crime. You don't get a lawyer. You don't even get a jury. High Justice is the King's business, and he's going to give you the business before lunch." The captain made a face and shook his head, in the classic style; I always like to see someone who really understands the Lore. "You're an illegal mage, *imbecil*. Well, that's what the King's going to decide. Unless I get something that will convince me that you're not."

"You think I fear death? I know death, *opopo*. I know lots of deaths. Maybe I'll know yours, ah?" Perez's accent had thickened, but he was talking big; I could see his hands scrabbling in the handcuffs built into the interrogation chair. So did Lucas; he raised an eyebrow, then smacked one of Perez's hands with a book. Not enough to hurt, but enough to smart.

Both Perez and Gannon started, and looked at Lucas. He shrugged. "Looked like he was trying to start building a spell. Not that I'd know anything about that."

"You going to let him do that to me?" asked Perez.

Gannon shrugged. "Citizens and visitors to New California are to provide reasonable assistance to the authorities in the subduing and extradition of illegal mages. He could have hit you with a mace, if he thought you were casting another spell. Do you get it yet? Is your situation grinding its way into your brain? If you want out of this, you start talking."

"I said I don't care if you kill me. Just get on with it. I am done with you."

"Well, that's a shame." Gannon sipped his coffee. "Because we're not done with you. And you have us all wrong; we're not going to kill you. We're not going to harm a hair on your head. We'll just give you up to the Dominion, like the treaty tells us to."

The two ATSE artisans were out of Perez's field of vision, but not mine. They looked unhappy, but not mutinous. It might have been different if Perez had been born here, but a foreigner who'd probably killed one of their own already? Besides, maybe Gannon was bluffing. It's a hell of a thing, throwing a mage right into the Dominion's maw. Even one that had just tried to blow up an exorcism.

It was a good shot, but it didn't hit Perez like it should have. He was still acting like he knew something that we didn't. Maybe we should tell him that he didn't know everything, either? So I grabbed a chair in front of him, lit a cigarette, and contemplated the smoke for a second. Gannon smoothly made room; I was going to miss him, when he finally retired.

"You're thinking about this all wrong, chum," I said cheerfully. "And by 'chum' I mean 'shark bait.' There's a mechanism in place for these little affairs. What happens is, the King makes the decision, and then the King tells the Dominion, and then the Dominion comes for you. They got a place right outside of Cin City to make the drop-off. And, here's the funny thing: the Dominion ambassador ain't involved at all in the affair. Something about how his bosses want to make sure that he's not making little deals on the side with renegade mages."

Ooh, that struck a nerve. I went on. "That's half of it. The second half is, there are no mages in New California, right? So when we get one from outside, and we hand one over to the Dominion, we gotta do that without magical defenses. It's a long walk to the spot, you know? But hey, you don't care if you die, right?"

Perez looked real uncertain now. I smiled, to cover my own sour stomach. If this was a regular punk using a cheap knockoff artifact, or a mage that threw a fireball instead of pulling out a knife, this wouldn't be happening, and the punk and the damfool mage would know it, too. Hell, even with a demon-related crime on the docket, some people out there would still hate giving up somebody to the Dominion. Not enough to riot, but enough to maybe make a fuss.

Behind him, Eddie was scowling, but I was pretty sure that was because he just got reminded that a fellow union member was still missing. Next to him, Daisy quietly said, "You can take John Perez's name, but you're not him." I've never heard her voice sound that bleak before.

And that did it. 'Perez' slumped in his chair. "What do I need to do?"

"Talk," Gannon said. "Start out by telling me who you work for. We'll go from there."

"I do that, I die."

"You don't do that, the Dominion will kill you. Very slowly. You have to give me something that will let me tell the King he needs to start reading with his left eye, you understand me? No? Fine, we'll start small. Where's the real John Perez?"

"In an alleyway between here and his apartment. I was rushed for time, so he might even still be alive; I needed his papers and a bit of his hair. And it was easy for me to get both," 'Perez' sneered. "You people are like children when it comes to security. The Flatfoot supposedly guarding him didn't even arrive until after I was done! And entering this station of yours was just as pathetically easy."

"We care more about making it hard for bad guys to get out," said Gannon. "Which you discovered. So, that's how. Let's keep going: why did you want Bernardo Verdugo so bad?"

"Who?"

"The guy possessed by a demon."

"Oh, him. He's not important. A very useful idiot, once. But not needed anymore. I thought you would simply kill him, eventually, while I made my escape. You were obviously luckier than that."

You get a lot of arrogance in Cin City, but this guy could teach workshops in it. Handcuffed to a chair, clearly telling us the bare minimum needed to keep him from being handed over to the Dominion... "Hey! Quick question: how long have you been working for Wolfie, anyway?" As his eyes flickered over to me, I shrugged. "Pretty obvious, since you didn't start sweating up the place until after we told you the ambassador's out of the loop in this. He clearly owns you."

If I hadn't thought 'Perez' was a foreigner before, I would have now. You don't call a New Californian a slave. But this guy actually smiled. "You could say that I was inherited from the previous ambassador's estate," he jeered. "Who owns *you*, Shamus?"

I sighed. "Somebody go get some ice, please? We're going to need it in a second." As I turned back, 'Perez' looked almost entertained.

"What are you going to do with that ice? You have some little game that you are just dying to play on a prisoner? I have faced worse than you, Shamus."

"You do not want to speak that title again, demon-lover," I rumbled. Daisy put a towel and a bowl full of water and still-cracking ice chips by my side; she didn't say where they came from and I didn't ask. Not that the door was getting opened until we had proper wards up anyway.

"Oh, a threat! Tell me, in so much detail: just what are you going to do about it, Shamus?" – and then 'Perez' stopped, shook his head from side to side, and started to gibber and howl. His handcuffs rattled as he tried, unsuccessfully, to clutch at his tongue.

"It was more like a warning," I said helpfully, as I dipped the towel in the ice slurry and scooped up a generous bit. "Some places are great places to be a demon-lover. Cin City ain't one of them. Somebody grab this idiot's arms, please? And his head?" They got hold of 'Perez,' and I managed to get some of the ice into his mouth. "He's gonna be useless for a few hours, Captain. Sorry about that, but I didn't do it."

Gannon looked unconvinced at my excuse, but he still stood back to let the ATSE prepare the prisoner for a presumably warded cell. As they hooded and bound 'Perez,' the Captain murmured to me, "He knows more than he's saying."

"Yeah. But we know more than he thinks. Like who the target was."

"Well, sure. The demon was after you. Guess you figured that out, hey?"

"That's my job. If he was just trying to shut Verdugo up, there were ways to do that. But that dazzler he had? That would have gotten everybody in the room blinking and stunned long enough for the demon to find me. I'm flattered." And I almost was. Always nice to see somebody noticing the work you're doing.

I shook Gannon's hand. "Keep him on ice. Try to find out 'why,' Joe."

"Hey, don't tell me my job. Shamus." He touched his tongue gingerly, then smiled. "Guess I don't need to worry about keeping the wrong words in my mouth."

"What, a captain who doesn't worry? Unnatural." I looked around. "Lucas! We gotta go see a man about a thing."

Lucas was talking to Eddie in a low voice; the elf handed over a small pouch, shook hands, was surprised by a quick hug from Daisy, and then came on over. I gave him a look as we headed for the door. He shrugged and said "Membership dues."

"What, joining the local group on the ass end of beyond?"

Lucas rolled his eyes. "Okay, yeah, sorry about that. Look, the guy's a jackwagon, bless his heart, but he had a point about memberships. If I'm staying here for any length of time, I should be in good with the ATSE."

"And the Syndicate."

"And the Syndica– Wait, them too?"

"You won't have to join. You can't join, if you're with ATSE. But you had better stay sweet with both. You never know when you'll run into one– hey, Rose!"

The 'cleaning lady' smiled and waved back at me. Looking over Lucas, she rattled off something in Spanglish so archaic it was more or less Old Spanish. Lucas clearly couldn't quite catch it, and half-glared at me when I laughed. As we climbed the stairs, he said "Well?"

"What? Oh, Rose just said that if you were looking for ways to get in nice and tight with the Syndicate she could think of a few. She'd be real happy to show you them, too."

"Ah." I think Lucas actually blushed a little, at that. "Quick subject change?"

"Sure."

"What was the deal with that 'start reading with his left

eye'? It sounded like a saying."

"It is. Back in the day, we had a time where the Dominion was a lot more hard-assed about trying to get our mages – which was a problem, since we don't have any mages. This was just after they broke Deseret in half and took the better part, you see. So the Dominion forced a real big slave-taking one year, went away – and the year after, the ambassador at the time summoned the king at the time to 'attend for further instruction'."

"Now, that king was Ronnie the Third, and they'd had to cold-cock him the year before, so he wouldn't order the army to attack the Dominion mage-catchers instead of letting them grab people. He knew he had to let the Dominion do it, but when the day came he just couldn't let it happen, so a few retainers knocked him out and then reported themselves to the dungeons for *lese majesty*. So you could say Ronnie was *motivated* to kick up a ruckus. And there was something he *could* do.

"When the day came, Ronnie showed up, with his entourage leading him, and wearing sunglasses. When the ambassador handed him the order from the Dominion telling him to get another batch of mages ready, King Ronnie took off his glasses. One eye was swollen shut – by the same retainers who had knocked him out the year before; that was their punishment – and the other had been plucked out by Ronnie's own hand. He held the paper up, said 'I see no such decree,' and was walked out."

"And that stopped the Dominion?" asked Lucas.

"Yeah. A ruler sacrificing his eye for power and wisdom is old magic. *Really* old magic. That's straight up Lore of Lore, and the Dominion didn't want to touch any of it. At least, not until they share a border with us, and could overpower land-magic like that with giant armies. Anyway, ever since that day we say 'reading it with your left eye' when we mean 'you damn well didn't see nothing'."

CHAPTER TWENTY-ONE
Raisin In The Sun

"Right," said Lucas. "So, what's the thing, who's the guy, and where's the place?"

"I'll tell you the last one right now," I said, and whistled for a carriage. "It's somewhere the horse-cars won't go. Hope you aren't carrying anything you don't mind risking."

"If I have it on me, Shamus, it's meant to be used. I take it we're going to the rough part of town?" The approaching cabbie heard that, and abruptly sped up. I gave Lucas a glare; he looked sheepish. "Sorry."

I shrugged. "If they'd spook before hearing the destin-ation, they'd spook after hearing it, too. Somebody will want the fare." And the next cabbie did.

As we rattled down the street, Lucas repeated, "So. Rough part of town?"

"Yeah. We call it Redtown. It's small, but it makes up for it in nasty. 'Wretched hive of scum and villainy,' to quote the Lore. Only it ain't that refined."

"Doesn't sound too bad," Lucas said. "I've been to the Thief's City of Vana, dark crown jewel of the island of Belegdor. Scum and villains can be all right, if you're careful."

"Not these ones," I muttered.

I could tell that Lucas had begun to change his mind after we entered Redtown proper. You could tell the exact point where Cin City gave up trying to keep up the streets; hell, the city painted red lines showing the border, which was more a warning to the Reds about the limits to their tolerance. On the other side: drab, busted, shabby, and listless. We got a good look at all of this because the cabbie wouldn't go over the red-line, and I didn't try to convince him otherwise. Good thing we didn't have far to go.

As usual, none of the Reds were happy to see us. You got the ones that didn't care, and the ones that cared too much, and you couldn't really tell the two apart unless you could see their eyes. It wasn't smart to stay too long; it wasn't really smart to stay at all, but there was a chat I needed to have.

"Vicious, but skinny," murmured Lucas. "Worst-fed people I've seen here. Is there a reason why?"

"Yeah. They live in Redtown."

"What if they don't want to?" asked Lucas.

"They can leave," I said while keeping my eyes constantly moving. "We try to get them to leave. All they have to do is agree to live by some basic rules. Like 'stuff belongs to people' and 'it's wrong to take stuff that isn't yours.' We get a few every year who decide that sounds good. The rest stay here."

"Right, but how do they live?"

"Poorly."

"You know..." Lucas, being smart, decided to use my name "...Tom, people do steal for a living in the rest of Cin City."

"Yeah, but they know that it's a crime. This crowd doesn't. Which is why we're not staying long... ah, here we are."

Where we were was a dive, and not in a good way. There wasn't any garbage around, but only because nobody throws anything away in Redtown. Vermin, ditto. But it smelled the part, all right. I asked Lucas, "You know the good cop, bad cop wheeze?"

"Sure. But is that wise? I mean, I don't know all the strings I'd need to pull on to intimidate people here."

I looked at him. "Who said you were going to be the bad cop?" And then I kicked the door open.

#

There was a bouncer, naturally. Large, greasy, and slow. He was still getting up when I punched him in the gut, smacked him on the back of the head as he bent over, then kicked him two or three times in a sensitive spot as he lay on the ground.

"Hi!" I said brightly to the rest of the smoky, poorly-lit room. "I'm looking for Chewie. Get him, please."

I was slipping the brass knuckles off my left hand as I said that, because there's always one wiseacre who thinks this is supposed to be when the fight starts. I spun and threw the knuckles right at the head of a volunteer getting ready to charge me with a pool stick; he went down in a clatter. I put my extra pair of knuckles back on as I surveyed the room. "Tsk, tsk," I said. "Such a shame that everybody's suddenly deaf. Guess I'll have to be louder."

Redtowners ain't cowards, but they don't think for themselves much. The trick is to keep them from collectively making up their minds, and it helps a lot if you smash up the first two or three people who look like they can start swinging on their own. But you have to keep going, once you start.

Right about then Lucas stepped in front of the doorway, and the room's mood shifted again in the course of thirty seconds. He was now moving like a man wearing chain-mail under his jacket, and there were a couple of short swords in his hands that I didn't remember him having earlier; but most importantly he just looked like a stone-cold killer.

And then Lucas grinned. "Come on, guys! If your name ain't Chewie and you didn't like these two, what do you care? And if you did like these two—" (Lucas casually tossed one sword in the air, and while it was still spinning, snatched a coin purse off of his belt, threw the purse on the bar, and then grabbed the blade out of the air again.) "—then you can help 'em drink their headaches away. On me." His grin showed some teeth at that point.

Without looking I pointed to one side, where I was hearing a little bit of almost-stealthy commotion, and said, "Stop him from leaving." And perforce, they stopped him from leaving. My pointed finger became a beckoning one, and somebody kindly marched Chewie over. "Thank you." And I dragged Chewie back out into the daylight, more or less by the scruff of his neck. Lucas watched my back with a sneer that probably made him no friends, but who needs a friend in Redtown?

Chewie was short, sported greasy, unkempt hair kept at bay with a truly ugly hat, and tried to pull off a beard and mustache. Tried and failed. He wasn't exactly a police snitch; it was more like nobody told him anything unless you wanted everybody to know it, and sometimes that included the cops. Right now he looked almost resigned to this little meet of ours, and I appreciated that.

I still shoved him up against the wall around the next handy corner. Chewie was one of those guys who wasn't living up to his evil potential, because that was too much like work. Good whiner, though. "Come on, Shamus! I didn't do it!"

"I haven't told you what you did yet, Chewie."

"I know that game! I'm not gonna guess! Hey, who's the knife-ear?"

A sword blade suddenly slammed into the wood, right by Chewie's left ear. A greasy lock of hair fluttered silently down into the street.

"Elf. I meant elf."

"He's helping me clear this Case, Chewie. Yeah, that's right. Guess where we just came from, Chewie?"

"All-day *Loteria* at the Vertigo Club?"

"Nah, that's Sundays. Today we came out of the precinct house, just after some *imbecil* tried to set free a demon in an interrogation room. The cops are pissed, Chewie. They're real pissed. The demon knocked over the *donut* table, Chewie. They're not gonna rest until they avenge their pastries."

"That's a crying shame, Shamus. Tell you what, I can give you a few simoleons and you can tell 'em I said it's a pity what happened-" I did another loud, but again not painful, slamming against the wall. Lucas had caught the stylized nature of all of this and was now doing a full swaggering bravo-bodyguard routine.

"Nice try, Chewie. The guy that got possessed? He's from the University, Chewie. He's one of those Uni know-it-all brats who think that they're all 'down with the struggle' and 'fellow travelers' and the rest of the crap that Redtowners feed 'em along with the drugs." That was a guess, but Verdugo did have a UNC ID card on him so I figured it was worth taking the shot there. "He's gonna be singing like a canary as soon as he finds out he's all caught up in the High Justice. So start practicing your scales."

Chewie had gone a little pale at the 'High Justice' part. I nodded. "Demonology, Chewie. You know how *reactionary*," I continued, to use his own swearwords, "the Castle gets about that. So start chirping. What the hell are the Uni cells up to?"

Damned if Chewie didn't almost relax. "Shit, man, why didn't you say? Fuck those deviationist splitters!"

"Lay off the religious talk and cut to the chase, Chewie."

"Fine, fine. Those assholes at Uni act like they don't want nothing to do with us anymore anyway. The cells there got themselves mystified up by some new group, and suddenly it's supposed to be just business. They buy the drugs, they give us the money, and they're all 'fuck you, exact change now.' Nothing extra for the Struggle." Chewie looked like he was most outraged about that.

"Ain't that a shame, Chewie. Who's the new group?"

Chewie looked calculating. "What's it worth to you?"

"You get to swing on their ankles, after the Castle's done with them?"

"That doesn't help the Cause, Shamus."

"Chewie," I said, flatly. He looked at my face, and visibly decided that it wasn't worth pushing it further.

"Fine. The new fuckers are tied in with the, and this is flat-out crazy, Shamus, the Dominion ambassador! There's about five or six of them, and they're this entire cell, right in the heart of the aristocrats. We tried to reach out to them, but they said they didn't need our drugs or our dialectic, the stuck-up assholes. Fucking Haidans."

Gotcha, I thought. "Haidans, huh? Try harder, Chewie. What the hell would they be doing, working for the Dominion?"

"I'm telling you the truth! They got some weird thing going on with the Dominion embassy for years. I dunno, maybe they're doing something under the table. Wouldn't be the first time, right? But, yeah, they got that fucked-up magic shit going, and then they've got the brass balls to lecture us about how it's really okay and we're the ones who ain't conscious enough."

He'd have blathered more, but I started shaking him a little to give myself a moment to think. Haidan knife and Haidan cell associated with Elizabeth's dead friends meant that, crap, we were back to liking Wolfie for the murder. Although if I could link the Ambassador to no-fooling demon summoning, that would get the Dominion off of our backs. If only because none of his bosses would forgive Wolfie for getting caught.

"I said, no religious talk," I said. "Okay. You got some names?" Chewie had one or two; I memorized them – and hopefully so did Lucas. "Great. Always nice when somebody from this part of town contributes to the civic safety of Cinderella. Now amscray. Go tell the Hood that the coppers are going to be descending on wherever he's lurking this month, just as soon as they roll up the Uni cell. He might even be grateful." I said that last bit to Chewie's retreating back.

I turned to see Lucas's raised eyebrow. He asked, "Did that go well, or not?"

"It went great. Chewie's real reliable that way, for a weasel. And a snitch."

"You mean, he's like a guy who's about to go tell the crime lord whose people you beat up earlier that now you're wandering around the streets of Redtown by yourself?"

"But I'm not! I've got you coming along this time, Lucas."

"Yay." Lucas didn't look happy, for some reason. I figured that I should reassure him as we started walking towards the nearest edge of Redtown.

"You got to understand the way this stuff goes," I explained. "Some 'rad from the bar already went to tell the Red Hood we were here, and now Chewie's gonna go tell him that our schedule's clear. I'm not here with the cops, so it's time for the chat. And maybe they'll try to ambush us later. Just for the look of the thing."

"Fair enough," allowed Lucas. "How long do you think we need to wait here?"

"Eh," I said. "Redtown ain't real big. He'll show up anywhere from five minutes from now to five minutes ago."

"What, you think this 'Hood' of yours could be already here?"

"Yes," said I – and so did somebody from the shadows, at pretty much the exact same time.

CHAPTER TWENTY-TWO
Getting A Crew Together

"You were told to drop this case. You do not hear well, worm," said the latest Hood. This one moved like he was old, and he smelled a little old, too. Baked in, like he'd been living rough for a while and there's just so much baths can do. From the way he walked as he came into view, the Hood wasn't all that physically strong, either. A little creaky, even.

That actually worried me more. You don't wear the Hood long if you can't keep ambitious Redtowners from removing it, along with your head. What was this Hood's special trick for staying alive?

From the way Lucas was glancing around, he was looking for the shadows that weren't moving right; from the way he was tensing up, there were too many to suit him. I thought about it. Maybe now was a time for a little bit of charm?

"What's that, gramps? Still got some ringing in my ears. Your guys scream real high when they get kicked in the rude place." Well, sure, it was time for charm, but I didn't actually have any to spare right now.

Hard to tell from the, you know, hood – but I got no reaction from that trenchant observation of mine. Not even a sneer. "Silence, and be grateful I have decided that you are needed alive after all."

"But not wanted? It's nice to be wanted."

The Hood snapped his fingers. Out of the shadows whistled a throwing star, presumably aimed for my hat. It got slapped out of the air by one of Lucas's throwing knives. Lucas went back to casually leaning against the wall. I grinned, while only gibbering a little inside.

"We done dancing on this? You want to tell me something, Hood, tell me. Here." I tossed a small pouch of simoleons on the sidewalk. Mind you, it was just about the last of the Castle's money anyway. "Congratulations. You've just robbed from the rich. Now you can gloat a little, say your say, and we can all get the hell out of here."

"Silence," said the Hood again. I contemplated that, decided that interrupting would waste *my* time too, and shut up. He said, "Good. There are answers in the Abomination's lair." Which meant the Dominion embassy: Redtowners hate the Dominion, but for all the wrong reasons. He went on, "You will find answers which you will not understand until it is too late; and hopefully a good deal of pain there as well."

I was still shutting up, so I had to suggest that I was laughing in his face without actually doing it. When the Hood figured that out, he stiffened a little (this guy *really* didn't like people laughing at him) and reached into a pouch to pull out a key. Lucas relaxed again as the Hood threw it at my feet.

"That is one of the keys to its lair."

Well, that was different. And surprisingly helpful. A key to the embassy would get us in. It might even keep one of us safe. So it had to be a trap.

I still took it. If the Hood enjoyed seeing me stoop down to grab the key, he didn't show it. And if he had, I would have done it anyway. I'm here to clear the Case.

However, I did think it smart to ask, "So why the gift, Hoodie?" And damned if that didn't get a reaction out of him, either.

"You annoy me, worm," he said. "But since you are so difficult to kill, I might as well get some use out of you. There is an item in there that I require, and you will fetch it for me."

"As usual," I said, matter-of-factly enough that Lucas cocked an eyebrow at me. "What's the MacGuffin?"

"The what? Speak plainly, insect."

What was this guy, a foreigner? "The item you want," I patiently explained. "What does it look like, what does it do, and how do I keep it from killing me?"

"It is a small statue, shaped like a winged monster of vaguely anthropoid outline, with an octopus head. It will not harm you to touch it. And what it does is my business."

"Sounds like it's my business, too," I replied.

"I do not care," said the Hood. "You will retrieve it. Leave the embassy without it and my pawns will swarm you and all whom you care for until everyone except me is dead." Well, that was clear.

"Fine," I said.

Lucas looked at me. "Really?" he said.

"Look, getting the key saves time," I said. "If Hoodie here wants some loot from the Ambassador, fine, that's on him. You planning some kind of play against Wolfie, Hoodie?"

"Oh, yes," said the Hood. He sounded like he was looking forward to it, too.

I beamed. "See? We get in, he gets his doohickey, he'll send some mooks to kill us after, *they'll fail*—" (I glared at the Hood) "—and we can all get on with our lives. You're an Adventurer, don't you do this kind of thing all the time?"

"Yeah, sure," said Lucas. "Only we don't just come out and say it."

"I figured that we should cut to the chase," I said. "So, Hoodie: that's it, right? MacGuffin found, MacGuffin handed over, sudden yet inevitable betrayal, something burns down?"

"I will remember your scorn, slug," said the Hood. "You understand the tasks set for you, yes, but it amuses me how little you comprehend the reasons for them. You will not realize why until it is too late, either."

"Glad that you've got something to look forward to there, bub," I said.

"Not just that, worm," said the Hood. "With even a little good fortune, one of you will likely still die inside. And more painfully than from just failing to get in." Then the Hood did that retreat back to the shadows thing that some criminals do.

Lucas murmured, "Leave now please?"

I was already heading for the nearest redline. When you leave Redtown, walk firmly, with speed, and never run. Running tells them who to aim for first. Lucas openly kept his throwing daggers in his hands at this point; about half a block from the redline, he tossed one at a windowsill. There was a sudden flicker of motion there, as if somebody was hastily ducking out of sight. When I looked at Lucas, he shrugged minutely and said, "I didn't like the shape of that particular silhouette."

We didn't really relax until we were about four blocks on the right side of the redline, and out of sight. Lucas shook his head. "I must say, I am disappointed in Cin City's Thieves' Guild."

I laughed. "Don't let the *real* Thieves' Guild hear you say that." And then I laughed again when Lucas tried to figure out whether I was pulling his chain.

#

When we got back to the precinct house – just outside Redtown ain't a great place to get a cab, either – the place was buzzing like a wasp's nest after the stone hit it. Lot of patrols that should have been out and about were instead milling around just outside, glaring at everything and carrying their mad on their sleeves. Lucas tensed a little; hell, so did I. Cin City cops don't rile easy but when they do, look out.

None of it looked aimed our way, though. And damned if Lt. Foster from the Castle wasn't coming up to us. She deigned to acknowledge me with a "Shamus"; to Lucas, she said, "I'm Lt. Foster. You both were at the Verdugo interrogation." It wasn't a question. "This way," she said, and that wasn't a question either.

We followed her. Well, I followed her and Lucas followed me, which was smart of him. "How bad is it, anyway?" I said as we went inside.

"Bad," she said, still looking ahead. "But it isn't dead-cop bad. Yet."

Damn.

#

We were back at Sgt. Shauni's stomping grounds, and it wasn't going to be a happy visit. There was more blood on the walls than I remembered. Not to mention the smells of things that don't normally cook, and a few things that shouldn't be allowed to burn.

Shauni wasn't dead yet, at least, and there were a couple of paramedics working on keeping her that way. It looked pretty bad, though. There was an ugly gash in her gut and burns up and down her uniform. This wasn't a regular fireball, either. Those usually flash up so quick that even if you get hit with one straight-up you might just end up knocked on your ass. Whoever did this spell liked it when people whimpered in pain.

Judging from our Mr. Perez, though, Sgt. Shauni didn't whimper. It looked like he had started melting the bars to his cell; his corpse was slumped through the hole he had made, one sightless eye staring at the scene. I say 'eye' because someone had jammed a large wooden stake through the other one.

Sgt. Shauni stirred, feebly. "Nobody had better walk off with Mr. Pointy," she said. "That's, like, a family heirloom and everything."

I glared at the lead paramedic. "Why is she still awake? And why are we even here?" I don't know much about medicine but even I've heard of germs.

The paramedic shook her head. "Same answer for both, dude," she said. "The cop said you needed to hear what she had to say, and it couldn't wait."

That sounded like it involved the Case, so I enhanced my calm and crouched down so that she could see me. "I'm here, Sarge," I said. "Tell me, so you can get some sleep."

"About time," Sgt. Shauni said. "That reject, he, like, first told me to let him out of the cell, or he was going to roast himself a pig. And I was all, *whatever*, and then he pulled off the special cuffs he had on like they were vines or something? And then there was this blast and zap and I'm on the floor and everything."

Shauni coughed so wetly I was surprised not to see any actual blood. After a moment she went on, "So I'm like, trying to get up and I see that he's melted this hole in the bars, and he's heating them all up more because his hands were totally all red and he sees me moving around and then he tells me that it's my own fault for being a total bitch and I was like, *whatever* again and that's when I threw Mr. Pointy right through his stupid eye. So he starts screaming and I'm like, no, *that's* me being a total bitch and then he, like, got stuck on the bars and stopped moving."

"Okay," I said, for lack of anything better to say. "You know, Sarge, you could have told me that later."

Sgt. Shauni thought about laughing, and settled for shaking her head. "I've got, this completely gross *hole* in my *stomach*, Shamus, so there may not be a later. And it was a really cool thing to say! I mean, I, like, totally threw that right back into his face and everything! No way am I gonna let him be the only one who ever heard that."

Lucas spoke up. "That's fair. Hell of a good shot, by the way." He said it as an expert in stabbing people through the eyes would have, which I guess is something that the Adventurer's Guild might test for.

"Well, *duh,*" said Sgt. Shauni, but she smiled when she said it. She went on to me, "Make sure they give Mr. Pointy to Mom. And Shamus: like, if they don't patch me up? You make sure that you clear the Case fast. My Mom's gonna *freak* when she finds out what happened." Her eyes fluttered; the drugs were finally winning the fight. As Shauni went unconscious, she managed to say, "She isn't, you know, *civilized* like me..."

#

"What the hell happened?"

Under different circumstances, it'd have been fun to see Gannon and Foster going at it; he's got more rank but her connections are fresher. Local cop against the Feds: the Lore's full of stuff like this, and it's great to watch it on the stage. In real life everything gets a bit more antsy.

I couldn't blame either one. Lt. Foster had needed 'Perez' to squeal some more, and she was blaming the local cops for letting him get killed. Captain Gannon had a cop in the hospital, and he was blaming the Flatfoots for letting 'Perez' sneak into the city. Both of them were mad, which was fair. But they were ready to take it out on each other, and that was going to get in the way of the Case. So I cleared my throat. "Okay, so everybody screwed up," I said. "Can we get past that? Because I got better things to do today."

That got me a glare from both of them. *Nice.* When in doubt, piss people off. That's what the Lore says, anyway. "Fine," said Gannon. "You got any *helpful* suggestions, *Shamus*?"

"Sure," I said. "Trash the cell; see if it was messed with. Then check the cuffs and the hood. See if *those* were messed with." A line from the opera I had seen crossed through my mind. "Or you could just sit around, and glare."

Ah, the classics.

#

Yeah. After everybody did some checking, the tone in the room got a lot better. Before, both Foster and Gannon thought that the other had screwed up; now, they both knew that they had screwed up, too.

Including me. I mean, I had *seen* fake-Perez messing around earlier with the restraining gear that ended up getting put on him, but it went clear out of my head and the ATSE artisans', too. Real easy to slip out of handcuffs when you've broken the lock earlier.

As for the cell? Well, the ATSE artisans wouldn't even let us directly *look* at a certain piece of metal they had hacked off of that cell bed. We got shown an actual photograph instead.

The photo showed a set of scratches in the metal; even secondhand they looked ugly and wrong. And deeper, somehow, than they should have been. "Okay," I said. "What am I looking at?"

Lucas took off the darkened glasses that he had put on the second he saw the photograph, *after* turning over the photo itself. "It's a trap," he said, then blinked as the New Californians all chuckled.

I waved it away. "Long story. So, it's a magical trap?"

"Yeah," said Lucas. "You get these sometimes, out in the ruins. Especially if you're anywhere near the Dominion. We call 'em Amok Bombs: basically, they pump a mage full of juice, then mess up his head until he thinks that everything can be solved with a fireball. Oh, and that anybody who isn't with the Dominion is secretly a lizard person waiting for the mage to go to sleep so they can eat him."

"Jesus," said Gannon. "What's the point of *that*?"

Lucas shrugged. "To keep mages out of the ruins. And I guess sometimes they get recruits coming in, after a mage wakes up from the slaughter. I mean, viciously killing the rest of your party is one hell of a bridge being burned, you know what I mean?"

"That doesn't explain how it got in the cell," Foster pointed out. "How often do those cells get used?"

Gannon looked at a sheet. "Last special case in there was four weeks ago. Domestic dispute, nothing major: she got drunk and made the family dog able to talk." At my raised eyebrow, he went on. "It was a Gran Pomeranian, so you can imagine how *that* conversation went. We stashed her in a cell until the booze and the spell wore off. I don't think she's our perp."

"She ain't," I said. "That list's just for special cases, right?" Gannon nodded, then swore under his breath as he figured it out. "Yeah, they use that cell for regular criminals when it gets busy out. Remember that bum from a couple of days ago? He was in there."

"Crap," said Lucas. "He was working with 'Perez,' then? No, wait, that doesn't sound right."

"Given that this bum of yours sent 'Perez' on a rampage," said Lt. Foster, "I'd agree." She frowned. "But why? Are they running a long con?" Foster looked to me for an answer that one.

"I don't *think* so," I said after a minute. "Long cons work great in the Lore but not real good in real life. Maybe the bum has a grudge?"

Then it was my turn to swear. Tall, old, smelly in a weird way – the last time I was talking to somebody like that, he was wearing a red hood. But if the latest Red Hood was a mage?

Hoo-boy, this would get ugly, fast.

#

Lucas, bless him, didn't blab about the Hood when he saw that I wasn't going to, either. He just followed my lead, right out the door when it got clear that the discussion was going to switch over to serious cop stuff. It wasn't any of our business and what we didn't know wouldn't hurt us.

The station was already busier when we left. All over the city, the word was going out: somebody had carved up a cop. When that happens, pissed-off cops like to spread the hurt feelings around. It was not going to be a good night to be brash about breaking the law.

"You got a plan?" asked Lucas as I hurried down the steps. "You look like you have somewhere you want to be."

"Nope," I said. "I just want to clear the area, that's all."

That puzzled Lucas. "Why? You seem to get along good with the cops here."

"I do, kinda, with these cops," I said. "But we've gotta go do something." I hoped that this would be enough of a hint. Blessedly, it was; Lucas shut his mouth until we ended up at Garapenna's.

He didn't care for the pie, either. Putting down his fork, Lucas asked, "So why *aren't* we letting the cops know about the Hood?" I looked at him with actual surprise. He said, "What? Isn't busting 'perps' their job?"

"Yeah, sure," I replied. "But there's icemold involved, and it's mixed up in this Case somehow. There's an angle I'm not seeing yet, and I want to see it before the cops find out that the Red Hood's a mage and use it for an excuse to smash up Redtown."

"Why do you care?" asked Lucas. "That place is an eyesore. You'd be doing the people living there a favor if you burned it to the ground."

"We've tried getting rid of Redtown. Cops can't do it. Hell, an army couldn't unless they went in ready to hang anybody. These days the city settles for keeping them penned in."

"Don't tell me, let me guess," said Lucas. "The cops are going to assume that a Red Hood who's a mage is going to tip this delicate balance you guys apparently have?"

"Got it in one," I said. "Redtowners aren't what you call thoughtful but they know what happens when mages get hooked on icemold, which they make down there. They also get that even if the cops can't clean out Redtown, they can damn well knock it in the head a few times and call it a day. So the Redtowners don't let mages be Red Hoods."

"Right," said Lucas. "But have the cops figured out about the icemold angle, yet?"

I swore. "Not yet. But they will. They got two murder victims, both with icemold found on them." I drummed my fingers on the genuine imitation Formica top. "The cops won't care either way if the icemold was planted; they'll still try to raid the usual suspects. So we gotta raid them first, see what they know." And they had to know *something.*

"How big is this 'we'?" asked Lucas. "I mean, sure, I'm down for hard knocks and hard questions, but it goes better with some more muscles."

"We'll get a proper bunch of extras. Your boss has to have some behind glass, in case of emergency." I looked at Lucas. "He won't mind. Hell, if we get there before the cops, we'd be doing Kermie a favor."

It took Lucas a second, but he got it. Kermie the Frog didn't run icemold, but he knew the people who did. If the cops were gonna be busting mold dealers, it would be in Kermie's best interests to have somebody to go through the place first and see if there was anything, you know, *awkward* lying around. Everybody would appreciate that, including the cops. Can't bust what you can't see, right?

Hey, it's Cin City.

CHAPTER TWENTY-THREE

Tom Vargas And The House of Flying Monkeys

But Lucas was not thrilled with the idea of breaking into the Ambassador's house first. "I thought you told Kermie that going in there wasn't a smart idea. He said you used the word 'suicide'."

"Which it is," I said, happily. And then I held up the key. "Unless we have this."

"So, that's real?"

"Oh, yeah, Lucas. Can't you tell? Oh, right, you couldn't." At his frown, I went on. "You know how we don't have any mages in New California? Right. So who maintains the embassy's spells?"

"The... Dominion?"

"The Dominion is over a thousand miles away, Lucas. Officially, their mages put in the spells when they founded the embassy and they've never needed fixing since then. Unofficially?" I shrugged. "The Dominion has expectations and the Castle provides 'salvage' which meets them. Like, say, magical keys. And nobody opens their big mouth." At least, not this century. A really ambitious ambassador could make trouble for New California by pushing the Dominion's prerogatives; it was kind of weird we had two in a row who didn't try real hard.

"What? I can't believe the Dominion would trust their site security to illegal mages," Lucas pointed out.

"They don't," I replied. "But they're not going to work the key itself to take an enchantment, either. That's apprentice work, and they don't let apprentices come this far south."

"Because the chains won't stretch so far?"

"Exactly," I said. "Besides, the little spell already put on it that tells the world this is an official Dominion embassy key? The Dominion likes that. They think it's a warning and a brag. Fair enough, it usually is. New California doesn't want anybody messing with the embassy."

"Except us two."

"Except us three."

Lucas wasn't dumb. "Right. You heard from Elizabeth again."

"She'll be coming by later." There came a knock on the door. "In fact, here she is." Hopefully.

As I opened it, to indeed see Elizabeth standing there, Lucas murmured, "You really do have lucky timing."

"I visit a lot of garbage heaps, too. It evens out."

#

It wasn't hard to convince the manifested shade of a woman viciously murdered by an evil mage that we needed to break into the murderer's house to find evidence. Go figure. Shucks, we almost had to run, just to keep up with her.

As we went through the streets, Lucas asked, "So what is your thing, Elizabeth?"

"I don't know," Elizabeth said over her shoulder. "Vengeance?"

"Nah, that's your current goal in life," said Lucas. "What's your *thing*? Are you a ghost, or a construct, or something like that?"

"I have no idea, Lucas." Elizabeth laughed. "It doesn't hurt, at least. And I'm not *hungry*, either. I know you were wondering about that."

"Yeah, well, you understand my professional concern," said Lucas. "People come back from the dead, there's usually a problem. Otherwise everybody would do it."

"Oh, there's side effects," said Elizabeth. "For one thing, it takes a lot out of me to keep fully solid. I can only really manage it with the Shamus around."

I blinked at that. "You might have said, Elizabeth."

"I just did," said Elizabeth. "Anyway, I'm still figuring out all of this. But even around you I can't concentrate forever."

"What happens when you stop concentrating?" asked Lucas.

"I get fuzzy and drift," said Elizabeth. "Until I remember that somebody murdered me, and then I get solid again. And before you ask: I don't know how long I can keep doing it. It's not really hard to keep myself together yet, but I can kind of see it from here."

"Gotcha," said Lucas. "So, why aren't we showing her to the mages that you guys don't have?"

"What makes you think they'd have any idea?" I responded.

"Isn't that their job?"

Elizabeth snorted. "What's happened to me is absolutely outside any regular magician's understanding how magic works," she said. "Take it from me."

"Yeah," I said. "And they'd waste too much time trying to figure it out. Elizabeth's condition is Shamus business." I looked ahead on the street. "Crime, and payback."

"Sounds almost religious," observed Lucas. "Speaking of which, why not call in Father Mike?"

"Two reasons," I said. "First, Mike's a good guy but he's also a priest, and his religion has a strict limit on who gets to come back from the dead. He'd just dump holy water by the gallon on Elizabeth and send for the Pope-in-Exile's finest exorcist."

"Which wouldn't work," observed Elizabeth.

"Which wouldn't work," I agreed, "and we don't have time to wait for a convoy from Quebec City. But even if Mike wouldn't freak out, he's not around anyway. He went off with the army to Sonora."

"Really? What brought that on?" said Lucas.

"The concert last night, I guess. Mike told me afterward that he had to go and minister to the troops." I'd pointed out that maybe half of the army wasn't part of his religion and it was sure as his Hell that all of the enemy weren't; Mike laughed and told me not to bother coming up with more reasons to go.

"He left with them this afternoon," I went on. "He's got a smart assistant and some really formidable *abuelas* running the parish; they'll work it out." And I figured, so should we.

#

The embassy was smaller than you'd think. But then,

there was only ever the one person in it. Magic apparently did all the housecleaning, so there were no staffers from the Dominion, and the Dominion didn't trade with anybody, didn't play nice with anybody, and absolutely didn't let anybody visit them unless it was permanent. The Ambassador was there to relay threats and sneer enviously at our entertainments, so he didn't need much.

We got pretty close before I noticed something that wasn't there, but should have been. Again, not a mage, but: "Where are the go-away wards?" Go-away wards are usually really, really loud. They're even loud enough for non-mages to hear.

Lucas sniffed the air. "Oh, they're still there," he said after a moment. "They're just really old. Ms. Hernandez?"

"Elizabeth is fine," she murmured. Apparently the wards were more visual for her, because she started to peer closer, then caught herself at the mortal habit. "They *are* old. I don't think that these particular wards have been renewed for years."

Very strange; the Dominion hates having people over. Almost as much as we hate visiting them. Even though these weren't the *real* defenses, just the ones set up to keep people at arm's length, it was still weird. "Wolfie hasn't been here that long," I noted, then looked up at the darkened house. "And why isn't he there now?"

Elizabeth shrugged. "I don't know. All I can tell is, he's not inside Cinderella itself."

"Which is why we're here. Lucas, how do we sneak in?"

Lucas showed the key in one hand, and a clipboard in the other. "We don't. We walk inside the gate, casually stroll around to the back, and let ourselves in. Anybody sees us, they'll assume we're supposed to be here, because what idiot would break into a Dominion embassy?"

And that's what we did.

#

I was expecting something more impressive.

I shouldn't have been; I had been back earlier to talk to

Trixie and Slye, and they had given me a pretty thorough debriefing. The two had only ever seen the front door, the hallway, and Cackle/Wolfie's bedroom/bathroom, and they weren't thrilled by what they did see. As Slye put it: "It looked like it should've smelled of old man, but it didn't because magic." But that was the living area. The rest of the mini-mansion should have been more ostentatiously tacky.

Maybe it had been, but not now. There were plenty of rooms, sure, with all sorts of bling. Priceless artworks looted from us New Californian natives, that sort of thing. But there was dust on it all. The kind you get when you don't dust regular and then only on the obvious spots. I wondered how often Wolfie walked through his own house.

Luke stopped in one room, and blinked. "Wait," he said. "This guy has a television?" I looked; sure enough, he did. Dusty, too. If there was an enchantment on the house to handle this, it had long since expired.

"What, you never saw one before?" I asked. Lucas shrugged a bit.

"Not in working condition." He looked at the walls. "This entire place is wired for electricity, isn't it?"

Elizabeth spoke up. "Yes. I can feel the energy moving along the wires around us." She frowned. "Which is new for me."

I carefully decided not to touch anything that looked like metal. "Yeah, Lucas, this is one of the two places in New California that gets to have electric." Officially.

"What's the other?"

"The Billy. The opera theater," I elaborated after seeing his look of confusion. "The Dominion only hates it when other people have electricity and gasoline. Dominion mages can use all they want."

"Greedy bastards."

"It ain't even greed, Lucas." I peered at the shelves of Old American movie crystals, then swore. "But 'bastards' hits it right on the nose. Some of these flicks even the Loremasters don't have. And the Dominion won't share."

Lucas looked at the collection with renewed interest. I shook my head, with regret. "Even if Wolfie never watches them, he'd still know if they got taken." And that was a lurch; there was a crystal there for the complete 2079 *Lensmen* series. We have maybe forty, fifty minutes of it. And there it sat, gathering dust on a mage's bookshelf.

I hate the Universal Dominion.

The rest of the house was the same. Dust, disused spells, and dull. But there was a second level, complete with the winding stair you'd expect. Before we opened the door at the top, I looked at Elizabeth. "Any sign of him being in range?"

She shook her head; I looked at Lucas. "Do your stuff." He nodded. I thought about telling him not to get greedy, but I figured that I didn't need to tell an Adventurer not to be an idiot.

Yeah. Yeah, I knew that was a stupid thought at the time.

#

Twenty minutes later, we were all running back to town. While trying not to laugh. It was just too absurd: the son of a bitch had flying monkey sentries.

That shouldn't be funny, sure. Those monsters were terrors in the 23rd Century, back when the Dominion was taking over the center of the continent. Back then they killed people in job lots. But the Dominion stopped using them for two reasons, and only one was because they had better constructs now.

The first sentry monkey had done its damnedest to gut us as we entered Wolfie's sanctum. But it missed my stomach – by a lot – on its first leap; and by the time the monkey turned around Lucas had already closed and slapped the sword out of its hands. The monkey didn't like that; but it was slow. The damned thing was so muscle-bound that it lumbered. That was the other problem with flying monkeys: they rarely aged well.

Elizabeth stepped up and touched the monkey's shoulder with one hand. It suddenly froze, then collapsed into a heap. Elizabeth blinked. "That was very strange."

Lucas brushed himself off. There was dust everywhere here, too. "Energy drain spell, Elizabeth?"

"Not a spell." She looked worried. "I could see the magical energy inside of it, and when I grabbed it, I just absorbed it all. God, what if I'm a vampire?"

"Hmm." Lucas looked like he was seriously considering the situation. "Can you see my magical energy?"

Elizabeth peered at him. "No."

Lucas brightened. "Then it's not a problem!" He looked around. "But the dust here is. Isn't this supposed to be the ambassador's magical workspace?"

If it was, he hadn't visited it in a while. I shook my head, while trying to cram the monkey back on its pedestal. It wobbled a little, but stayed on okay enough. If you squinted. I also tried to shove the sword back in its hand, but that just wasn't happening.

I said, "Look. You two. Do your stuff. Your thing. Get your magic on. We don't want to be here when Wolfie gets back. He's not coming back, right, Elizabeth?" She shook her head – then bit her lip as the damned monkey's hat fell off. I jammed it back on. "Come on. We don't have time—"

"To monkey around with this?" innocently suggested Lucas, as he expertly popped locks and flipped through drawers. We all ducked as a shower of mummified monkey parts tumbled out of a bin. You could tell that this one was originally made to fight as some kind of swarm of monkey bits, but by now they were mostly just fighting each other.

"Be nice, Lucas," replied Elizabeth, eyes closed. I guessed she was looking for whatever monkey piece was controlling the whole thing. "No need to tell any more howlers."

"Why, you think Tom'll start gibboning if we do?" asked Lucas as he started kicking the pieces into one corner.

It was at this point that the flying monkey clattered to the ground again. Loudly. "Real funny, you two," I half-snarled as I tried to rearrange what I hoped was a corpse. As I turned, I felt something tug at my foot. I looked down, and saw a paw gripping the cuff of my pants. I tried to pry it off, but the damned thing's fingers wouldn't open. "Elizabeth!"

She opened one eye and murmured, "*Dos monitos*." Elizabeth smiled as I groaned, and Lucas raised an eyebrow.

"Nah, no rush," I said. "I've only got an undead monkey clinging to me."

Elizabeth opened both eyes, and frowned. "No."

"No?" I replied.

"No." Elizabeth pointed. "*That's* an undead monkey."

We looked. And yeah, that was a skeletal winged monkey, all bones and tattered skin, crawling out of a cabinet at the other side of the room. It kept trying to fly over to us, only to keep falling to the ground with a clatter and a rattle as pieces popped off. The third time that happened, the piece that flew off must have been an important one, because the whole thing just sort of fell apart.

I think we all found it kind of disappointing. I mean, if you're going to face off with an undead monkey, it shouldn't fall apart before the fight even starts. But then the damned monkey's paw spoiled the moment by trying to climb up my pants leg, and Elizabeth rushed over to drain the paw's magical energy.

"Thank you," I said as all the skittering monkey parts shivered and went still. "Lucas, got anything useful?"

"Nothing here," said Lucas as he went back to checking the last drawer. "And if the Ambassador's ever used this lab, I'll eat my fez."

"You don't have a– right. Elizabeth?"

"I have to disagree with Lucas. The Ambassador's reek is all over this place."

I looked at the dust. "How?"

"What makes you think I know?" said Elizabeth.

I shrugged. "Mystic spiritualist connection with the Cosmic All?"

She gave me the fish-eye. "You want to steal that Lensmen crystal, don't you?"

"What, rob the Dominion of what our ancestors considered to be the greatest cultural achievement of the Old

Americans? If I could figure out how? Absolutely, Elizabeth. Dammit, it..."

"...belongs in a museum," we all said in unison. Even Lucas, who blinked at my and Elizabeth's mutual look of surprise.

"What?" he said. "That's just a thing we say in the Guild. Is it important?"

#

"There's *got* to be more here," I said. "Even if it was just that thing the Hood wanted. Anybody see it?"

"There's this," said Lucas. "But it's not what we're looking for."

"Okay," I said. "So why do we care?"

"Because it's broken, reeks of death energy, and it's inside the monkey skeleton?" said Lucas.

That was a fair reason to look at something, so the two of us joined Lucas. The monkey skeleton's ribcage was hinged, and inside was what looked like a broken glass egg. It was hollow, and the inside surface seemed kind of pitted and cloudy. I started looking around for the inevitable acid-spitting monstrosity as Lucas poked at the cavity and shards with a short stick.

Elizabeth shook her head at my assumptions, once she figured out what I was doing. "This isn't like that, Shamus."

"Tell it to the Lore, Elizabeth." Was it under the desk? Hiding in the vents? Would even bullets have killed it?

"Shamus," Elizabeth patiently repeated. "*Tom*. Stop it. You're making me jumpy. I know what this is."

"Okay?" I decided to humor her. Besides, I figured I could keep one eye on her and another out for the monster.

"It's a life-egg," she said. Lucas furrowed his brow for a moment, then visibly got the reference. I did not.

"So what's that?" I asked.

"It's the one form of necromancy the Dominion practices," Elizabeth said. "They keep a part of their body's life energy in the egg. If they die suddenly, the egg 'hatches' and uses the energy to keep the mage's soul in her body. It also does some emergency healing. Enough to keep the body alive, at least." She shuddered. "We don't use the spell because it's real nasty to cast."

"Huh," I said. "Is it Wolfie's?"

Elizabeth shook her head. "No. It feels different than the rest of the room. I don't think he's even ever touched it."

"So it must have been the previous owner's," I said. "And since it's broken, then it... worked?"

Lucas picked up on that first. "Hey! Think Cackle's now wearing a Red Hood?"

"That's one way to bet, Lucas. Guess Wolfie really was sent to take him out. But it didn't quite stick."

"And now Cackle's ready to get revenge." Lucas thought about it. "Works for me!"

Elizabeth and I looked at each other. Lucas wasn't wrong, really, but if Cackle was the Red Hood, we'd *really* need some kind of hold over him after all of this was done.

And now I couldn't keep the Castle updated, either. They'd been making noises about me slowing down all along, once Wolfie'd claimed he did it. They knew they couldn't touch the Dominion ambassador, so why rush to the awkward part where they had to let him go? Hell, maybe he'd confessed just so he could gloat when he got off the hook.

But... had he been bluffing, and Elizabeth'd been murdered by *Cackle*? That could make sense: her friends had gotten themselves linked with the University Haida cell *and* with Redtown icemold dealers. Cackle might've thought that underground weather-mages would spill the beans to Wolfie's pet demonologists – or Wolfie himself, when Elizabeth went to the Castle. And there'd been no sign of a struggle at the murder scene; to do that to a mage takes a lot of arcane firepower. One of the regular mages we don't have could've done it, but not covered their tracks from Tia Leila. So that left Dominion powerhouses like Wolfie or Cackle – and if Wolfie hadn't done it, he might 'confess' to save face, sic his demon-summoners on me in case I figured it out, and gone to find Cackle and fireball him a few more times.

Which was a problem, right there. If Cackle himself was under a death sentence from the Dominion, that Wolfie'd already tried to carry out, then the court would drop everything to give him asylum, and never mind whatever murders or drug-peddling he might have been up to in the meantime. Fine: the Castle had their own priorities.

But I'm a Shamus, and I have mine.

I shook off my thoughts. "Fine," I said. "We'll worry about the Hood later. For right now, let's find his damned item."

"What did it look like?" asked Elizabeth.

"Some kind of weird octopus-crab statue with wings," I said. As I walked, my foot hit a certain spot on the floor; it creaked, a hatch popped open, and a flying monkey came barreling out, paws burning and flame coming out of its ass. Couldn't steer at all, though; I instinctively smacked it out of my way and right into a giant metal vase. I raised my voice over the rattling and crashing: "Made out of stone, I guess. I figure it's linked to the ambassador somehow. Also, that the Hood will try to kill us as soon as we hand it over to him."

"I've never really gotten why we're *going* to hand it over to him, then," said Lucas. He looked at the rocking vase, nodded, and started shoveling monkey bones into it. There was a loud snap, and Elizabeth's face scrunched up in distaste as the rocking stopped.

"I told you," I said. "I figure that he wants to use it against Wolfie, and that's fine. You can't expect a Red Hood to *not* try to kill you when he no longer needs you. It's baked into the damned cake with those guys. I'm not even gonna get mad about it."

"Well, sure, you can't get mad at people just for them trying to kill you," mused Lucas as he started looking for secret drawers or whatever. "It's the job, these things happen, and... bingo!"

He looked at me and Elizabeth, and noted our lack of reaction. "Sorry," Lucas said. "That means 'I found something'."

We looked it over: yup, it was a hairline crack in one wall.

Just the right size and shape to be your standard secret door. Elizabeth spoke. "Two spells, both *very* faint. One on the wall, one on the inside. The one on the wall looks like a shock spell."

"Fatal?" said Lucas.

"Not now."

"Got it," said Lucas. "But better safe than sorry." He pulled a brass pry bar out from one boot, jammed it into the crack, and jimmied it open in one quick movement. There was perhaps a spark.

Inside the vacant space now revealed was, huh, nothing. Elizabeth sighed. "That's the second spell. Invisibility." She reached out, and maybe went the tiniest bit brighter as she absorbed the spell.

Inside was a hastily piled collection of luggage and travel gear. Elizabeth put one hand on Lucas's shoulder as he moved closer. "The defensive spells are *considerably* stronger on those."

"How much stronger?" asked Lucas.

"Lethal," she said, and concentrated. There was a flare, and she staggered. "And now they're not. Augh, that hurt."

"Dammit, Elizabeth!" I said. "Don't take risks like that!"

"Well, I won't *now*," she said. "Besides, I'm the second edition, remember? I don't mind getting written on."

She opened one of the satchels before either Lucas and I could do anything. And lo! There was the Hood's MacGuffin. Lucas whistled. "Damn," he said. "Is that authentic Old American resin? That's gotta be worth some money, right there."

It certainly *felt* old. Older than me, older than New California, older than the Mountain Herself. It had watched a breakup of an empire and the end of the world; I wondered how many hands had touched it. Although mine wouldn't, and Lucas had sensibly put on gloves before he wrapped it carefully in a cloth bag we had brought. I felt like there was *something* caught up in the statue, but I didn't have quite the right senses to figure out what.

The room did go still as I took the bag from Lucas, though. It felt like there was something significant happening... and then the vase with the monkey parts in it started to smoke. Guess those two particular monsters didn't get along.

Plugging the hole seemed smart, so Lucas and I grabbed the first monkey and shoved it on top of the vase. Then we ran for it; Lucas stopped for a moment in the first room as we left, muttering something about dropping another no-scry-me on our way out the door. I didn't think it'd help, but I didn't say anything. If nothing else, it made him feel better, right?

CHAPTER TWENTY-FOUR
Lair Raid

The handover went about as I expected, but nothing like the Redtown knife-gang did. We had set up the meet in a crumbling shack by the docks; Lucas paused by the door outside, closed his eyes (I did the same), and tossed in some kind of flare-up. We then cleared the door, to discover one of their troikas still trying to blink away the sudden screaming pain in their eyeballs. I smacked the closest guy all the way into unconsciousness with a hand-chop to the back of the head while Lucas amused himself by placing the tips of his two swords on one throat each.

"Howdy, 'rads," I said. "This is getting to be a habit." I tucked the bag into the patched pouch of the unconscious Redtowner, trying not to gag from the smell. "We're gonna leave now, and you're gonna take your 'rad here back to the Hood with the statue. Don't leave him behind; they got a strict trash policy up here. We clear?"

"I think that the guy on the left isn't clear about this, Shamus," Lucas said easily. "He's thinking about going for the shiv he's got hidden in his left boot."

"And the other one's got a single-shot zapper around her neck," said Elizabeth. "Sorry, she had one – oh, that tasted horrible! You're lucky, *senorita*; that would've blown up too soon if you used it."

"Two fingers," I said to the male Redtowner with the hidden shiv. "Take it out, nice and slow." And he did it! Dropped it on the ground, too. "Good job, 'rad. Now stop being dumb. You got the artifact. You ain't getting us, and you never were."

They might have still argued it, even then. They were supposed to take us out, you see? And the Hoods ain't known for liking excuses; but they never got the chance to give it one more try, because right then the last damned flying monkey came smashing through the roof. And the crates. It made a pretty good dent in the wall, too.

That was enough for the Redtowners; they grabbed their unconscious chum and stayed not on the order of their coming. We never saw them again, either. You'd think that I would have – but I guess they didn't survive the Hood, once he had what he needed.

The three of us stuck around, though, more out of horrified curiosity than anything else. Although in my case there was a certain amount of civic feeling involved. What if it wasn't broken? You can't have flying monkeys wandering around and killing people.

But it looked broken, or inert, or whatever the word is that mages use. The impact had left it halfway into a wall, head first.

Elizabeth was the first person to speak. "Are those... stockings that it's wearing?"

"Yup," said Lucas. He was busy looking among the wreckage for something.

"And some kind of... harness?"

"Yup."

"Oh, and those are heels." Elizabeth stared at them, confused. "Why would a flying creature need heels?"

"Why would a flying creature need fetish gear?" responded Lucas. He now had a fairly long stick in one hand, which he used to start poking at the flying monkey. It didn't move.

Elizabeth winced. "Do you *have* to poke it in the panties, Lucas?" she asked. "It's... rude."

"I have to poke it *somewhere*," Lucas said reasonably, "and all that pink makes it easy to aim. But yeah, I think it's broken."

"Yes, of *course* it's broken," said Elizabeth. "I can tell that it's broken from here. There's no need to poke the dead fetish monkey in the bum with a stick."

"Come on, just because there's no *need...*" began Lucas. At this point I felt it obligatory to interrupt.

"The question is, why was it shadowing us?" I pointed out. "And will there be any more?"

There was a pause. After a few moments, all of which

remained remarkably free of the appearance of any more flying monkeys, Lucas said, "I guess not?" We waited a few more moments. "Nope, that was the last one, probably. It must have activated as we left, and just now caught up to us."

Well, he was the Adventurer. They know these things, right? And since none of us really felt like explaining this to any of this to a night guard, we left.

I kept expecting it to make the papers, but it never did. Guess there's some stories out there that *nobody* expects the readers to ever believe, huh?

#

"So," Elizabeth said, "Was that a bust?"

We were back at Garapenna's. We were out of expense money, but I figured that we all needed something besides the swill they sell elsewhere. I don't dare ask what Tolva puts in his omelets, but they're good.

"Maybe," I said.

"And maybe not," said Lucas. "What kind of mage doesn't mess with his lab?"

"The kind that has another one somewhere else," said Elizabeth promptly.

"Or who doesn't do the kind of magic you do in labs," I added.

That got me a look from Elizabeth. "He's definitely a mage," she said. "He was throwing enough fireballs at me."

"Sure, sure," I replied. "But fireballs ain't exactly what you'd call *esoteric*, right? You were throwing 'em right back, and you weren't trained in some kind of Dominion slave-school. Wolfie's aim sucked, too. That's weird."

"So maybe Wolfie isn't all that skilled after all?" asked Lucas. "Maybe he's a fake? That'd be helpful."

I thought about it. "Nah," I decided. "We sent word back to the Dominion that he had shown up, and they didn't go nuts at the news or anything, so that's probably Wolfie. But they always send us somebody who likes to mess around with magic, the nastier the better." That's even a requirement for anybody who wants to get anywhere in the Dominion. Nice guys and gals don't make it out of the first Circles.

"So we can figure that at least Wolfie's rusty at using the usual Dominion spells," mused Lucas. "That's something."

"Yeah," I agreed. "I just don't know what it is. Something the matter, Elizabeth?" She was looking a little less solid, but she rallied quick.

"Sorry," she said. "I'm feeling a little unfocused."

"Hold on." I fumbled in my pouch for her lightstone. "Try holding this." And damned if it didn't work: I could see her settle back in as she held its bright light in her hands. After a moment she gave it back.

"I shouldn't use this too often," she said. "I'm draining it every time I touch it." She frowned. "I also can't see it when you have it, Shamus."

"Probably the spells your Aunt Tia put on me," I said. "She warned me that they'd block friendly magic, too. Why were you pushing yourself?"

"I was trying to get a feel for the ambassador's location. He's headed," she paused, "not this way. Looks like he's flying above the Bay, of all places."

"Good," I murmured. "I still don't want to be anywhere near the Embassy when he comes back, in case he does notice something. I mean: you ever see a Dominion mage go ape?"

I'm a bad man.

#

But I'm not bad enough to take Elizabeth along on the icemold raid, far too early the next morning. Oh, hell, why lie? I wasn't sure what we were going to face, and despite what she said, the effort of keeping herself solid looked like it was getting to her. I didn't want Elizabeth straining and grimly holding on before the Case got cleared.

I put that from my mind and looked over again the Brute Squad that Lucas had put together for tonight's little jaunt. Kermie liked them either big or little for his crew, and since we weren't going to be wriggling through many narrow spaces,

Lucas had opted for guys who opened locked doors by punching them down. I did recognize one, though. It was my brawling friend from a few nights ago.

"Hey, Jimmy!" I said, with a big smile on the face and my hand outstretched. My right hand, just in case he was still a little mad. Barbies get a bad rap in Cin City sometimes, but kens *can* be a little, you know, moody.

But Jimmy wasn't sore; we engaged in a manly handshake that didn't break any of my fingers. "I hear this is about Shauni, yeah?" he said. I'm surprised he didn't rumble; the other kens in the raiding party were tight-faced and unhappy, and even though none of it was aimed in my direction I– actually, I didn't mind. I wasn't happy about what happened to Shauni, either.

"Yeah," I said. "She a friend of yours?" It could be. He was a decent looking guy.

That got a laugh from Jimmy. "Ha! Naw, she much too, ah, high-up for me. Her family is from, ah, you would call it the 'Veranos' tribe. Big mojo. *Real* big mojo. Maybe if I was a chief."

"Gotcha. Well, we got a lead on the assholes that her attacker ran with. I wanna have a chat with them before the cops show up with the cuffs and magestickers."

"All of them?" said one ken. No, wait, that was definitely a rumble. One that promised an avalanche later.

"Nah, I just need a couple with enough teeth to talk. But no massacres! With that crowd, if we run into a mage he'll know death magic." That got grunts from the extras, but they were the smart grunts that professionals give when they get what you're telling them. "So smack 'em on the head when you can. If they keep throwing up later because of it, that's on them."

"Especially if you dodge out of the way," Lucas said cheerfully as we headed for the door.

#

The place we were going wasn't in Redtown itself: it was on the docks, north enough of Kermie's hangout so that he didn't have to strain too hard to not notice it. I had talked to him briefly about that, beforehand. It went about as I expected.

"Don't push it, Shamus!" he had groused. "They were making that witch's brew before I got here, and they'll be making it after I'm gone. Long as your mountain pisses out schmaltz, some natural-born damned fool will come along to cook it up. It's gonna happen. You all set it up that way."

Which was entirely true, but I was still pissed. "Fine, Kermie, I don't tell you how to do your business..."

"Smart fella. Because you'd suck at it," Kermit interrupted.

"...But this is a Case." I manfully refrained from smacking the table with my fist. Or maybe I just didn't want to annoy a crime boss in his lair. "The icemold thing's gotten out of hand, and now there are people on the slab, okay?"

"Icemold always puts people on the slab, Shamus," said Kermie. "It's just that this time some of them are sober citizens. I'm shocked there's not more. The supply dried up, did you know that?"

"Yeah," I said. "Weedy said something about that before he died."

Kermie's face lost a little righteous indignation. "Yeah. Damned shame about that. And about the people you're trying to avenge. But on the street? When the drug went scarce, we went from moldies being a pain in the ass to being half-crazed nutjobs stabbing each other for a fix. Who clears *their* Cases, Shamus?"

"I ain't got a broom that big, Kermie." I wished that I did, but wishes ain't cheap and there's no quality control on them these days. "But maybe next time don't wait three months before telling me about something going down with the icemold supply?" I'd have to forgive him for that: Kermie wasn't raised New Californian. Somebody from here would know to tell a Shamus about what was going down with the icemold.

"That's fair," allowed Kermie. He held out a clawed, slimy hand that I shook without hesitation. "And, yeah, that place you're going to is overdue for a smacking. Try not to get too many of my crew killed, Shamus. Oh, and you, too."

#

It's not too often that I'm on the giving end of a Brute Squad. Gotta say, everything looks different from that angle. All the hassles in your way suddenly look a lot more breakable. The trick is to make sure that you're only breaking the right stuff.

Oh, and not do everything yourself. Let the big guys take point. That's their job, and they don't want to punch, stab, or shoot around you anyway. I was there to aim them in the right direction and free them from thinking about what to do when things went sour.

Moldworks are smelly, nasty, filthy pits in the ground that need a lot of undrinkable water and some vicious chemicals to work, so the moldmakers had gone the obvious route and used a tannery as the cover business. There were three employees above ground, and I guessed that at least two of them were supposed to raise an alarm if necessary. Maybe all three. Moldmakers aren't what you'd call trusting.

They also didn't hire the best people. Me and Lucas went in by ourselves; the Brute Squad was for when sneaky was no longer an option. "How are we doing this?" I asked as we walked up to the door.

"The usual! We improvise," said Lucas as he went in first. "Plans at this stage are so pointless, don't you agree?" he chirped brightly at the 'cashier' propped up on the counter. I also spotted an 'assistant' lounging by what was probably the basement door and the 'tanner' himself poking at a pile of smelly jackalope furs.

The cashier said "Huh?" as Lucas approached the counter. The smile on Lucas's face never slipped as the elf reached out suddenly to grab the cashier by both ears, then slam the guy's face into the counter two, three times. "Could you hold this, Shamus?" Lucas said as he let go with one hand, reached into his jacket, and pulled out a few throwing knives.

I grabbed the cashier's head myself and kept it against the counter. Lucas said, "Thanks! Just give me a minute." Three of the knives spun out: two pinned the sleeve of the assistant as he reached for what looked like a bell-pull. The third slammed into the wood so close underneath the crotch of the assistant's jeans that I winced in sympathy. Lucas was already moving to meet the tanner, who had pulled a warhammer out from underneath the pile of jackalope furs and was roaring.

Warhammers are great for messing people up. If you can hit them before they can hit you. When you got somebody with a blackjack who can duck under your swing, well, wear elbow pads. The tanner wasn't wearing an elbow pad. Or anything to protect the back of his head, which is what Lucas hit next. Tanner went down in a heap.

I looked at the two remaining. "Cashier's still awake," I said as the guy kept trying and failing to get traction. "Assistant looks like the dumb one."

"On it," said Lucas. He slapped some goo on the assistant, who went slack-faced and sloppy pretty much instantly. "I'm gonna be the bad cop this time," Lucas said conversationally as he walked up to the counter, short sword in hand.

"That's fair," I said. I looked down. "Although I think our guy here isn't going to give you any time to play."

#

Whaddya know: I'm a prophet! There's a pun there about me and my bank account, but it only works in Court English.

Our friend manning the counter was more than happy to tell us the passwords, countersigns, and secret handshake that his fellows downstairs were supposed to use to keep mean bastards like me and Lucas from just popping in. He seemed almost disappointed to find out that we only wanted to know how many were down there (a 'bunch'), whether they had a mage (yes, dammit), and whether there was something else besides the bell-pull to sound the alarm (nope). I could almost sympathize. Why bother coming up with a secret handshake for security if the bad guys will just kick the door in?

"All right," I said after the cashier started repeating himself. "Slap the goop on this mook and let's go on down." By now the room was starting to fill up with Brute Squad and the clock was unwinding. I wanted to be underground before things started going wrong.

I did check to make sure everybody else had on their cotton breath masks. Lucas quirked an eyebrow above his as he saw I wasn't wearing one. "What, you immune to icemold?"

"Yes," I said.

"Fair enough." As we moved to the door, Lucas asked, "How evil-evil is this bunch?" His tone was curious, almost detached, but I could almost see the Adventurers reflexes start to kick in.

I thought about it. "Take surrenders," I said to the Squad. "Except the mage; put him down right off the bat. Save survivors for the cops. But Kermie did a head-count before you left, and he wants me to bring as many of you back as I can, without any pieces missing. So don't do anything stupid, either."

"I've heard worse house rules," Lucas said as he readied his blades.

#

Icemold makes people do dumb things. The stuff rots the brain, okay? Anybody on it for too long starts taking knocks to the old noggin, only from the inside where you can't wear a helmet. Old moldies are – well, dead; but before then they can get pretty stupid.

And so can moldmakers; gloves and masks only do so much, and anybody who toils in a moldworks for long enough is gonna get a taste for their own supply. When that happens, the poor dumbass usually gets the chop quick and they bring in some other poor dumbass who can do the job and disappear easily. The turnaround time is usually maybe four, five months? So there's a lot of turnover in moldworks, is what I'm saying. And they ain't well trained. And none of them are what you'd call buddy-buddy with their coworkers.

You can imagine what happened to the first two or three that ran into the Brute Squad. Sorry: the Brute Squad ran into *them*, and it wasn't the Brute Squad that bounced. Because we were, after all, getting in before the cops did and wanted to leave them people to interview, the Squad was using clubs and knuckles.

Only thing was, these were all kens from up north, so the 'brass knuckles' were one-handed dumbbells and the 'clubs' were barbells with one half knocked off. I didn't even see the first guard except as a blur in the air as he smacked into the wall, still dropping teeth behind him. His buddy got enough time to look shocked before he folded over the club to his gut, but the blow knocked all the air out of him, not to mention his breakfast. Two down, no hue and cry sounded. These were clearly ken ninja.

I didn't even bother to hope that we could keep the streak going, because things started getting seriously hairy right after that. Smacking people against the wall is *loud*, and moldmakers are naturally jumpy about violence. The bastards just started showing up and wading in. That's how we lost two Brutes off the bat; they weren't looking in the right place before they got stabbed with skimming knives.

And oh, yeah, there weren't a dozen moldmakers. There were more like two dozen. And they all showed up at once, it felt like. Lucas told me later that we were better off that way, because we were a group and they were a mob, but when some *bastardo* comes out of nowhere and is trying to carve you up with a skimming knife, you don't want to hear how this was nothing like that time in Lost Orleans, hey?

Nah, you just want to keep the knife away from your softer bits while you figure out what to do. In my case, I went with the classics; knee to the groin. Guy was wearing a cup, but I was wearing a knee guard under the suit, so it evened out. And it at least put him off guard long enough for my head to meet his nose.

And I wear protection under the fedora, too. At least, I do when I've gone to the rumbles. He went slack enough that I could make him drop the knife; then a quick one-two in the gut made him decide to drop, and with only a slice or two for my troubles. Nothing nasty, for once, but I figured that the spell on my suit was probably gone by now.

Damn. I should have had Father Mike tell me who had cast it originally. Well, I could ask around.

The fight was beginning to wind down as I knocked out my guy with the skimming knife. Which made sense; kens know how to clear an underground space. But, just when it looked like things would get resolved nice and clean, the mage showed up.

The good news about the moldworker mage was the same as the bad news; he was a damned moldie himself. Hell, half of these guys were from being around the stuff. But *they* didn't know how to throw magic around.

We were lucky that the mage wasn't so mold-raddled as to try to toss off some fireballs, because those are bad indoors and the backblast don't play favorites. But he also knew how to shoot steam out of his fingers, and hit us with a wave of the stuff just as we were regrouping from smacking the fighters around.

You ever get a shot of live steam in the face? The kind that the really Old Americans used to have? It's not good. It scalds and blisters and even if you don't lose an eye you're gonna be blinking and blind for a little bit, and the mage got half the Brute Squad in his first attack. One unlucky Brute was inhaling at just the wrong moment, too, and that wasn't a great way to go. Even the ones that weren't in the blast still got so tangled up in the surprise. Or so I figured out later; me, I was blinking and blind.

If the moldie mage was smarter, he'd have run then. Nobody good enough to hold off a Brute Squad by himself would ever be in a moldworks, and he had a decent path to the door. But the icemold in his blood was doing the talking, and it said to keep shooting kens in the face with live steam. He really piled it on, too. Panic and no sense of preservation will do that to you. Besides, mages on icemold can hold it together longer than regular moldies could, until they suddenly can't. Until then, it could get real hard to get spells to land on their living flesh, not that we had our own 'specialist.'

But the moldie mage's real problem was that kens – well,

it's a nasty lie that barbies don't feel pain the way we do. That's something that *cabrones* say so they can feel smug about looking down their noses. But a ken ain't going to let something like being scalded half to death keep him from going and messing up whoever's doing the scalding. It's one of the things that keeps the barbie tribes alive and kicking up north, so why change what works?

My buddy Jimmy was one of the guys who almost lost an eye, so he couldn't see a damned thing. But he had a sword, and he knew where the steam jet was coming from, and that to him was enough. To hear him describe it later, it was a mighty blow that cleaved the vicious sorcerer form from navel to sneering chin. I didn't say anything, even though when I finally could see again it was obvious that Jimmy had just ripped out the moldie mage's guts. It's his story, not mine.

#

So, we had three guys dead and eight hurt, five bad enough that we needed to get them upstairs and looked at by a real doctor. They had about fifteen guys dead, eight or so knocked out one way or another, and two, maybe three who could talk. That was better than what I figured going in, but these moldmakers were real sloppy. A couple of them were even upset that we were there.

"You're gonna pay for this," one of them started to say, just before I shoved a rag into his mouth. He and his buddies all glared at me, but didn't do anything else. The ropes and handcuffs all three were now sporting probably helped with that, though.

"Now, don't say anything you're gonna regret later," I said with more calm than I felt. "This isn't a smash-and-grab; the cops will be by later to capone you all good and proper. Or were you gonna go yell for Kermie?" I leaned against a handy table. "Go ahead. Yell for him."

"Sorry, he's busy," called Lucas from the next room. "Can I take a message?"

I spread my hands. "See what I mean? You three are out of

a job. Keep it up, and soon you'll be out of sunlight for the next twenty years. I hear the Castle gets really upset when moldmakers don't pay their taxes." Odd little quirk of the laws: you can possess icemold, but can't make or sell it. And if you get caught selling it, you're on the hook for the taxes you didn't pay. The whole thing's a political wheeze so old it predates the Lore.

One of the two ungagged moldmakers looked smart enough to follow along, in a seedy kind of way. "'Keep it up?' What, we have a choice?"

"Sure," I said. "You tell me what I want to know, and I'll cut away enough of the ropes to let one of you escape before the cops show up. Just one of you, though. I ain't a charity."

"Which one?" said the other ungagged guy.

"Whoever impresses me the most," I said.

And with that they were off. Even the gagged guy was ready to talk, at that point.

#

Poor old Weedy hadn't been lying: the supply of icemold *had* dried up. Somebody was buying up all that the moldworkers could make, and he hadn't taken no for an answer.

The guy I had gagged turned out to be the best squealer. Typical. Knock loose the bluster and the words come spurting out: "They were doing this when I started working here," Third Guy whined. "They told me that we needed every drop, even the crap gleanings that got sold to the real junkies. That wasn't fair. I got promised that we could do a little on the side, right?"

"Screw you, *culero*! You got paid fine!" shouted Second Guy.

"No!" yelled First Guy, "*You* got paid fine, because you were putting your hand in my pocket and it came out holding my money!" Well, at least they weren't trying to show solidarity. I looked at Third Guy, who was keeping his mouth shut. If I was gonna feel sorry for any of them, it'd be this guy because he looked dumber than the other two. Some people get sucked up, you know what I mean?

"So, who was the buyer?" I asked Third Guy. First Guy

laughed at that, real nasty-like.

"He won't tell you crap. He can't even spell it." And Third Guy didn't like to hear that at all, probably because it was true.

"Piss off! Yeah, I know things," said Third Guy. "That guy buying from us? Don't know his name, but I know he was a sorcerer."

"Really?" I said, and decided to take a chance. "That's funny, because I heard that he was a noble prick from the Castle. You dumb enough to tell me another lie?"

Telling a whopper like that is a gamble; a smart guy can pick up that you're trying to make him mad enough to prove you wrong. Third Guy here wasn't smart enough to catch that. "Screw you, smart-ass," he said. "The way he talked, he wasn't no noble or from the Castle, either. That sorcerer your pet sliced up? That was one of his people. And real scared of his boss, too. Only thing that scares a sorcerer is another sorcerer."

Yeah, sure, Third Guy had a point there. "You ever see this 'boss' do magic, though?" I asked.

Second Guy interrupted there. "Yeah, I saw him cast a spell once." First Guy started telling him to shut up; Second Guy raised his voice. "Screw you, he already knows. I want out of here before the pigs show up. Yeah," he said back to me, "the first time the buyer came for a shipment he did some spells over the barrels, all glowy lights and crap. Said he wanted to check to make sure they were all good."

"Were they?" I asked, idly. Really idly, for once.

"Well, yeah. Mostly. There was this one barrel, maybe it wasn't so good." Second Guy gulped at the memory. "He did a spell and one of the guys on the floor walked up to the barrel, opened it up, and shoved himself in, head first. Then the barrel lid flew up in the air and nailed itself back in. Right after that, the screaming inside started, but none of us moved until the buyer told us we could."

"Right," I said. I didn't bother asking if they had passed off a crappy shipment after that. Some things are too stupid even for moldies to do. "Where did the shipments go?"

"He picked them up," said First Guy. "One guy followed him, one time. He didn't come back. We got the hint."

I stood up. "Yeah, you guys don't know nothing." I started walking to the door. "Say hi to the cops for me."

"Wait!" shouted Second Guy. I turned back. He said, "One time he was here, he dropped a snot-rag. We grabbed it, kept it on ice. For insurance, you know? It's in that cooler."

I looked in and grinned. There it was! And in an authentic-looking Old American zip-box from just before the end of the world, too. Those things really did last forever. "Consider your insurance policy paid out." I cut most of Third Guy's bonds. When Second Guy squawked at that, I looked at him like I was wondering how hard I could punch him without knocking his chair over. That shut him up.

I turned back to Third Guy. "Take your winnings and get the hell out of New California. Or at least somewhere they ain't got Shamuses. Or don't. Your life ain't my problem."

Lucas was waiting for me by the door. "You done?" I asked.

"Yeah, we're good." Lucas didn't say any more, and I didn't press him for it. "What you got there?" he asked.

"A snot-rag of whoever was buying the icemold," I said. "It was a mage with mage lackeys who isn't from around here and who likes to kill those who disappoint him for the last time. Sound like anybody we know?"

And that was actually it, for the day. I dropped the snot-rag off with somebody – never mind who – who could do some discreet checking, but that was about it. Sometimes exciting things don't happen one after the other. You always wish that those moments would last, too. But they never do.

#

The next day, Lucas and me grabbed either a late breakfast or an early lunch at Garapenna's. We were between shifts, so I waved the replacement cook back to his siesta after we got our sandwiches. I didn't want anybody listening in, anyway. The papers were full of the raid on the moldworks; I looked to see if any of the informative Three Guys were mentioned in the article, but I guess they ran. If they're smart, they'll keep running until they're over the border. Any will do.

"So," Lucas said with his mouth deplorably full, "there's a bunch of Haida mages working for or with Wolfie? Or the embassy in general? It seemed a little vague, even when you don't include the icemold."

"Yeah. We call 'em 'redmages' because they got a lot in common with the Redtowners. They have this really messed up way to explain away magic, because using it is against their religion, only they hate it even more than Redtowners when you call it a religion. Redmages do *all* the dark stuff, too. What I can't figure out is why Cackle hired them in the first place. Or why they stuck with Wolfie. Or why they even took the job. The Dominion and the Haida hate each other."

"What if they didn't have a choice? Do the Haida have politics– what am I saying, of course they do. So maybe this crowd lost a fight and Cin City was just far enough to run."

"Yeah. Maybe. But they're behaving themselves. That's the really weird thing. What does Wolfie have on them?" I contemplated my coffee. "Guess we'll ask them, when the cops round 'em all up. One of them will know something about the murders. A shame we won't be able to pin it on Wolfie himself, but that's life in Cin City."

"You persuading me, or yourself, Tom?"

"Neither. You know how it goes. Even if they give Wolfie up, or we pin him to the icemold, he's got diplomatic immunity and all that happy crap. But he'll get recalled, once word of this gets back. He was walking a tightrope already by killing a bunch of mages instead of snatching them. The Dominion wants its mages alive and kicking. But using the Haida? And just for drug deals? Yeah, that'll get him in all kinds of trouble. Maybe even the kind that gets you dead."

Famous almost-last words.

#

I reconstructed it, after. I was assuming that I was safe from fireballs, because spells weren't biting on me right now.

Nothing to aim at. And Lucas was safe when he was with me, because he was dropping those no-scry-mes everywhere. So as long as there wasn't anything on him to track, everything was all right, right?

Well. It's a good thing that Adventurers have instincts and Shamuses have our screwed-up luck; both saved our lives. Lucas and I had just walked out the door when the explosive fireball hit the storefront a few seconds later. Something must have warned Lucas, because he went from walking to diving in nothing flat; the bastard who was using Lucas as a quick-and-dirty aiming point still couldn't quite lock on to us (we have *very* good cleaning ladies in Cin City), so the blast just sent him sprawling into a wall and me rolling into the street.

I rushed over to Lucas, winced at the broken legs and arm, and started to do first aid. He weakly slapped my hands away and mumbled, "Suspended animation stone. Top right pocket." I scrabbled around in the pocket, pulled out... an Old American movie crystal.

I looked at it, then said, "Dammit, Lucas," as I started looking further in his pockets.

"Sorry," said Lucas. "I wanted it to be a surprise." He coughed in a way I didn't like. "Surprise!"

By then I had found what I guessed Lucas was actually looking for: a pale blue-grey inscribed stone, cold to the touch. I stuck it in his grasping good hand. The blue-grey flowed down from the stone and across Lucas's body. I could see him relaxing in relief, just before he stiffened into sparkling immobility. I started to stand up to check on any other survivors, only at that point a brick fell on my head.

Just my luck.

#

No matter how bad it got, we never did forget how to doctor in New California. Hard to forget to wash your hands, boil everything, and keep You oranges around; but other realms managed to lose even that much medical know-how, so yay us. Chapman General Hospital can do everything that you can do without the Old Americans' electricity, and it's rumored that, down in the sublevels, you can find a few of those gadgets, too. For sure that's where they'd keep the magical healing, if the Old Chap admitted to having any.

They wanted to keep me for a week, and were willing to compromise for overnight. I made them rush things even more. I might not have, except Dory showed up to berate somebody; I would apparently do, in a pinch.

"The Hell, Tom? This is not what we meant by quiet!"

"I'm glad to see the both of you too, Dory." I was still a little woozy from the scientist's brew that the doctors had whipped up for me. I was assured that it would kick in any second. I couldn't wait.

"What? Yes, thank God you're alive. But what did you do to the Ambassador to make him throw fireballs in public? Once, we could ignore. But there's a burned-out shopfront in the middle of town now. The Castle won't pretend that didn't happen."

"Wolfie's running scared, Dory. Scared like a bunny– oh, hey, did the cook get out?"

I tried to focus; Dory looked like she was about to say something, then calmed down. "Yes, Shamus, the cook got out."

"Oh, good." And then the wave of grinding pain hit. "ARRGH!" Quick as a flash, Dory caught me.

"Tom! *Tom!* Do I need to call a nurse?"

I blinked away tears. "No. No," I said more firmly. "Whatever they put in me just started working. Damn, but that's the stuff."

The Old Americans knew their medicines; after a minute I could stand, and start rummaging for my shoes. "Here's what's happening, Dory. We caught Wolfie with his hand in the damned cookie jar. He and the guy before him were hiding mages from us and the Dominion. Nasty ones, the kind that summon demons. Somehow a bunch of people from the university found out, and Wolfie had them killed, and then Elizabeth found out, because those were her friends. So Wolfie had *her* killed when she went to the Castle to tell somebody. We're golden here, Dory. The Castle's golden. The cops sweep up Wolfie's secret mages, and we wave them around until the Dominion yanks Wolfie back home. He tried to kill me before I put it together, but it's too late. He's probably already running."

I was very proud of all of this, but Dory was not. She pointed to the window. "I don't think that he's running, Shamus," she said.

I looked out the window. Above, in the air, was something out of the Lore: huge letters made of clouds, hanging in the mid-afternoon sky. The words read **SURRENDER SHAMUS** – and an arrow, pointing straight at Mount Jeannie. It took me a moment to regain my composure at that insult.

When I did, I managed to evenly say, "Dammit, 'Shamus' doesn't have three syllables."

CHAPTER TWENTY-FIVE
Surrender Shamus

Sure I went – after I checked up on Lucas. He was in a room nearby, splinted up in that way you see when somebody's going to sneak in later and make the splints redundant. Out like a light, too. The Old Chap has its little ways when it comes to accumulating stuff to knock patients out, and Lucas was Castle business right now.

Shame, though; I wouldn't have minded backup on this one. But Lucas was gonna need some days to recover – and when I asked, the nurses made it real clear that I had gotten all the miracles that the Old Chap had in stock. That's Shamus luck for you: I was back on my feet and on my own. Or so I hoped Wolfie thought.

No, I didn't even try to get one of the Gonzalezes. Too far away and this was strictly my kind of business, anyway. Lucas would have been pushing it as it was. And I might not have gone and gotten Elizabeth even if I could have contacted her. There are places to do on-the-fly magical research: the top of the Mount ain't one of them.

Getting to Mount Jeannie is officially hard, because it's a damn glacier in the middle of the Gulf of California and it's brass-monkey territory at the top. But unofficially it's easy, because illegal mages and Shamuses have been coming to the Mount for four hundred years. You want to arrive quick, there are ways to do it. In this case, Dory got me the loan of an antique motorboat from the Castle's collection. It smelled like french fries and it was loud as hell, but it was also faster than rowboats and I wasn't trying to sneak.

I was troubled as the boat puttered along on the bay. Wolfie hadn't been reacting the way I expected at any point in this Case, although seven murders argued that he was prone to bad decision-making. But the truth was, we did have a treaty with the Universal Dominion. We were supposed to hand over our mages. We just didn't, and the Dominion was a little too far away to make us.

But the Dominion was closer to our borders now, so was that Wolfie's angle? Because if his plan had worked, he'd be in a great position to be pushing New California around. Only the scheme went bad.

Okay, that happens. But the guy was still an ambassador, which meant that Wolfie had access to more resources than he was using. I'd seen his place; he barely was using the stuff he had. He wasn't even using the stuff he brought *with* him. It's like he didn't want to.

Hell, he didn't even try to summon any backup from the Dominion. So why didn't he? Was the problem all those Haida mages? Sure, the Dominion hates those sons of bitches (even if it's for all the wrong reasons); Wolfie could have pinned the blame on his predecessor for them, once he killed 'em so they couldn't tattle that he'd continued the arrangement. It'd even be fair.

Was it something about the local mages? But what made things different now? Sure, they were 'illegal,' but illegal mages aren't rare on the ground here. Hell, they're what makes the kingdom function. Without them and Mount Jeannie, New California would be a dusty peninsula in the middle of nowhere. Good thing the Mount couldn't be stolen.

And that's when I stopped. Because I'd just figured out what the angle was.

#

There's not much to see on the Mount itself, at least at the bottom. Somebody carefully carved holes for a quay and stairs, which gave me something to attach the boat to and a direction to go. The breeze off of the Mount was nothing like I've ever felt before; there was an interloper on Her summit, and I fancied I could taste the anger and outrage in the air itself.

There's a combination storage shack and observation station at the very top, right underneath the hovering stars that keep every boat in the Gulf from crashing into the Mount at night. That's where I headed, because that's where I knew things would go down. Why? Because I'm a Shamus. It was inevitable. And things were going quick, which meant things were pretty awful.

I could smell copper and iron (and icemold, which was *bad*) even before I saw the bloodstains on the floor of the vestibule leading to the main room. One of the Flatfoots assigned by the Castle to guard the place and shoo out the canoodlers; he had gotten his nightstick out, at least. From his grimace, the Flatfoot had died quick but not easy; there was a certain set to his corpse that suggested that he had been smacked around a little after, like a cat might push around a dead mouse and wonder why it wasn't playing anymore.

I reflexively pulled my piece out. And the moment I did, I could hear disembodied laughter. *"Brave, but very foolish,"* went the voice in my head. *"I have no fear of guns. And it is not even loaded!"*

"But this is," came a voice from behind me.

A guy stepped out from the shadows. I remembered him after a second; he was the moldie I fought in an alley, right before I cut off a hunk of his hair. But even if the face was kind of forgettable, the stench of icemold wasn't. I felt an irrational spike of anger towards the mage probably waiting above for us; even a Dominion mage should have more of a heart than let a moldie near the source of his addiction. The poor bastard probably chewed on the mops people used to clean up the place. His eyes were still clear, though. Clear enough to aim the crossbow he had pointed at me.

"Hands up, Shamus. Nice and slow. We're going to go see the Master. Isn't that nice?" I recognized the accent: the same as that bastard fake-Perez. And when I didn't move right away, his hands started to twitch as he raised the 'bow. "I said *hands up*."

"You're the guy with the crossbow," I said agreeably as I put my piece back in its holster, then raised my hands. He didn't like how casually I did that, nor the look of amused contempt I was giving him. As he opened his mouth to say something, I added, "Aren't we supposed to go see your Master, chum? Up the stairs and into the big room at the top. Don't worry, we won't get lost: I've been here before."

I'm pretty sure I heard one of the moldie's teeth crack under the strain. Poor bugger was closer to the end than he looked. Not that I mentioned that as we climbed the stairs. In fact, I didn't say a word as we went upstairs and I calmly walked into the main room. I think the moldie was expecting more of a fight, but I wanted to go up there anyway. Best to get this over with.

As I said, I've been here before. The room's normally pretty clear, with a nice picture window for people to observe stuff and some desks for them to write it all down on. Whoever it was who'd designed the place a century and a half ago had a real weakness for neo-Heinlein decor; even the hurricane lamps were made up to look like atoms. You could tell that the designer ached to put some boxes full of real random blinky lights along the sides, but had to make do with colored glass and salvaged burnished aluminum.

But now the room looked like it came out of a bad play about a wizard's tower; I knew that most Dominion mages wouldn't know good taste if it beat them around the head a few times, but this was something especially awful, in every way that the word meant. There had been another Flatfoot up here, and Wolfie had used his blood to draw all over the walls and floors and even the damned ceiling. It shaped words that I think were supposed to be burning holes in my brain, although I decided not to mention that I wasn't real impressed.

And absolutely worst of all were the barrels of icemold everywhere. Some of them were even open, and the idea that all of it was here, *here*, made me ready to boil over. I kept it all in, though. Now wasn't the time.

I gotta say that the mage was definitely in his element, though. He was standing there, looking out at the bright lights of Cin City across the Gulf. As the mage turned, I noted with some satisfaction the fading bruises and burns left from his rooftop battle with Elizabeth. Good luck getting another mage to help anybody wearing Dominion robes in this town, buddy.

"Ah, Shamus." He actually sounded not particularly hostile. "We meet again."

I grinned, in a way precisely calibrated to piss off the moldie. "Hi, Cackle."

#

This got a real, amused chuckle from Wolfie/Cackle. "You impress me, Shamus! Or should I call you Tom?"

I thought about it, and decided that he was warded against what happened to his minion in the cells. "Tom. Definitely Tom."

"Fair enough. I do not subscribe to your odd little faith, after all. When did you figure it out?"

"Which part?" I said. "Who you are, or what you're doing?"

"Start with the first one," said Cackle. "You're probably going to get the other one wrong." It was weird, how he *didn't* sneer there. You'd expect a sneer, right?

"See, it's things like that," I said. "You did a great job pretending to be Wolfie when I ran into you the first time, but you just ain't the right kind of nasty for a young evil mage. An old evil mage, sure, but the real Wolfie would probably have tried to burn down half the city by now. Or just tried to kill me directly. Or, you know, anything else just as stupid."

"Oh? You know Dominion mages that well?"

"Nah, but I know entitled young assholes just fine."

That got another laugh. "Fair enough, Tom. But if it makes you feel any better, I wasn't really *invested* in trying to kill you. Not even after you interfered in that odd fight I had with that random mage-girl. Oh, I was annoyed when I got a face full of alchemical garbage; but I decided to treat it as a learning experience, and make sure you got one, too. And you seem to have handled yours very well!"

"Tell it to my accountant," I said. "My doctor's bill is gonna make me hide from the mailman."

"Pshaw. I wasn't even aiming at you," said Cackle. "I will admit to being mildly peeved that the *clever*, if greedy, Mr. Coltrane managed to avoid dying, but I'm a fair-minded sort of fellow. I will allow him to flee this land, once he's out of the hospital. As long as he's reasonably quick about it."

"Big of you."

"It is, actually!" Cackle looked sincerely rueful, for some reason. "Or at least it's self-corrective of me. Normally I've found simply killing off annoyances to be a perfectly reasonable life strategy, but it doesn't seem to work all that well in New California. One reason to finish up my plans here, really.

"But a little business first," Cackle went on. "You have two things: one that belongs to my servant here, and one that I will take possession of myself. The lock of hair and your magical deterrent, please."

I shrugged and tossed them both on a table; the scryguard skittered and rattled a little as it settled. I told the moldie, "If you want my advice, chum, burn that hair just as soon as you can."

He sidled over and grabbed his lock of hair without taking his eyes off of me. "Piss off, wrecker," he said. Heh. Guess even icemold can't erase a guy's religious beliefs.

"Tsk, tsk," said Cackle. "Neither of us subscribe to your even odder little faith. Speaking of which, let me take care of yours, Tom." He spoke a few Words of power and I felt something like a spell go off. And, just like that, a connection that I didn't even know I possessed was sundered.

Cackle almost sounded apologetic. "I just interrupted your spiritual connection to the city. Interrupted, not destroyed; even something like me cannot break a bond that strong without some work. But I can't have a fully functional priest wandering around here, either. Oh, yes," he said, I guess in response to my look of slight surprise, "I understand that you are a priest. Not the oddest thing I've ever seen, but odd nonetheless."

He spoke a few more Words, and I could feel the outlines of a compulsion spell settle about me. "And that's to keep you placid while we finish things up. After all, you still have physical skills, as a few of my servants can attest. At any rate: do you know what the great flaw of New California is, Tom?"

When I didn't reply, a frown moved across his face for a moment. Then Cackle gave a small shrug and said, "Interesting. It worked better than I thought. Yes, you may answer questions and converse with me."

I immediately replied, "Sure. The Padres haven't won the World Series in four hundred and thirty-four years."

Cackle grinned. "That's better! I was afraid the compulsion spell had burned out a piece of your brain. No, the problem with New California is not your puerile version of baseball–"

"Yeah, but we haven't even made the pennant," I interrupted.

This time Cackle glowered. "Don't interrupt, though." I readily stopped. "No, Tom, the problem with New California is the way you treat your mages. I could understand it if you enslaved them! The Dominion wouldn't tolerate it, but I'd understand it. But this entire ridiculous setup that you have makes no sense. They don't rule, but they're not outcasts. You never admit to having them, but you can't live without them. They work, but you pay them."

After a moment, I judged he was finished, so I shrugged. "Sounds like, if we had mages, we'd treat them like regular Joes and Janes. People. If we had mages."

"Would you believe me if I told you that I respect that, Tom?"

"Only if you told me to."

"Fair enough. I respect that, but it's still not sensible. Magic is either your master, or it is your slave. It can never be your partner. None of you seem to understand that."

The spell didn't even try to protest when I looked around. "And you're gonna make us understand?"

"Exactly." Cackle waved a hand. "What I've done here is a makeshift magical working, but I'm sure it's obvious even to you. You have a marvelous array of magic spells here. A whole iceberg, preserved and constantly reformed out of the sea! It's almost a miracle. I'm going to break it."

CHAPTER TWENTY-SIX
Somebody's Got To Take The Fall

I very, very calmly looked at Cackle. "So *that's* what this all about," I said, just as calmly. "You don't care about the mages here. You care about the Mountain."

"I told you you'd get the other one wrong," Cackle said. Again, no sneer. I would have liked a sneer.

"I would have gotten it wrong," I calmly – *so* calmly – replied. "But why blow up the Mountain? And why use the ice-mold?"

He shrugged. "This mountain is in the way," said Cackle. "I've looked into how this 'icemold' of yours is made. It's a fascinating substance, although it's very, very bad for those with magical powers. Bad enough that infusing the entire mountain here with it should rip through the local spell infrastructure like TNT through a butter sculpture. Ah, forgive me, but TNT..."

"I know what TNT is," I said without thinking. At least I didn't say *It's in the Lore*. Fortunately, Cackle didn't notice I had interrupted him.

"Really? It's always remarkable to see what ideas do manage to survive. Anyway, without your 'Mount Jeannie,' the entire area will inexorably fall apart. Your mages will be blamed, because it will be safer than blaming the Dominion. And as your kingdom grinds them down, I will be there to gather the wheat from the chaff." He smiled. "First I will draw from the ATSE. And then I will bring in the hedge witches and folk magicians. Not all of them. The sensible ones, the ones who chafe under this ridiculous system that your people use.

"After that?" he went on, "I take over. New California will eventually become uninhabitable, but there's plenty of land across the Gulf. Sonora's falling apart and the orc tribes won't have the right kind of magic to fight us."

"While the Dominion just sits and watches?"

"While the Dominion praises 'Wolfie' as the man conquering the south on the cheap. By the time they realize that I've merely created my own mage empire, it'll be too late to stop me. And I will be most accommodating to them! Mages will rule here; loot will flow north. All will be well.

"And when the time is right," went on Cackle, "I will take the fighters and the mages and the armies that I have gathered from a dozen shattered lands. We will assemble; and we will march north through Old California, and the Dwarvenwood, conquering as we go; and we will smash utterly the Haida; and only *then* I will have had my revenge on those slave-mongering mortals."

The last piece of the puzzle fell into place. "Ah," I said. "You're not really 'Cackle,' either." He shook his head. I asked, "Then what should I be calling you?"

"I have many names," Cackle said. He then looked mildly disappointed when I didn't seem to have any idea what that meant. "Oh, 'Legion' will do. Let me simply say I came here from the mysterious West. Asia, if that means anything to you?" Checking the compulsion spell, I thought it safe enough to nod. "Yes. Out from the mountains, up that coast, across the ice bridge in the far north, and back down again. Jumping from body to body made it easier, but it still took a remarkable amount of time.

"And then I discovered the Haida – and I did not enjoy the experience." Legion's face showed a hint of the interloper living inside it. "Later, neither did they. Be grateful that they are not nearer neighbors; I am no stranger to the barbarities of those who heed the words of the ancient Marx, but this particular snake cult is remarkably cruel about it. They thought nothing of enslaving me – me, who remembers The World Before! – for far too many years. But they have the usual weakness of their kind: cults of personality. I simply made my own cult, and used it to free myself."

"And then you moved down here? Avoiding even going near the Universal Dominion, because everybody else does?" Legion grinned at that, and I think honestly. I'm telling you, *everybody* hates the Dominion. "And when you got here to Cin City, you decided to swap bodies with the local ambassador. Because Cackle was powerful, but had no friends."

"Exactly. Alas, he was also older than I wanted. I thought about having 'myself' killed and forcing the Dominion to send a replacement, but fortunately they decided to replace 'me' with Wolfstone. Or 'Wolfie,' as you will never call me again. Nothing personal, but it's not appropriate in public."

"But you're still short one ambassador– right, they expected Wolfstone to kill his predecessor?" I managed to not say 'Wolfie' in time. The timing on this was going to be tricky.

Legion shrugged. "I didn't bother to ask," he said. "I barely let him drop off his bags before performing the switch. Frankly, he seemed like a very unpleasant person, and I saw no reason why I should tolerate his company for any length of time. Besides, he might have realized that I was not what I seemed.

"After I switched bodies and disposed of the old one, I went through the correspondence Wolfstone had carried with him. His superiors didn't order any assassinations; but didn't forbid one, either. I suppose his superiors in the Dominion decided that the new ambassador slew the old one secretly, and then dropped the body in the ocean. Which is almost what happened, at that."

"And the rest of them?" I asked, carefully. Legion looked confused for a moment, then got it. He laughed again, only this time a bit more nastily.

"Ah, yes. The researchers. I needed their assistance when it came to the spells surrounding this mountain. Not enough to master them, but from them I learned how to break the enchantment. They were very helpful; it was a shame that one of them had a friend who knew just a little too much about the ice-mold business. One of my now-deceased employees made the mistake of storing a barrel or two at the researchers' warehouse, and that meant I had to have it all cleaned up."

Legion sighed. "It wasn't a mistake to use the drug on the Haida redmages; it made them tractable, or at least quiet. But it's wasteful to use on anyone that you'd like to keep around, so I compartmentalized things. Not well enough, and for that I blame your society. Most places are better at keeping their criminals at arm's length."

"Most places don't have the Dominion paying attention," I shrugged. "If one set of laws are stupid, what about all the other ones, hey? At least we still get pissed off about murder."

"So I've noticed," said Legion dryly. "At the time I decided that the researchers were more dangerous to me alive, and able to tell people things about icemold, than they were dead. Still, I went to a lot of trouble to kill them quietly, you know. But then *I* made a mistake." He smiled at my look of surprise. "Yes, I admit to mistakes.

"Here," Legion went on, "my mistake was thinking that the young woman involved with that group of mages wasn't worth the trouble of either recruiting, or disposing of. I really should have known better, but I took for granted her friends' own unconscious assumption that anyone from outside the City didn't *really* need to be brought into the fold. It nearly undid my plans; by the time I found out that she had made a connection between her murdered friends and the Dominion ambassador, she was on her way to the Castle. I had to be more direct.

"If it's any consolation," Legion said, "I would have liked to preserve her for my later plans; she was very intelligent, and would have been very useful with the proper conditioning. I just didn't manage to take control of her body long enough to allow my servant here to set the control wards." The mage shrugged. "It's happened before, which is why she was already immobilized with a daze spell. When the control didn't work, I had my servant stab her before she could fully come back to her own body."

I flickered my eyes over to the moldie, giving him the once over; yeah, he was short enough to have done the actual murder. I decided I had no reason at all to warn him about how stupid a decision that had been.

"You have him arrange the body, too, or was it all him?" I

asked.

"Oh, that was me," said Legion. "It seemed the sort of thing 'I' would do, if you take my meaning. The Dominion's ruling class is thoroughly wretched that way."

I didn't want to agree with him out loud. Instead, I said, "Wait, you can take possession of more than one body at a time? Split yourself?"

"I only wish," said Legion. "When I take possession of a body, its old owner ends up in my former one. I can switch between the two freely, but you get one soul per body, always. And the only way to break the link is to have it die on its own. Which is why I always kill the prior one when I'm making a permanent switch. A successful transfer knocks out the old body – it makes disposal easier, or I can switch back after someone's properly conditioned."

"Wow. You were pretty quick to tell me that," I noted.

Legion shrugged. "You'll be *my* new priest; you'll need to know these things. I really am trying to get into the idea of not killing inconveniences. If I hadn't killed the mages, I wouldn't have encountered the girl. If I hadn't killed the girl, I wouldn't have encountered you. I don't know what killing *you* might spawn, so it seems smarter just to stop the cycle here, if I can.

"Besides, as you can imagine" – he waved a hand at the moldie, standing there with what I now realized was helpless, frustrated rage at the world – "my current crop of servants are rapidly becoming useless. Icemold makes them pliable, but it also makes them far too brittle. I'm happy that your police are hunting them all down, really. It will make things easier later."

"So you want me to be your new priest?" I thought about the offer. "No," I decided. Legion shook his head.

"I'd say I was disappointed, except that I expected you to manage to refuse, even under a compulsion spell. No matter; I'll just take you over long enough for a proper obedience implantation. Don't worry, it won't make you any dumber. Just pliable. Look at me," his voice intoned, and I could feel my consciousness begin to drift out into the abyss that was his eyes–

–and I floated there, for a few moments, only to drop back into my own body. Legion frowned. "That happened *again*? Damn it." He actually looked mildly regretful. "Well, nobody can say that I didn't *try*. Hold still, please, while my servant kills you."

"No," I said again, and turned to the moldie. I still didn't have a reason to warn him, but the Lore demands that the good guys have to give the bad guys a chance. Dammit. "**This is the part where you run away**," I quoted.

The moldie hesitated. I assume that he was planning to say something – only the lock of hair that he had taken off of me earlier rushed out of his pocket and started spinning in the air. Quick as a flash it had turned into a miniature cyclone, with his neck in the eye of the storm. And then the storm contracted into a tight ring of hair, choking the life out of him as he flailed about the room.

I winced as I dived behind a console, while Legion tried ineffectually to save his minion. I mean, I *had* assumed that 'Tia Leila' planned something special in mind when she 'borrowed' that lock of hair I'd cut off of the man earlier, but I wasn't expecting this. Then again, turns out the moldie had personally killed her honorary niece, so I who was I to judge? Or more importantly, complain? So I turned back to Legion, who was just now starting to process what was admittedly one of the stranger ways to see a man die by magic.

"Hey, Legion," I said, "Turns out I got a couple of things to bring up, too. First: did you know the name of the mage you killed was Elizabeth?"

Legion blinked, said, "I don't care," and started to pull eldritch energy from the air.

I shook my head, sadly. "I wasn't finished, bub. Second question: when you jumped into your current body, did you destroy the old one's brain?"

That stopped him. "What? Why would I do *that*?" Legion asked, as I hastily reached into my pocket, and lobbed out a brightly-glowing key. It landed on the ground, and flashed into nothingness. Well, I wasn't going back to the ambassador's any time soon anyway.

"Because Dominion mages aren't what you call trusting!" I helpfully explained over what sounded like an approaching din. "They like to have one last defense, just in case somebody, you know, shoves a knife into them, and drops their body into the ocean! Why the hell do you think we never try to kill the bastards? Even head shots don't always work!"

Just then a transcendently infuriated old man (still wearing the Red Hood) came smashing through the window in a blaze of arcane light and barreled right into Legion. Wolfie-in-the-Hood was now here, and looked a lot more powerful than he had earlier. Guess that statue – which I just realized was from *Wolfie's* bags – was some sort of magical insurance of his own. I ducked back down to let the two work out their issues.

And then I found it smart to hide behind a cabinet; wizard duels are messy, loud, and real dangerous in enclosed spaces. I felt something tug at my sleeve; I looked down, and saw the hair-cord that had just strangled the moldie to death. As I gazed at it, it spread out into the word 'Soon,' and then collapsed into a random pile of bloody hair.

I nodded, swallowed my gorge – *It wasn't really black magic*, I told myself; she was just manipulating the hair, not animating it – and started feeling for the wind. Now that the masking artifact was off, anybody with magic could track me, and that meant one entity in particular, riding the wind and bringing the storm with her. It was time to clear the Case.

I looked around. The two mages were in what looked like a slow-motion use of arcane energies, as if they were trying to force the other down through the sheer use of magic alone. It wasn't smart to move around them too quickly, though; the first time I popped my head up, a bolt of greasy wrongness blasted my hat off and across the room. I kept well down after that, and circled around the two carefully, making sure to touch each barrel of icemold as I passed it.

Would Legion's plan have worked? Maybe, if he hadn't

brought a Shamus to the exact place where I could feel the Mountain beneath me, and focus Her attention on each barrel of icemold long enough for the corruption to boil away. Shamus luck, again: now that She could perceive through me what the threat was, the icemold wouldn't *be* a threat. As long as I didn't die in the middle of a wizard's duel, of course. That's also Shamus luck.

Which was why I was looking for the emergency rescue box, and there it was. Quietly, I popped the hatch open, and carefully removed the ice axe. Good, solid work; not as light or strong as what the Old Americans had, but it'd do. It was also balanced for throwing, which is something the Old Americans didn't care about, but we do. And then I stood, pouring my righteous anger at the desecration of this holy place into the axe. It took it all and asked for more, so I gave it more until my own balance was right.

I listened to the song of the wind, getting louder and louder, until just the right moment. And then it was just the right moment. I stood, yelled "Legion! Catch!" and lobbed the fire axe. Legion's head snapped back, with a look of surprised gratitude in his face (it was all I could do to keep my face even neutral at that), grabbed the axe, and swung it down at Wolfie-in-the-Hood's skull.

And that's when Elizabeth showed up, and grabbed them both.

There were four people in the room, at the center of a magical mountain, and three of them weren't in the bodies that they were supposed to be. Legion had no right to *any* body here; Wolfie had a claim to his original body, now stolen by Legion; and Elizabeth existed in the world of spirits and the world of matter at the same time, thanks to– her being somehow tangled up with Legion, I guess? She was also a living conduit of magical energy, and there was just too much sorcery around to be contained.

The easiest way for things to fix themselves was for Wolfie to flow through Elizabeth back into his true body, and for

Legion to be forced back into the only body present where he had an uncontested connection – just in time for the blessed fire axe to smash through Legion's just-taken-back skull, and right into the brain. No resurrection in the angry sea for *this* spirit.

End of the line, Legion, I thought. *Go back to the Hell that spawned you* – yeah, I got the Biblical reference. I'm just not a Christian.

Wolfie slumped down, dazed, but I had eyes only for Elizabeth. She looked at me, sadly, as she started to fade (what need for a second edition, now that the first had been avenged?) – then she saw me frantically waving at her. She tried to speak, only no words came out. I didn't try to explain; there was no time. Instead, I frantically pulled out her lightstone and threw it at her.

She instinctively grabbed it, and I could see all the magic of her childhood pour out of it and into her. It wouldn't last long, not that it needed to. There was too much sound for her to hear, so I waved in the direction of the summit of the Mountain. "GO," I mouthed, clearly and forcefully, and hoped that she would take the hint.

Elizabeth almost didn't realize – but, thank Her, Elizabeth suddenly brightened, both in expression and form, and started to travel in the direction I showed. I could see her form grow clearer as she drifted through the room. But not fade away. The Mountain took Elizabeth in, with a touch as gentle as a grandmother's soothing a child. And wasn't She Elizabeth's grandmother, in Her way? Weren't we all Her descendants?

That was a nice thought, only the Case wasn't quite cleared yet. I turned at the sound of Wolfie scrambling to his feet. His face was full of vicious petulance, and badly-hidden terror, and promises of slights avenged in blood and screams. "Three months," he ranted. "Three months of being trapped in an inferior, decrepit body, while all around me feral mages went about their days. Three months of trying to survive on the dwindling power of a dying husk. Oh, there will be changes here, and I will enjoy making them happen."

I sighed. And was impressed, in spite of myself: Legion had done a good job imitating this bastard. "Afraid not," I said. "Look down." He looked down, and saw that I had drawn my piece on him. "Somebody's got to take the fall for all of this," I explained. And before he could even sneer, I tightened my finger on the trigger.

Dominion mages are always fast. They have to be, given how many scorpions they cuddle. But you show a Dominion mage a gun, and they show you how good their reflexes really are. You see, they all learn that one spell that makes gunpowder explode, and they learn it *hard*. Wolfie beat my finger on the trigger by a good half-second, and he grinned as he cast the spell that would detonate all the gunpowder it found.

The room erupted in light and noise. Wolfie looked down, aghast and already paling, as he slumped over the spreading redness on his robes. "But," he managed. Green sparks fizzled from his fingers as he vainly tried to fix the mess that used to be his gut.

"Yeah, Wolfie. It was a real shame about how you went nuts, left the old ambassador for dead, then started killing anybody who got too interested in you. But you had to, right? Because you were a fraud all along. You weren't really a mage, by the only definition that the Dominion respects. You got killed by a damned *pistolero*." I shook my head.

Wolfie had a hurt look, like this wasn't what he'd been promised. "Magic?" he quavered.

"Nah, Wolfie. Not magic. You weren't here for this, but your predecessor over there figured out that I'm a priest. What he got wrong was that I'm not a priest of the city: I'm a priest of the Mountain. In fact, you're on my holy ground." I considered the gat. "Anywhere else, this piece is for exorcising demons. Here, the bullets work just fine, even without gunpowder." I thumbed back the hammer again. Two in the head should do for whatever life-eggs *he* might have, and it'd be over quicker for Wolfie that way.

"I'd say it's not personal, but why lie?"

CHAPTER TWENTY-SEVEN
I Dream of Jeannie

The thing about Dominion mages is, they always leave a mess behind.

Cleaning up the Mount Herself was easy enough – or at least we knew what to do. Send in teams of artisans and cleaning ladies to scour the place, as much as they could, and then let the Mountain do the rest. You don't need to know what got done along those lines. Don't get upset about that; it's just the way it is.

The bodies were tricky. The Castle promptly sent word to the Universal Dominion, all properly deferential and oily and ever-so-apologetic that the two mages had decided to fight to the death in our miserable little village of a settlement. The Castle also sent Cackle's corpse back with the ice axe still embedded in its brain. We didn't dare disturb it, you see. Perhaps the Dominion could even now do something? On the other hand, Wolfie's body was returned completely without any kind of honors, and packed in salt. And the Dominion said nothing, since by their own beliefs the three bullets in Wolfie's body and head was proof that he wasn't a mage in the first place.

Dory later told me that the circles were in an uproar over that; the ones that sponsored Wolfie got a black eye, and the ones that didn't were eager to keep swinging. It's not a civil war, because New California isn't that lucky. But it ain't happy magic fun time over in the Dominion right now, either. We haven't even gotten a new ambassador, *yet*. Although I bet the next one ain't gonna be quite so slack about things.

But right now it's still good news. Both for us, and Sonora. Oh, yeah, they're still holding on up in the north, with Old Tucson as the new capital. Turns out that the general they found for themselves was pretty good, after all – and wasn't she shocked to have a New Californian relief force show up, just before a really important battle?

But not as shocked as the orc chiefs were. More infantry

they might have handled, but the flying carpets spooked them, hard. Dory said that for some strange reason the orcish horde had it in their heads that the Dominion was helping out the Sonorans, and having no-fooling magic cavalry show up convinced them it was true. Now that's the genuine New California razzle-dazzle for ya: smoke and mirrors, so you don't have to pay in sweat and blood.

Well, we paid some. Remember Carlos, from the rug races? The flying carpets had to go after the siege engines first thing, and the orcs had them protected pretty good, if not good enough, and, well, Carlos didn't make it back to the victory parade. Like I said, he was a good kid.

But we still won, or at least won enough. We broke the siege, and then we broke enough of the enemy that the rest retreated. The border's shifted a lot, but not enough that our forts are now facing down orc hordes. And damned if Sonora isn't still being grateful about it, either. It's enough to shake my faith in human nature.

It's not all sunshine and light in Cin City now, though – well, sure, it is, but you know what I mean. The cops managed to sweep up most of Legion's old network of secret mages. The ones that the cops grabbed didn't survive the arrests, which was damned awkward but less so than handing over live mages to the Dominion. Instead, the Dominion got sent little urns full of ashes. Which is probably safe enough, unless the Dominion suddenly develops a taste for necromancy. Which it won't, thank whatever god you like to thank.

Lucas got woken up a couple days after things were straightened out, and was back to walking around normally about three days after that. A week later, he was off to do some strange sort of crazy dig with Remy and Sofie up in Old California. Something about an ancient Masonic complex in Pasadena being rediscovered. Mind you, that was pretty firmly in barbie country, but that's why you bring muscle to an archaeological dig. I'm sure that they're all doing fine with each other. And if they're not, well, it's not my business anyway.

And did I get paid for all of this? Yeah. Fifty simoleons a day, plus expenses. Oh, and a little box containing a genuine *2079 Lensman* series crystal showed up on the Billy's front doorstep one morning. Don't ask me, *muchacho*: I have no idea how it got there. And if I had known how much trouble it'd end up putting me through– but that's another story.

So, that's the end of this Case. You go through a lot of them, in my line of work. Mind you, most of them aren't as hard to clear as this one was.

And I guess that's it.

CHAPTER TWENTY-EIGHT
Epilogue

Oh, all right.

There's a thing that Shamuses do. What I did was, I went back to my office and poured myself a glass. You always do that, after a Case. You drink to – and remember – the dead, because sometimes nobody else will. There were a lot of people who died whom nobody else will remember, because they were in the wrong place and had the wrong abilities and attracted the attention of two very evil men. So I drank to them, and then I put Elizabeth's old lightstone in the same place that I put all the other mementos of a cleared Case.

That night, as I slept, I saw Elizabeth. She looked good. She looked like herself. We spoke, a little. She now served the Mount as I do, willingly, and faithfully. The Mount had put her in charge of making sure that the farmlands got the rain they needed, which meant that her days were now spent dancing on the breeze and tickling clouds. Elizabeth was almost perfectly happy.

"Should I let them know something of their daughter survives?" she asked me, almost diffidently.

"I don't know," my sleeping self replied. *"Does she?"* From Elizabeth's smile as she left for her tasks, I had answered her question satisfactorily. And I was pleased, but I had more pressing things to attend to. Like paying court to my goddess, who sustains me as much as She sustains the rest of New California.

I woke up the next morning with a smile on my lips and my dreams undisturbed. It was another beautiful day in New California. I had a good feeling about stuff.

I wondered how long *that* would last. After all, I do live in Cin City.

ACKNOWLEDGEMENTS

Who helped me with this book? Good heavens, who didn't?

First off, there's Jamie, my wife, and my kids, who took all of this in good humor, thankfully. My wife's also my alpha reader; man, you should have seen the first draft! My beta readers were Michael LaReaux, Phil Smith, and Jeff Weimer; man, you should have seen the *second* draft!

Then there was all the feedback I got from other writers. Ursula Vernon was happy to answer stupid technical questions, and M.C.A. Hogarth has written a book on how to make good business decisions when you're an artist, and wasn't *that* invaluable. Beth McCoy structurally edited my book for me when she was just supposed to be *copy*-editing it (yeah, I noticed). This would have been a nonexistent book without their help. I lucked out with the artists, too. Shaenon Garrity did stuff with the cover I didn't even know I wanted until I saw it, and it's embarrassing how bad my ad hoc city map was until Robert Altbauer took it away from me and turned it into something believable. Both were a pleasure to work with.

Finally, I want to thank me — sorry, I had a little egotism flare-up, there. More seriously, I have excellent readers (Sheryl Sahr and Anda Olsen in particular get mentions). Their encouragement, support, and occasional boot to the rear helped immensely.

#

Special Thanks go to my Kickstarter backers: Aaron Pollock, Adam Nemo, Allen Hueffmeier, Amy Kimmel, Annette Bennett, Anonymous, Arioch "The Question" Morningstar, Azri-el, Bagofcats, Bill, Blodwedd Mallory, Brent Cochran, Brian, Brian Bolinger, Caitlin Barthold, Caleb Howe, Charlotte, Chris, Christopher Guilfoyle, Craig Cicero, CS Fitzgerald, Dan McLaughlin, Daniel Wallace, David L. Jessup, Dewy, Disillusionist, Donald Dohm, Dsroelandt, Duncan Harris, Elal, Eric Burns-

White, Eric Narges, Esther Whitlock, Francium, Gayle "Butterfly" Chin, Gregory Roth, ibguy, James Huang, James Morphew, James Saffell, Jeff Niles, Jeff Weimer, Jennifer Flora Black, Jim King, Jimmie Bise, Jr., John Fiala, Jon Saul, Joshua Seckel, Jowen, Kathleen Sobansky, Katie Kenney, Kemberlee Kaye, Kevin W. Patterson, Kevin Wadlow, Lady Alicia of Cambion, lambentower, Laura Wilkinson, Loch & Myf, Mark Erikson, Mark Garbowski, Mary Cosgrove Lane, Matt "Spud" Armstrong, Matt Trepal, Matthew Blackwell, Matthew Heimiller, Michael Emerson, Michael Ganschow-Green, Michael M, Michael Nutt, Michelle Detwiler, Mija "acat" Cat, Moria Trent, Neil Stevens, Nicholas Sylvain, Nick Robbins, Orla, Pat Lennon, Patches, Paul Leone, Paul Sudlow, Phil Smith, Randy Cox, Ranten N. Raven, Regina Holmes, Reno, Richie & Preet Bassi, Robert E. Maurer, Robert Nealis, Royce Day, Russell Sprague, Sam, Sean, Shannon Rodriguez, Spencer Colmenares, Susan Taylor, Taryn Mateyka, Ted, Teri Bolke, Thanks Will!, The Hallock family, Tom Abella, Travis Foster, Unsafecrayon, and Walter Milliken.

CAST, SETTINGS, AND PROPS

In order of appearance

Tom Bannion Vargas: A Shamus. Hero of the story.

Shamus: A type of investigator, unique to New California.

Mount Jeannie: A magically-sustained iceberg, found in the Gulf of California.

New California: Kingdom, located in Baja.

Lore: The accumulated wisdom of the Old Americans, collated from their books, music, movies, television programs, and direct-sensory stories. Shamuses are traditionally steeped in the Lore.

Old American: Members of the former continent-spanning empire ruling over North America. Collapsed at the beginning of the 22nd century AD, after the return of magic.

Lightstone: The magical equivalent to a light bulb.

Adventurer's Guild: A mythical criminal organization specializing in exploring and looting abandoned ruins.

Cin City: Cinderella, capital city of the Kingdom of New California. Formerly the town of San Felipe, Mexico.

Sonora: Republic on the other side of the Gulf of California. Currently fighting orcish barbarian tribes. Notable Sonoran cities are **Hermosillo,** the former capital of Sonora, recently razed by orcs; and **Old Tucson,** A Sonoran border city, located in the north part of the country.

Flatfoot: A not-entirely-ceremonial guard for the Castle.

Castle: The palace and primary court for New California.

Simoleons: Currency used in New California. Types of coins/bills include nichols, gippers, chaplins, monroes, grants, and orsons.

Case: When capitalized, it's the current mission of a Shamus. His or her job is to Clear it, no matter the cost.

Barbie/Ken: People originally from the barbarian kingdoms of Old California. Often used as an insult.

Grand Panama: A southern empire centered around the still-functional Panama Canal.

Deseret: A theocracy in the north, currently half-conquered by the Universal Dominion.

Dwarvenwood: A decentralized nation-state located in the Pacific Northwest.

Court English: One of the two languages spoken in New California.

Spanglish: One of the two languages spoken in New California.

Schmaltz: The magical stuff that comes off of Mount Jeannie. When it curdles, it can be made into icemold.

Sasquatch clock: Like a cuckoo clock, but with fewer birds and more furry hominids.

Dorothea Fleming Toro (**Dory**): The Court Producer (grand vizier) of New California.

Remy: Head Cin City coroner.

Elizabeth Gonzalez-Hernandez: A secret mage of New California. Murdered.

Hawaii: Refers to a refugee area, and is either 'refugee camps' or slums, depending on who you're talking to and how they feel about it.

University of New California (Cinderella): The main campus of the UNC system.

Alliance of Theatrical Stage Employees (**ATSE**): Absolutely not 'The Mages' Guild.'

Universal Dominion: A magical empire, centered on Grand Moingoana (the former city of Des Moines, Iowa). Thoroughly unpleasant.

Wolfstone Aconite of the Ninth Circle: The current Dominion ambassador to New California. Thoroughly unpleasant. Quickly nicknamed "Wolfie."

Florence: Cleaning lady. Not a witch.

Rose: Cleaning lady. Also not a witch, is that clear?

King Ronald the Ninth: King of New California.

Queen Salma: Queen of New California.

Lt. **Sharon Lenina Foster**: Castle Flatfoot.

Haida/Haidan: A Marxist dictatorship found in the Pacific Northwest. Less powerful than the Universal Dominion, but just as unpleasant. Regularly uses demonology.

Vancouver: Capital of Free Canada.

Elhai: Dock region in Cin City. Not quite the poor side of town, but not the best.

Gran Pomeranian: A dog bred up from the Old American Pomeranian breed to be a guard/war dog. At some point in the last fifty years, someone bred Mini Gran Pomeranians.

Tijuana: A city on the northern border of New California.

Esmerelda: A city on the western shore of New California.

Kingdom of Virginia: A fabled land on the east coast of North America.

Atlantis: A ruined city in what is now the Elf-lands.

San Felipe Church: A Roman Catholic Church located in Fond.

Fond: A working class neighborhood.

Tourista: A poor neighborhood. Many are Freemasons. The movers and shakers in Tourista are known as the Five Hundred.

Father Miguel (**Mike**): An orcish Roman Catholic priest.

Orcs: A race of large, green-skinned humanoids with tusks.

Redtown: The worst part of Cin City. Residents are called Redtowners or Reds. Not actually linked to redmages, but there's parallel evolution.

Red Hood: The traditional ruler of Redtown. High-turnover job.

Thieves' Guild: Not the Adventurers' Guild. Possibly a minor religious order.

Frederico Baldwin-Cuaron (**Freddie**): A secretly reputable minor nobleman.

Estaban and **Diane Puma**: A married couple. Murdered.

Syndicate: Officially the *Sindicato Nacional de Trabajadoras del Hogar*, or the cleaning ladies' union. And that's *all* it is, you see? No hedge-witches *there*.

Billy: An unfortunate fellow with unfortunate friends.

Rick's: It's THE bar.

Grackle Toadstone from the Nightmare Stalkers: The former Dominion ambassador to Cin City. Often called Cackle. Presumed dead, or gone, or nobody really cares what else.

King's Bookie: A valued member of the New Californian court.

Cottonton: The town closest to the Gonzalez farm.

Enchanted Mountains: Just to the west of the Gonzalez farm.

Diane Hernandez: Elizabeth's mother.

George Gonzalez: Elizabeth's father.

Leila Cordova Parsons: Head of the Syndicate. Absolutely, positively, make no mistake about this, NOT A WITCH.

Icemold: A drug. Do not touch. People who use it are moldies. Created in a moldworks.

Dwarfs/dwarves: It's an entire thing with them.

Weedy Randy: A respectable dwarf, dealing in cannabis.

Stonefaces: A dwarven term for police.

Tourista Landfill: A potter's field, where the unclaimed dead are buried.

Joe Gannon Lacy: A precinct police captain/Castle Flatfoot.

Garapenna's: The restaurant on the cover.

Tolva: The guy on the cover tending the grill.

Variety, Union-Tribune, El Vigia, La Cronica: New Californian newspapers.

Al and **Sancho**: Two Flatfoots.

Puerta Verde: A modeling agency of negotiable virtue.

Trixie and Slye: Two models at the Puerta Verde modeling agency.

Jimmy: A ken working for Kermie the Frog.

Big-Eye Sam: Kermie the Frog's right-hand man.

Kermie the Frog: A reputable businessman from the Second Republic with no ties to the Adventurer's Guild, ayup.

Second Republic: Claims to be the last remnant of the old United States. Located in the northeast. Its inhabitants have been thoroughly cursed by the Dominion.

Lucas B. Coltrane: An elf from the Elf-lands.

Elf-lands: A disorganized realm located in what used to be the American South and the Caribbean.

Infernalism: A term for enchantments made with demonic magic.

Satanspawn: An elvish term for anything with demonic magic involved in its creation.

Vertigo: Bourgeois neighborhood. Very tacky.

Galivant: Rich neighborhood.

School for Research Archeology: Dedicated to enthusiastic dungeoneering.

Benefactor Sofia Huston Redgrave (**Sofie**): New Californian high noblewoman.

Cold-Lands: Mountain West region. Unpopulated, rich in monsters and lootable sites.

Free Canada: Military/commercial republic, centered on Vancouver Island. A cross between Venice and Malta.

Greens: The polite name of one faction of New Californian nobles, primarily descended from the invaders from the north, led by King Ronnie the Great.

Greeks: The polite name of one faction of New Californian nobles, mostly descended from the people living in the area when the 'Greens' invaded.

Clancy: A cop studying to become a Flatfoot.

The Five Hundred: The collection of families, descended from Old American refugees, who informally run Tourista.

Shauni Buchannon Quinn: A policewoman with barbie heritage.

Saint Jackie: A mythic hero from the days of the Old American.

Rune-monkey: Current slang term for somebody who can keep the enchantments on a flying carpet functional.

Carlos Reyes O'Malley: A rug-racer from the good side of town.

International Film Preservation Foundation (The Lore-

keepers): A guild of sages and academics.

Cin City Special: A light, one-handed crossbow, enchanted to re-cock itself. It still requires reloading.

Bernardo Campa Verdugo: A fellow under a problematic obligation, with an unpleasant "roommate" in his body.

John Williams Opera House (**The Billy**): The premiere opera house of New California.

Carmalita Prinze Perroni: A noblewoman prominent in New Californian opera.

Povenmire and Marsh: Fabled classical composers of the Old Americans.

Tomas Garcia Garcia (**Mr. Gee-Gee**): Chief Loremaster, aka Chairman of the IFPF.

Sonoran Expedition: An army from New California, sent to reinforce the border forts and free up more experienced troops to help Sonora against the orc tribes. Air units (flying carpets) were recruited at the same time, but sent with the forces going to Sonora.

Eddie Cazals: An artisan of the ATSE.

Daisy Fukunaga Araujo: An artisan of the ATSE.

John Perez: An intern in the ATSE.

'John Perez': A mage in Legion's service.

Vana: Capital of the elf-island of Belegdor. Formerly Havana, Cuba.

The Redline: Painted between Redtown and the rest of Cin City, the redline marks the division between 'don't burn the rest of the city down' and 'we will arrest you if we catch you doing crime.'

Chewie: Redtown snitch.

Vertigo Club: A social club in, naturally, the Vertigo neighborhood. They have daily pastimes such as cards, trivia questions, and Sunday Loteria.

Mr. Pointy: Sgt. Shauni's family heirloom, a large wooden stake.

Veranos: A high-status barbie tribe.

Moldworks: Where icemold is refined from schmaltz.

First, Second, and **Third Guys**: in over their heads.

Redmages: Haidan mages. It's generally considered ethical to kill them on sight. The name has a parallel evolution with Redtown's, but Haidan mages are not Redtown residents; their belief systems clash in a 'more pure than you' fashion.

Chapman General Hospital (**The Old Chap**): the best hospital in Cin City.

Neo-Heinlein: a retro-retro-futurist school of design popular in the 24th Century.

Legion: He has many names.

Made in the USA
Middletown, DE
20 December 2020

29054725R00154